Small Crimes

in an Age of Abundance

Also by Matthew Kneale

English Passengers

Matthew Kneale

Small Crimes
in an Age of Abundance

DOUBLEDAY CANADA

Doubleday Canada and colophon are trademarks.

Library and Archives Canada Cataloguing in Publication

Kneale, Matthew, 1960–
Small crimes in an age of abundance / Matthew Kneale.

ISBN 0-385-66138-X

I. Title.

PR6061.N37S63 2005   823'.914   C2004-906786-9

Book design by Fritz Metsch
Printed and bound in the USA

Published in Canada by
Doubleday Canada, a division of
Random House of Canada Limited

Visit Random House of Canada Limited's website: www.randomhouse.ca

10 9 8 7 6 5 4 3 2 1

To Shannon

CONTENTS

Small Crimes

in an Age of Abundance

1. Stone

NONE OF IT would ever have happened if Tania had not become best friends with Sarah Spence. One moment Tania's parents had hardly heard the name, and the next it seemed like they heard nothing else: Sarah Spence knew where to buy the best second-hand clothes, Sarah Spence had a CD by a fantastic new band, Sarah Spence said Friends of the Earth were just old hippies. At first Tania's parents were happy enough, as Sarah Spence—an unexpectedly plain yet self-possessed girl—always treated them politely. But Tania's father, Guy, began to lose patience when Sarah's reported achievements were extended to travel. The Spences, Tania explained triumphantly, "were really adventurous," going to exotic, faraway places all by themselves. Sarah's father was a "totally brilliant linguist" and would learn Latin American Spanish or Bahasa Indonesian "just like that" so they could buy tickets and find hotels as they went. "Sarah says it's the only way to travel," Tania insisted, "as you can really see the country and make friends with the people."

There was no mistaking the criticism of her own parents lurking in Tania's praise, and Guy Winter found this especially annoying as he was rather proud of his family's holidays. Yes, they went with a tour firm, but this was no ordinary tour firm. For some years Guy's family had booked with the High Style Travel Company, to Rajasthan, India, Tanzania, Indonesia, and elsewhere, and not once had they been disappointed. High Style lived up to its name, taking them to atmospheric, offbeat spots alongside the standard tourist sights, and choosing characterful hotels. Most of all, High Style had a knack of attracting just the right sort of person to their groups, which never seemed to include the loud boors or complaining oldsters Guy dreaded. He and his wife, Chloe, had met some fascinating people on their trips from all kinds of interesting professions, and they had remained good friends with a number of High Stylers even long afterward. For that matter Tania herself had loved all their High Style holidays, and it was only now that she had treacherously decided they were inferior to the Spences' DIY efforts. The Spences? Guy did not think of himself as a snob, but there were some people he simply had no time for. Didn't Geoff Spence run some sort of fitness club? Guy had met him at parents' events and had thought him a silly-looking man, with straggly hair and an overeager, gap-toothed smile.

What really decided matters, though, was Michael Chen. Chen was a buyer for one of Hong Kong's larger jewelry stores who passed by Chloe's shop during a visit to London and stepped inside, professionally curious. He ended up staying for more than two hours, examining piece after piece. "You should come to Hong Kong and show these to our manager," he told Chloe. "Of course I can't promise anything, Mrs. Winter, but I like your designs and I'm sure he'll like them too. And believe me, Hong Kong people like buying jewelry."

He left an impressive-looking business card, which she showed to Guy that evening. There was no denying it was a good opportunity, but a round-trip flight there seemed an expensive outlay when nothing was certain, and Guy remained doubtful. "You might go all the way there and then find this man Chen had just got overexcited. People do that when they're on a trip."

"What if we combined it with our next holiday?" wondered Chloe.

For some time Guy and Chloe had been tempted by High Style's Cool Cathay tour of China, but had always decided against it because of the country's poor record on human rights. Chloe, the family moralist, was firmly opposed to visiting countries with reprehensible regimes, insisting that "spending money in that sort of place is like giving presents to criminals." Guy was rather proud of her stand on such matters. Not that he was morally unconcerned himself, but he represented the safe, sensible side of the Winter marriage, while Chloe represented the passionate and committed side. Although he had discovered she could be more practical than he expected. He had not taken her jewelry shop seriously at first, regarding it as more a hobby than a real business, and quietly hoping it would not make too much of a loss, but after a couple of slow years it had done surprisingly well and now brought in a handy addition to his own income. It had also introduced them to a more exciting circle than they would ever have met through his City colleagues. For that matter, they had first heard about High Style through one of Chloe's clients.

"China's getting a lot better these days," Chloe considered. "I saw something in the paper about it. They still have a long way to go, of course, but things aren't nearly as bad as they were. Perhaps we should give it a try."

Guy and she had looked up the High Style brochure only to find a problem. The Cool Cathay tour did not pass through Hong Kong but began at Beijing and left from Shanghai. Chloe was not put off. "What if we take the tour and then travel down to Hong Kong ourselves? We could even stop off at a few places along the way."

Travel independently? Guy found his wife's suggestion a little alarming, as Chloe's ideas often were, but he could see how it might be exciting. If the Spences could do this sort of thing, then why not the Winters? Then a problem occurred to him. "What about the jewels? You can't very well haul them round China."

"I don't see why not, so long as we get them insured. Chen mostly liked the rings and smaller pieces, so they wouldn't take up much room." She looked into it the next day, picking out a collection she felt was suitable, estimating the value—rather less than

Guy would have guessed—and found it was fairly straightforward to arrange a premium with the company that insured the shop. "They weren't interested in how I'd be traveling. They just wanted to know where and how long I'd be there."

So that was that. The next day she bought a map and a guidebook and began studying possible routes, and that weekend they told the children. Guy half expected Tania to turn up her nose at the idea—she was getting so hard to impress these days—but instead she surprised him with her enthusiasm, saying, "Wow, Dad, that's so cool," so he wondered if she too was involved in a little rivalry with the Spences. Her younger brother, Ben, was also excited, and more so when Chloe suggested they might visit the Baolin martial arts temple: Ben had been doing kung fu after school for a year now, and nothing could have been more appealing to him than a visit to Baolin. Tania, who was going through a mystic phase, wanted to see the huge carved Buddhas near Guangfaochu. Chloe cleverly managed to come up with a route that combined them both. The High Style tour ended with a long boat trip down the Yangtze River, and the Winters would simply disembark half a day early, take a train direct from the river port to Guangfaochu, then another train to the town below Baolin, and finally a third back to the main railway line south to Canton and Hong Kong. Chen confirmed their proposed date for a meeting, while High Style had no problem booking a return flight from Hong Kong rather than Shanghai. In a week everything was fixed and paid for. Guy took some pleasure in mentioning it to Geoff Spence at the next parents' event and seeing his surprise.

"China? That should be interesting. No, we've not done that one yet. I've heard it's quite a hard place to go traveling."

Guy smelled the whiff of sour grapes. "I'm sure we'll survive."

He even bought a language course in Mandarin Chinese, though the words and the strange system of tones were so remote from English that memorizing them proved laborious, and he was still only on page five when the time came to begin packing their bags.

"Don't you worry, we'll get by," Chloe told him breezily. "People always do."

The High Style tour proved disappointing compared with others they had taken. Famous sights such as the Great Wall and the terra-cotta army were impressive enough, but China as a whole seemed far less charming than Indonesia or India. The countryside could be picturesque, but most of the towns were depressingly industrial, and so polluted that the sun looked as if it were shining through gauze. The hotels, too, were not up to High Style's usual standards and were either modern and immemorable or grim, Soviet-era blocks, while even the new ones felt faintly run-down, with their dusty corridors, and at one place near Xi'an, Chloe decided against leaving her slim jewelry box in the safe, hiding it in her luggage in the room instead. She became increasingly irritated with the Chinese tour guides, whom she referred to as "the robots," as they always toed the official line and became quite angry when she asked them about imprisoned human rights activists or censorship of the press.

The main problem, though, was the other tourists. Most of these seemed tolerable enough at first, and Guy and Chloe got on quite well with a couple from Chalk Farm who ran their own PR firm, but little by little a gulf opened up between the Winters and everyone else. The reason was plain enough: their plans to travel independently after the tour. Guy was aware that he and his family talked about these a good deal, and sometimes he even found himself using phrases borrowed from Sarah Spence, about how this was the only way to see a country properly and make friends with the people. And why not? They were not showing off but simply voicing the excitement they felt. He became increasingly annoyed by the small-mindedness of the others: their weary looks and sarcastic replies. They were jealous, he and Chloe agreed. It was so unreasonable, too, seeing as there was nothing to stop them traveling alone themselves. As the days passed, he and Chloe found it increasingly hard to conceal the disdain they felt, and the coolness around them sharpened. By the third week even the PR couple were hardly speaking to them, and when the Yangtze boat finally docked, early one steamy summer morning, and the Winters assembled by the restaurant room with their luggage, nobody troubled to come and wave them good-bye.

"Good riddance," said Chloe as they shouldered their shiny new backpacks and walked down the gangplank to the shore. "Boring old farts."

Tania and Ben giggled at this disrespect.

The High Style guide tried to get them a taxi, but they seemed not to be available in the little port, and so the Winters walked the short distance to the railway station. In the event Guy was pleased they had to walk, finding it strangely exhilarating to be striding along the waterside of this foreign town, and breathing in its early morning smells, of river water, jasmine tea, and unfamiliar spices and foods. He was surprised he had never thought of traveling like this before, and even felt a grudging respect for Geoff Spence. How good it was to be rid of the baggage of guides and other tourists. Yes, he and Chloe had their planned schedule, but they could change their minds if they liked. He felt as if the whole of this vast country were unfurled before him like a great map: they could go anywhere they wanted, do anything they chose. In a curious way he had never felt so intensely free.

People were looking at them strangely, and one man almost fell off his bicycle. "I don't think many foreigners come through here," said Guy, pleased by the thought.

"It's like we're explorers," said Ben grandly.

The railway station gave them a moment of shock. Walking into the main hall, they were taken aback by a scene of seeming chaos. The Chinese written characters above each ticket window meant nothing to Guy, while the queues were alarming, with people shoving tightly forward against one another. As he and his family watched, angry shouting suddenly broke out from the far end of the hall, almost like a scream. Ben and Tania were looking nervous, and even Chloe seemed unsure. "Stay here and watch the bags. I'll deal with this," said Guy briskly. Everything had started so well, and he was not going to let it go sour. "What was the name of the place?"

"Guangfaochu," said Chloe.

"Guangfaochu," Guy repeated, adding a singsong accent to the word so it sounded pleasingly authentic. He chose the window with the shortest queue, waited his turn in the squash—actually it wasn't so bad when you were in it—and told the ticket seller one of the few phrases he had managed to memorize: "Wo shiang chu"—I want to go to—"Guangfaochu," giving the name his full Mandarin Chinese lilt. The ticket seller looked puzzled—Guy wondered if he had ever spoken to a foreigner before—and made him repeat the name twice but then held up eight fingers. Ticket window eight. The numbers were Western, fortunately, and Guy joined another slow-moving queue till finally it was time to repeat his demand, "Wo shiang chu Guangfaochu." A moment later he was walking back to his family, triumphantly holding up four cardboard tickets.

"Well done," said Chloe proudly. Even Tania looked impressed.

"It was easy," Guy said with a smile.

After that he simply showed their tickets to anyone wearing a uniform till they were on the right platform. Less pleasing was the sight of the train, with its battered paintwork and hard plastic seats. "How long does this take?" asked Ben doubtfully.

"Three hours," said Guy. "There are supposed to be really good views."

At least it was not crowded, and they easily found four seats together. Their mood began to improve as the carriage jolted into motion and they were on their way. And there was so much to watch. On the High Style tour they had traveled only on planes and buses, always cocooned with the group, and Guy was intrigued by the life around them on this Chinese train. Almost all the other passengers seemed to be eating something, from peanuts and strange fruit to chunks of chicken in plastic bags or rice in boxes. Leavings were simply thrown to the floor, which quickly became thick with husks, peels, and bones. Just as the mess was threatening to become oppressive, a large, uniformed woman appeared with a broom, bossily making everyone raise their feet as she swept everything away. She returned shortly afterward, now wielding a vast kettle, at the sight of which the other passengers brought out bags of tea leaves and tin mugs, which she carefully filled, their owners snapping tin lids into place to keep in the warmth.

"I feel distinctly underprepared," said Guy, making his family laugh.

"I rather like it," decided Chloe. "It makes a nice change from crisps and sandwiches from a trolley."

The one thing that troubled Guy a little was their speed. This was supposed to be a main line, and yet the train seemed in no hurry at all, trundling slowly past terraced hillsides and often coming to a stop in the middle of nowhere, halting for what seemed an age beside paddy fields or some broken railway building, where the carriage, robbed of its breeze, soon became like an oven. After two and a half hours Guy felt a need to check and asked a man behind him, "Guangfaochu?" to be answered with a finger pointed forward. He was met with the same gesture after three hours, three and a half hours, and four.

"I thought we were supposed to be there by now," said Ben grumpily.

"It must just be a slower train than the guidebook said," Guy told him.

"Or the guidebook was wrong," added Chloe suspiciously.

After four and half hours their neighbors took pity on them and gave them quantities of peanuts and fruit, as well as a couple of tin mugs for tea, for all of which they were very grateful as their own water and biscuits were long gone. After five hours the train rolled through the outskirts of a larger town, briefly filling Guy with hope, but no, it was not Guangfaochu, and what was more, the name was like nothing he could see on his map of China.

"This really can't be right," said Chloe.

"But it must be," Guy insisted. "Everyone says so."

After five and a half hours Tania had to go to the bathroom, and she returned pale and angry. "It's really horrid in there." After six hours Guy broke into a sudden panic that they had missed the stop and asked five different people, one after the other, "Guang-faochu?" only to be given the same forward-pointing gesture. After that he lapsed into a kind of uneasy resignation, too hot to worry. Chloe and the children fell asleep, each shooting him accusing looks when they woke and found themselves still on the train. After eight hours the carriage began to cool a little, breaking into new life, and their neighbors decided Guy's interminable cries of "Guangfaochu?" were hugely funny. After ten hours the joke had become undeniably stale. After eleven hours Guy had stopped asking, and almost ceased to care what happened. Did it really matter where they were? They were bound to end up somewhere, surely? He had been on this train for so long that he was beginning to feel reluctant to get off—it was quite dark outside while at least they were safe in here—and he jumped slightly when, after twelve hours, the man behind him tapped his shoulder and told him, "Guangfaochu." Should they just stay in their seats? But no, this was where they had wanted to go. Standing up, he found they had unwittingly become celebrities, and the whole carriage broke into good-bye waves and shouts of "Guangfaochu! Guangfaochu!"

Only a handful of other passengers got off with them, and the station building was ominously quiet. Walking outside, they found themselves in a long, poorly lit street.

"That man's looking at us," said Ben.

He was about the only person to be seen: a thin figure leaning in a doorway, leaning too much somehow, as if he were hinged at the waist. He was probably no more than twenty, but there was a seriousness about him that made him seem older. He stared at them with an undisguised curiosity.

"He's probably just not used to seeing foreigners," said Chloe.

Guy was frowning at his guidebook map. "I don't understand. There should be two hotels just across the road here."

There was nothing except a long, blank wall. By now their watcher was stepping cautiously toward them. Guy held up the guidebook to him, pointing to the Chinese characters beside the name. "Guangfaochu?"

"Meio." The man broke into a stern frown. "Guangfaochu."

"But that's what I just said." Guy was too tired for this. He pointed again at the characters. "Guangfaochu?"

"Meio. Meio. Guangfaochu."

It took four more tries before Guy finally understood. The words were the same but the tones were different: one Guang-faochu went up in the middle and down at the end, the other did the opposite. "Oh hell."

"So we're in the wrong town," said Chloe dangerously. "Well, I suppose that explains why the train took four times longer than it was supposed to."

"It's not my fault," Guy snapped. But it was, actually, and he knew it, as it was he who had bought the tickets. If only he had thought to show the written Chinese character name at the station rather than proudly trying to pronounce it, this would never have happened. He flipped impatiently through the phrases at the end of the book and found the word for hotel. This time the man understood at once and began leading the way down the road. At least there was one here.

"Where's Eeyore taking us?" said Ben, breaking into a giggle.

"Don't be rude," Chloe warned him, but even Guy smiled, as the name could not have been better suited to their guide with his long, unsmiling face. Fortunately Eeyore seemed not to realize he was the subject of the joke and led them on through dark streets, till finally they reached a small, peeling hotel. The receptionist, a bone-thin, shaven-headed man in a sleeveless vest, was slumped watching the television on the desk as it boomed out a kung fu costume drama. He looked startled by the sight of foreigners but then recovered himself, took their passports, and showed them inside. The concrete corridor was scattered with old coal dust, the rooms were plain and bare, and it all seemed a shock after their High Style hotels.

"It's awfully dirty," complained Tania, sitting on her parents' bed.

Guy was unable to resist temptation. "I'm sure Sarah Spence has stayed in worse."

"I can't believe they'll have a safe here," said Chloe wearily.

Guy, having brought them to this place, accepted the role of trying to make everything right. He examined the door, which did not have a proper lock but a thick metal hasp and staple, for which they had been given a padlock. "Actually, this looks quite strong," he decided. "If we had our own lock it would be pretty secure."

"I don't like it here," decided Tania.

"Eeyore does," said Ben.

He had followed them up and seemed in a state of doleful wonderment as he inspected the room, now carefully examining the empty minibar fridge, then trying the remote control to the television, which didn't work. Next he tried the buttons on the television itself, turning the volume high till the room was filled with its din. He looked faintly resentful when Guy switched it off.

"I'm hungry," said Tania.

They all were. Guy flipped through the phrase list for the word for restaurant, and Eeyore pointed through the window to a lighted doorway farther down the street. Chloe put the long, slim jewelry box in her daypack for safety, and they made their way down, peering through the door of the restaurant: a white-walled room, overlit by strip lights, so it seemed faintly like a swimming pool. At least it looked clean.

"It'll have to do," said Guy.

"Eeyore seems to be joining us," noticed Chloe. Sure enough, he was following them inside.

Guy was a little surprised. But then where was the harm? "I suppose he helped us and now he wants his reward." When they sat down, though, and Guy pointed at the indecipherable menu to ask what he wanted, Eeyore looked puzzled, and only after some encouragement did he order anything. When the food arrived, his turned out to be a simple boiled rice and egg, while he refused to take anything from their numerous dishes.

"I think he's just curious about us," said Ben.

"I'm getting tired of being so fascinating," complained Chloe. "We wouldn't be half so interesting if we were in the right town."

Guy slept heavily that night, and when he woke the next morning everything seemed somehow better. He had been faintly aware through his sleep of a rising noise outside, and when he peered through the curtains he found it hard to believe that this was the dark, lifeless place where they had arrived the night before. The street below had opened like a flower and was ablaze with colorful shops and crowded with pedestrians and cyclists. Even Chloe seemed revived, humming as she got ready to risk the showers at the end of the corridor. Opening the door, she broke into a laugh. "Guess who's here? It's Eeyore. He looks like he's waiting for us."

Guy had already forgotten all about him, and the name gave him a faint feeling of weariness. "D'you think he's been out there all night?"

"No. He's wearing a different shirt."

Despite his doleful presence, he was useful, and he helped Guy tackle the hotelman over the question of the two Guangfaochus. It seemed that matters were not as bad as Guy had feared, and that their interminable train had not taken them in completely the wrong direction from the real Guangfaochu but parallel to it, while the hotelman said it could be reached with one direct bus journey. "So we won't have to go all the way back," Guy told his family. "That's something." He slipped out to buy a large, black padlock for the door, and they put all the bags in his and Chloe's room for safety. After stopping at a dumpling stall for breakfast— surprisingly tasty—they set off for the bus station, Eeyore leading the way through the crowded streets. Guy's optimism faltered a little when they walked through the gate and he saw the long row of battered buses, with their cracked windows and balding tires, but at least there was no queue. He set to work questioning the ticket seller, this time taking care to point his finger at the Chinese characters in his guidebook as he pronounced each word. "He says the bus for the real Guangfaochu leaves at eight tomorrow morning," he explained at last, "and takes seven hours."

"Seven hours in one of those?" groaned Tania, who seemed to have lost all enthusiasm for Sarah Spence's notions of adventurous travel.

"I think it's worth it," said Chloe. "It'll be a bit rough, but then it'll be done, while otherwise we'll have to take the train all the way back and then another train from there. We'll lose a whole day."

"And we certainly won't have time to see the Baolin temple," agreed Guy.

That was enough to decide Ben. "Let's take the bus."

It was three to one. Tania sulked and Guy bought tickets. They had most of the day to kill and so began wandering back unhurriedly. Though there were no tourist sights here, Guy found he was more intrigued by this little town than by many of the sights they had seen on the High Style tour. The activity on the streets was fascinating, and one moment they found themselves walking by a healer applying heated glass cups to someone's back, the next they were passing a man selling poisons, with a line of dead rats displayed on the ground to show their effectiveness. Eeyore never left their side.

"D'you think he has a home to go to?" wondered Chloe.

Guy, too, was growing increasingly annoyed by the way Eeyore crowded them as they walked, staring importantly about and blocking them from the street stalls almost as if he thought he was their bodyguard. Or was he showing off to everyone else on the street, displaying his ownership of these exotic foreigners? When they stopped he would try to listen to Ben's Walkman headphones or would take Guy's camcorder from his shoulder and peer sternly at the display screen.

"I think he's creepy," decided Tania.

"He's not so bad," said Ben.

By now, feeling hungry, they had stopped by a small restaurant. Sure enough, Eeyore followed them inside.

"Does he always have to come too?" complained Tania.

"He has helped us," Guy reminded her.

This time Eeyore accepted the offer of food—more plain rice and egg—with a brisk nod. Though he could not understand what they said, still somehow his presence cast a silence over the meal, reducing it to a gloomy chinking of chopsticks, and by the end even Guy had lost his patience. "Thank you for your help. Shie shie," he told him as they stepped through the door into the strong sunlight. He gave a wave. "Bye bye now."

Eeyore regarded him with a blank stare, not taking a step. When they began walking, he followed.

"So much for that," said Chloe. Guy tried again at the hotel entrance but with no more success, and Eeyore followed them up to their room, where he set to work examining their possessions, showing particular interest in Chloe's hair dryer, peering curiously into the fan. Guy took it from him.

"I'm sorry, but we're tired and we have to rest. Good-bye now."

Eeyore seemed not to have heard and carefully picked up Chloe's cosmetics bag. All at once this freedom with their property was too much for Guy and he grasped one end of the cosmetics bag. "Look, will you please just go away and leave us in peace?"

Eeyore may not have understood the words, but he did the raised voice and Guy's angry stare. He regarded him for a moment, as if puzzled, then released the cosmetics bag, turned, and walked slowly from the room without a word. Guy felt a little unkind, but mostly he felt relieved to be free of this strange, clinging presence. They all did. After a brief rest Ben announced he wanted to go back to a kite shop that he had seen, and Guy and Tania decided to go with him, while Chloe, who was still feeling tired, stayed behind at the hotel. As Guy and the children walked out into the street, they saw Eeyore standing on the other side of the road.

"He's staring at us," said Tania.

"Take no notice," Guy told her.

They spent the best part of an hour in kite shops, buying several kites, and when they got back they found Chloe looking bemused. "Guess who I saw? Eeyore. I was walking back from the shower and there he was in the corridor, staring at me. I almost wondered if he was hoping to get a peek, though he would have been disappointed as I was all covered up with towels."

"I'm getting a bit fed up with this," said Guy. "It's like he's stalking us."

"He's harmless," said Chloe.

Guy was usually placid enough, but now his family-guarding instincts were offended. "I'm going to have a word with him."

"Don't be silly," Chloe insisted, but he took no notice and strode out of the room, causing Tania and Ben to cast each other glances, amused and a little awed by the strange sight of their father on the warpath. Guy marched along the corridor and down to the hotel entrance, then, slowed by the crowd, made his way back and forth through various nearby streets. There was no sign of Eeyore anywhere.

That night they went back to the strip-light restaurant. This was their first meal without Eeyore since they had arrived, and it was a cheerful evening, all of them chatting excitedly, as if lightened of some burden, and ordering far more food than they could eat. Guy even managed to hold a kind of conversation with the restaurant owner—a grinning, goading sort of man, stockily built like a fighter—and explained their disaster of the train to the wrong Guangfaochu, which the restaurant owner greeted with cackles of laughter. Somehow this led them to Ben's taking kickboxing at school, and he and the restaurant owner ended up shadowboxing by the door to the kitchen.

"You know, I'm beginning to think there is something to this kind of traveling," said Guy as they walked home. "It does let you get close to a place. When you're with a tour it's like seeing everything through a window."

Even Tania seemed to be coming back to the idea. "Yes, it can be fun. At least when nothing goes wrong."

They were all too tired to pack, so Guy set the alarm early. It was still half dark and he could hear the din of street life starting up outside as he stumbled out of bed and banged on the children's door. Walking back from the shower, he was puzzled to find possessions strewn across the beds; and Chloe and the children reaching among them, searching.

"The jewels," said Chloe tersely. "They're gone."

"You're sure?"

"Of course I'm sure."

From the moment they had left Britain, Guy had been worrying about precisely this, but now that it had happened he was more puzzled than anything else. "I don't understand. We always kept the room locked." He glanced at the hasp. "Nobody's interfered with the door. It would show."

Chloe looked at him a little awkwardly. "Unless it was that one time? When you were out and I was showering?"

He stared at her. "You didn't lock the door?"

Now she was angry. "I was only out of the room for two minutes."

"Chloe, you can't do that sort of thing in a country like this."

A wondering look came into Tania's eyes. "So it was Eeyore. I said he was creepy."

"We don't know that," said Chloe, though she sounded doubtful.

"It would explain why he was hanging around us all that time," said Guy. "And he noticed you take out the jewels when we went to the restaurant that first night. I saw him watching."

"I still don't think he would have," insisted Ben.

Nobody else thought so. Chloe was shaking her head. "So much for the meeting in Hong Kong."

Guy's thoughts were more on the insurance. "We'll have to get a police statement."

The hotelman looked alarmed when Guy pointed successively at the words for "robbery" and "police station," switching off the television and calling his wife from a back room to watch the desk so he could show the Winters the way. Guy had imagined the police station would be some modern block, but instead it was in an unexpectedly old-style building with a leafy courtyard. Three police were sitting in a row on a bench, drinking tea from little white cups, and they grinned at the unexpected sight of foreigners, one lifting the thermos invitingly. The smiles died, though, when the hotelman explained their presence. With a brief wave they were signaled to sit and wait on a bench.

"I suppose we'll miss the bus," said Ben gloomily.

"This is rather more important," Guy reminded him with a stern look, though in fact he was no less annoyed at finding their plans wrecked all over again. They waited on the bench, not sure quite what they were waiting for, Tania and Ben playing cards, and Guy was just about to try to ask what was happening when an anxious young man in glasses appeared.

"I am your translator."

That seemed progress. They and the hotelman followed him

into an office, where one of the three policemen was waiting. He broke into a frown when Guy explained that his wife's jewelry had been stolen.

"Police Officer Fan says you are mistaken," the interpreter translated. "Guangfaochu is an honest city and nobody here will steal."

"Somebody did," said Guy simply.

"What you are saying is very grave. Police Officer Fan asks, What is your claim?"

"I think we should be careful," murmured Chloe. "I'm not sure I like this."

"We have to make a report," Guy insisted. It was all becoming more complicated than he had expected. How could he explain? "All we need is a police statement saying the jewels have been stolen," he said to the interpreter, "so we can get our money back in England from the insurance."

Both the translator and the policeman regarded him doubtfully. Guy was wondering if he should try to tell them about insurance policies—did they have them here?—when the hotelman began hurriedly speaking, pouring out words in a rush.

"He says you put your own lock on the door so nobody could go inside but you," the interpreter reported.

The policeman was watching them, tapping his chin with his fingers. Guy was beginning to feel accused, and felt resentful of the hotelman, though he knew this was unfair as everything he had said was true. This was getting frustrating. They had to be believed or they would never get a police statement. For that matter, they might even themselves be accused of fraud. Or was that likely? "There was one time when we left the lock off by mistake," he explained to the interpreter. "My wife was taking a shower."

"Guy!" Chloe nudged him.

"What else can I tell them?"

The hotelman, looking anxious, broke into another long burst of words.

"He says there is an important thing you did not say," translated the interpreter. "You have a friend here who was always with you and in your room. He knows this friend, and he is called Jiao Zhe Yu."

It was strange to think of, but Guy had never heard Eeyore's real name till then. The policeman clearly knew it and closed his eyes for a second, as if he had swallowed something faintly distasteful. Was Eeyore a known thief? Perhaps it was no accident that he had been waiting outside the station? For that matter, his gawkishness could all have been an act.

"Police Officer Fan asks, Was Jiao Zhe Yu in the hotel when the room was not locked?"

Guy hesitated, feeling his wife's elbow jabbed against his arm. The hotelman was watching him with intensity. "All I want is a statement saying the jewels were stolen."

"Policeman Fan says please answer this simple question."

Guy saw no way out. "Yes, he was there. My wife saw him in the corridor when she came back from the shower. But that doesn't mean he stole anything." He watched the policeman make a note on a piece of paper.

"How could you?" hissed Chloe.

"What else could I say?" he hissed back. "It's true, after all." A thought came to him. "Besides, they might find the jewels on him. If they do, then we'll insist on dropping all charges."

Chloe glared at him. "I don't give a damn about the jewels."

The interpreter had turned to her. "Police Officer Fan asks, Please confirm that you saw Jiao Zhe Yu when you came back from the shower and the room was unlocked."

She breathed deeply. "All right, all right, I saw him in the corridor. But that doesn't mean he stole anything."

"Police Officer Fan says there is no need to be angry, Mrs. Winter."

Everything seemed to take forever. First they all had to wait while the hotelman was sent to fetch their passports. Police Officer Fan carefully wrote down all the details from each, then placed them one by one in a tin box on his desk. After that they finally began work on the statement, which was especially laborious as the interpreter had to write everything twice, once in English and once in Chinese.

"Should we sign it?" asked Guy, when it was finally finished.

"Not now," the interpreter told him. "First it must be checked by higher officers and made correct. Police Officer Fan says you will come back here tomorrow morning at nine."

"Tomorrow?" As the bus left early this meant they would be stuck in this town for yet another day. "But we can't stay here. We have to get to Hong Kong."

The interpreter looked at him strangely. "This is a very grave matter."

"Can't we at least have our passports?" asked Chloe.

"Tomorrow."

A gloom hung over them as they walked out into the street. "I really don't like this at all," said Chloe. "I mean, what d'you think they'll do to him?"

Guy shrugged uneasily. "What else could we have said? Everything we told them was true, while we made it quite clear that it might not have been him. Though I don't see who else it could have been."

They stopped at a restaurant and ate hungrily, having had nothing since they had woken. It was still only midday when they walked back outside, and though the thought of a free afternoon in this remote town had been exhilarating the day before, it now seemed oppressive. "I suppose we should make sure there's a bus the day after tomorrow," said Guy.

Nobody had a better idea, and so they made their way to the bus station, though it was a needless visit as the ticket seller simply confirmed what they had suspected: buses ran every day at eight in the morning.

"We won't get to Baolin Temple now, will we?" said Ben glumly as they began walking back to the hotel.

"I don't know," said Chloe distantly. "There's no rush to get down to Hong Kong seeing as I don't have any samples to show."

"You might still get them back," Guy reminded her.

Ben, his gloom gone, began counting days. "If we stay in the real Guangfaochu for two nights and . . ."

Something odd was happening. A short, stout woman with closely cropped gray hair was standing in front of them, blocking their way and looking at them strangely. Guy was just about to step round her when she waved a finger at his face and began shouting out at the top of her voice: a furious shriek of words.

"We don't understand you," said Chloe, with open palms, as if refusing money to a beggar. The woman, rather than being soothed, simply switched her attention to her.

"She's mad," said Guy uneasily. He walked away from her into the street, his family too, but the woman followed, shouting and jabbing her finger into their backs. "Let's just go home," he told them, shouting to be heard.

"Everyone's looking at us," said Tania. It was quite true; the whole street had stopped to watch as they marched along, their pursuer yelling behind them. Some of the looks were puzzled, others angry.

"What d'you think she's saying?" asked Ben.

"How should I know? Mad things." By now they were almost at the hotel and, as Guy hoped, safety, but when they walked inside she did the same, shouting behind them as they hurried up the stairs and along the corridor. They reached the room and Guy slammed the door shut, but she continued shouting from outside. The sound was strangely unnerving, and for a few moments the four of them stood there, not saying a word. Finally Guy shook his head. "I've really had enough of this," he declared, and opening the door, he bellowed at her, "Just go away and leave us alone."

To his surprise this worked: she shot him a furious look and then marched away down the corridor. But a moment later she started again, now from the street below their window.

"D'you think she's Eeyore's mother?" wondered Ben.

"I told you, she's just mad," said Guy.

"She looked a bit like him."

Eventually the shouts outside grew quieter and stopped altogether. When Guy looked out of the window she had gone.

"Perhaps we should go back to the police and say we made a mistake," said Chloe doubtfully.

Nobody said anything, and the moment passed. So they whiled away the afternoon, Tania and Ben silently playing cards, Chloe staring fitfully at the guidebook, and Guy cleaning his Swiss Army penknife. Only when it was dark and the street noise had fallen away to almost nothing did they venture outside. Guy had barely stepped through the doorway of the strip-light restaurant when the owner gave a wave of his hand. "Meio!"

Some part of Guy had been expecting this. He gave the man a stare, about to argue, but then changed his mind. "Come on, let's just go."

"But where are we going to eat?" complained Ben. "I'm really hungry."

"We'll find something."

"This is all because of Eeyore, I know it." Chloe shook her head. "Everyone in this town hates us."

"If they do then they're wrong," said Guy grimly. "It's probably just because we're foreigners."

They were saved by the hotel owner, who had his wife make them a large bowl of rice, meat, and green peppers. They ate hurriedly, greedy from the day's alarms. That night Guy moved the children's beds into his and Chloe's room, and he wedged a chair against the door handle as a precaution. But nobody came.

The next morning they made their way through the busy streets to the police station. The interpreter was already waiting.

"Some good news," he told them with a kind of smile. "Jiao Zhe Yu has confessed to this crime."

Guy felt caught off balance. Was this good? At least it made everything clear. "Have they found the jewelry?"

"Police officers say they are so sorry, still not, but the search will continue strongly. Jiao's confession shows that this crime is now solved." They followed him into Police Officer Fan's room, where Guy saw two neatly typed statements were waiting ready on the desk, with Guy's and Chloe's names at the bottom.

"Police Officer Fan asks, Will you take some tea?"

They all accepted small white cups. Guy glanced at the statement and saw that it had been changed and now began,

We are very grateful to the Guangfaochu police officers who have worked so hard and quickly to solve this grave crime. We also notice most strongly that this crime against visiting foreigners is not at all normal in honest Guangfaochu City.

Chloe had read further. "I can't sign this. It says I saw him walking out of the room with the jewels. That's not true. I just saw him for a second at the end of the corridor."

Police Officer Fan shrugged as if this were of no great significance. "Jiao Zhe Yu admits all these things in his confession," the interpreter explained.

Chloe shook her head. "I'm sorry, but this has to be changed."

The interpreter gave her a weary look. "Then you must come back tomorrow. If it is changed then it must all be written again and made correct by Senior Officer."

"I don't care."

The office fell silent, and Guy half closed his eyes. "Does it really matter, Chloe, seeing as he's confessed to it all anyway? I mean . . ." He felt a sudden, stifling exasperation. "Let's just get it over with." He reached for the pen and scrawled his signature.

Chloe stared at him for a moment. Everyone was waiting. She

gave a kind of shrug—angry and defeated—then took the pen and signed.

The policeman took the four passports from the tin box.

"Police Officer Fan says that because of your urgent traveling it is not necessary to speak at this trial."

"What will happen to him?" Chloe asked.

The interpreter looked away. "I cannot say."

It was all done. Guy pocketed his copy of the statement and they walked out of the building into the street, but then Chloe stopped. "I'm going back. This is all wrong."

The children were watching uneasily, and Guy gave her a look. "I don't like it either, Chloe, but what else can we do?"

"Something. There must be something. I'll say I made a mistake and that he wasn't there."

"Then they'll blame the hotelman instead. Chloe, we didn't make this happen. It's not our fault."

"I don't want to be any part of—"

Just as she stopped speaking Guy became aware of something out of the corner of his eye, swooping down into his line of vision, almost like a bird diving, but heavy. There was a sound that made him think of vegetables hitting a wall, and he saw Tania stagger, clutching her shoulder, as something clattered to the ground. It was a brick. Guy twisted round to the direction it had come from and saw that some people were staring at them, others were carrying on as before, peering at things in the stalls. There was no clue as to who had done this. Now Tania was letting out a wail. He and Chloe ushered her back into the police station, her ripped T-shirt smeared with blood.

"It'll all be all right," soothed Chloe, who had once done a first aid course, her eyes blinking in shock. "It doesn't look like anything really serious. You'll probably just need a few stitches."

The police were as horrified as the Winters themselves and broke into activity, one speeding to fetch bandages, another racing to get their van. In a moment the Winters and the interpreter were riding in the back, Guy holding on to the thick metal grille for balance. The hospital was not far, just outside the town center, and they were soon hurrying down a corridor past rooms that seemed somehow far too bare, like those in school dormitories. Chloe was allowed to stay with Tania while Guy and Ben waited outside with the interpreter.

"I am so sorry about this grave accident," he said unhappily. "Do you want to make a complaint to the police?"

Guy shuddered slightly. "No, no complaint."

Chloe eventually reappeared, looking pale. "She's very upset. I didn't like the doctor at all. It was almost like he wanted to make it hurt more."

Guy felt himself sag. "I'm sure that's not true."

The interpreter was watching them, looking awkward.

Chloe's voice sank to a whisper. "I don't care about any of this anymore. I just want to get out of this place."

It was not so easy. There was a problem with the stitches, some of which had to be done again, and the doctor was worried the wound might become infected. "He wants only best treatment for visitors to our town," the interpreter told them. "We are all very sorry for these terrible happenings."

The one good thing was that they were able to stay at the hospital: none of them had any wish to return to the hotel. The interpreter arranged for Guy, Chloe, and Ben to sleep in an empty room just down the corridor from Tania's ward. Guy asked about the simplest and most direct way to leave the town—all thoughts of Buddhas or kung fu temples were now quite forgotten—and the interpreter said there was a larger town just three hours away by train that had an airport and flights to Hong Kong. He even went to the railway station himself that same afternoon, returning with four tickets. When Guy took out his wallet, he waved his hand in refusal.

"This is a gift from Guangfaochu police officers to be sorry for these grave troubles."

Their time in the hospital passed quickly enough. By the next day Tania had got over much of her shock and played a few rounds of cards with her brother. Her shoulder looked bad with its huge bandage, but she said it did not greatly hurt. The doctor agreed that she could leave the next morning while the interpreter managed to arrange for one of the minivans that scurried about the town crammed with passengers to act as their private taxi. It arrived just on time.

"We won't be long," Guy told Tania and Ben as they drew up outside the hotel. "You can wait here if you like." Neither of the children wanted to be left alone, though, and so they all climbed out. The hotelman jumped up at the sight of them, calling out as they passed—greetings? sympathy?—but Guy had no time for either and simply passed him the money for the bill with a brief nod. The room felt strange, with everything just the same as they had left it two days before, the four beds crammed into the space. The four of them set to work scooping their possessions into their bags. Guy checked beneath the beds, pocketed the padlock from the door, and they all lifted their packs onto their backs. Guy was just about to step out of the door when something made him stop. "What's wrong?"

Chloe was standing in the center of the room, very still, as if trapped in indecision. Slowly she took off her backpack, opened it up, and reaching inside, pulled out a long, thin jewelry case. Guy let out a faint moan. Tania and Ben looked on, their mouths open.

"It was in that pocket between the straps and the frame," said Chloe slowly. "I must have put it there for safety. I only felt it when I put it on my back."

"Chloe." Guy slumped onto one of the beds, slowly shaking his head. "I really don't believe this. It just gets worse and worse." He closed his eyes. "There's nothing for it, we'll just have to go back to the—"

Chloe did not let him finish, staring at him with a strange, clenched look. "We're not going back anywhere. I'm not risking my children for another minute in this place."

Tania and Ben watched in silence. Guy opened his mouth to argue but then closed it again. He could feel the pull of Chloe's words. How good it would be just to be gone. All at once he had a picture of their home, with its large sitting room, the white sofas, and the view of the garden. For some reason he imagined them driving by the sea, and with his whole being he yearned to be home. If they could just get far away from here then none of this would matter, surely. None of it would be real.

"Very well," he said slowly. "Let's just go."

The children were out of the door before them, and they hurried downstairs, almost smiling now, buoyed up by the feeling of escape. They climbed into the minivan, and after just a few moments of creeping through the busy streets they reached a wider road and picked up a little speed.

Oddly enough, Guy felt he sensed the truck even before it came into view, as if in premonition. There had been other times in his life when he had felt that the worst possible thing that could happen—the thing he most dreaded—must happen, and always would, like when he had been dared to write graffiti on a wall at school and the very teacher he had chosen to insult had walked round the corner.

"It's Eeyore," said Ben, not understanding. "What's he doing in there?"

He was standing in the back of a truck just ahead of them with another man, and both of them had wooden signs hanging round their necks with rows of Chinese characters written in black. He had seen them now and was peering down toward the windshield with the strangest look, one that was hard to read, and could have been anger, or confusion, or even hope. Then it was all over. The minivan driver saw a gap in the traffic and slipped past the truck. A few moments later they were waiting with their luggage on the station platform. If the train had not been so late they would have been gone and Guy would never have heard the noise: a distant crack, like something snapping, so faint that he would have doubted he heard it at all except that Chloe flinched slightly beside him.

"He's dead, isn't he?" said Tania quietly when the train started moving.

Chloe had always been proud of the fact that she would discuss anything with her children, no matter how difficult or taboo. This time, however, she found no words. "I don't want to talk about it."

The journey south proved unexpectedly easy, and they reached Hong Kong the next morning. This gave them five full days in the city, far more than they had planned, but they were terrible days. What had happened pressed down on them all, and Guy was aware of a kind of pained numbness as he sweated his way through the hot, humid streets. Sometimes, when he was changing money in a bank, or showering in the hotel, Eeyore's face would appear, staring at him with accusing eyes. Guy's greatest distress, though, was his worry about his family. Chloe was withdrawn and short-tempered in a way that was quite unlike her. Guy had never realized till now how much she was the linchpin of the family, its rudder. It was as if she had left her post.

"You just can't do this," he told her suddenly one morning, as they stood unhappily on the deck of a ferry plowing its way across the harbor toward the dazzling skyline of Hong Kong Island. "It's not fair to any of us."

She did not answer. That afternoon she canceled the meeting with Chen's manager, and for a moment he worried she might throw away the jewels. Three days later, in the small hours of the night, the tension between them finally broke. "I just dreamed about him," she said, waking Guy with a nudge. "How could you make us go to that terrible place?"

"You were the one who said the damn things were lost," he

snapped back. Even as he let his anger out some part of him hoped that this might help matters, but the next day as they flew back, and she sat glumly silent in her seat, he knew this was not so: the air had not been cleared but simply stirred about. If anything the situation seemed to grow worse after they got home. Until then Guy had hoped that the children had not been too much affected, and were just upset by Chloe's moodiness, but now he realized that it was merely that their confusion had not had time to show. Ben broke into sudden arguments over trivial matters, and there were complaints from his school. The one who worried Guy most, though, was Tania, as she hardly spoke to them. Though she never mentioned Sarah Spence, there were other friends, new friends, and she spent ever more nights at their houses, as if she were avoiding her own, while on those rare occasions when she was at home for a meal, she barely looked at her parents. Guy felt he should talk to her but did not know where to start. He began to fear they had lost her.

Christmas came and went, and their unhappiness took on an aura of permanence. Guy never did quite understand why things finally changed. Perhaps it was the improvement in the season, or it was simply that time had passed. He noticed it one weekend in May, when he was in the garden inspecting the lawn mower and heard Chloe and the children in the kitchen, laughing: the sound seemed strange to him, like something new, and suddenly, in that one moment, he was certain that everything would be all right. And largely it was. Some scars remained, and even long afterward he sometimes found himself suddenly flinching at the memory of that small town in China. But over time he thought about it less often. Their lives went on, and even thrived. Guy was promoted at work, Chloe's business bloomed, and the children passed exams and went to universities. They bought a house in the Cotswolds for weekends. Little by little Guy felt closeness between the children, himself, and Chloe return, and sometimes he almost wondered if Eeyore—whom nobody spoke of—had in some way helped bring them together, as an experience, however disastrous, that they all shared. And so the whole business became much what he had hoped it would that moment long ago in the Guangfaochu hotel room. Something far away, that was not quite real, and that could not touch them.

2. Powder

PETER PELHAM WAS aware that something odd was happening as he walked Romulus across the common that bright spring evening. First there was the stranger, who was wearing quite the wrong clothes for exercise, who ran suddenly past him, bumping against his arm. Next, as if in answer to the question just forming in Peter's mind, there was the slow wail of a police siren. Peter Pelham was no vigilante, anything but. It never entered his thoughts to give chase, or even to complain at being bumped, and he merely frowned silently to himself, tugging at Romulus's leash to stop his barking. Only when the fugitive—or whatever he was—had safely disappeared behind a blackberry bush did Peter murmur, with sudden venom, "Stupid prat."

It was all over in a moment, just another small incident of London life, best left well alone, and it was already fading from Peter's mind when he stopped at a bench to sit and wait while Romulus struggled to defecate. Peter was staring at Romulus's graying muzzle and thinking vaguely of vets' bills when he heard a beeping sound from beneath the slats of the bench. It was, unmistakably, the ring of a cell phone, playing "Speed Bonny Boat." Peter let it ring once, twice, three times. On another evening he might have ignored it, but today for some reason he was curious. Glancing down he saw a black shopping bag, and reaching inside, his hand found the cell phone, resting on top of what felt like groceries.

"Hello?"

"Larry? Is that you?"

"Actually, no." Peter wondered how to explain this strange situation. Already his professionally trained mind was scanning for illegalities, but as far as he could see there was nothing against the law about answering an abandoned phone. "You see . . ."

The line went dead.

It was only then that Peter pulled out the bag and saw it was full of small plastic bags, each clear and filled with fine white powder like flour. He dropped the cell phone back in shock. Now finally he made the connection, remembering that the man who had bumped into him had been carrying one just the same. For a moment he was tempted just to shove it back beneath the bench and go, but he knew he could not. A lawyer might not be expected to play vigilante, but he should try to uphold the law, and so Peter got to his feet, picked up the bag, tugged at Romulus's leash, and set out for the police station. The bag was surprisingly heavy, and he shifted it from shoulder to shoulder, hand to hand. As he went he found himself troubled by the thought—which he knew was absurd—that he might be stopped by the police, and they would jump to all the wrong conclusions. His mind was still playing with headlines—"Solicitor Arrested in Drugs Haul"—when he was surprised by the sight of his own blue-painted front door. He had not gone to the police station after all but, from habit, had walked home.

He turned around, ignoring Romulus's puzzled whine, and stepped back into the street. So far he had done nothing remotely reprehensible, and it was only now that his behavior became strange. First he stopped on the sidewalk, standing motionless like a mannequin as he stared with great concentration in the direction of a No Dumping sign. A plane flew overhead, catching him for an instant in the blink of its shadow. Next he glanced up and down the residential street, almost like a criminal, to see if anyone was watching. Nobody was. And then Peter Pelham, dependable London solicitor, who had never broken the law in his life beyond the occasional parking ticket, walked round to the side of his house, unlocked the garage door, and breathing fast, swung it open and marched inside with his black bag of drugs.

Long afterward he would consider that this action was an aberration of character, entering a plea—to himself—of temporary insanity. But was this really true? For a long time there had been a discontent about Peter Pelham: the anger of one who feels that life has treated him unfairly. What made this surprising was that almost anybody would have agreed he was rather fortunate. Everything about him said so. He was a solicitor with a well-established firm, his wife, Harriet, worked part-time for a charity run by a baronet's sister, and they lived in one of London's more exclusive suburbs: a leafy ex-village with a pond, an old church, and a growing number of celebrity residents. And yet Peter did not think of himself as fortunate at all. He was constantly worrying about money. It seemed simply to pass through him like overspiced food, and hardly a day went by without some new sum being nibbled away. There were mortgage payments, pension payments, the children's school and university fees, household bills, private health bills, insurance bills, credit card bills. To say nothing of car tax, council tax, and of course, income tax. All in all it was a rare day when the Pelham current account was not overdrawn and accruing bank charges.

The root cause of his troubles, as Peter was only too aware, was his career. It was not that this had gone wrong so much as that it had stopped going right. Once—so long ago that now it seemed hard to believe it had ever been the case—he had been a promising new recruit to McLeans, a leading firm of solicitors, and he had gone to work each morning full of hungry confidence. But then something unconscionable happened: nothing happened. He waited patiently for the moment when he would be told the good news that he had been chosen as an equity partner, but somehow it never came. Several years slipped by, and he was still a lowly salaried partner, a temporary state of being, not really a partner at all. His panic grew as he saw others in the firm—others newer and younger than himself—slip past him, like so many queue jumpers. He could not understand it and would lie awake in the night angrily wondering why. Had he made some mistake? There had been a few, it was true, but nothing, surely, to warrant this? Had he offended someone? Did he have an enemy? Another possibility—that he was seen as a poor addition to the firm, unable to contribute to the general wealth—was too painful to consider.

"You haven't had much luck bringing in clients, have you?" remarked a colleague one day over lunch: a lunch that Peter guessed afterward had been set into motion by others. "That makes things very awkward."

Peter took the hint and reluctantly began looking round for somewhere less exalted to step down to. Blakeys seemed just the thing. It was not such a bad firm, and they assured him he would make full partner soon enough. And then, unbelievably, it all happened again: time slipped by and nothing happened. Peter veered between finding reasons—the economic downturn, the firm's troubles—and simple anger. How dare they? They had promised. They were liars and cheats. At night he sometimes dreamed of revenge—a gory massacre of Equity Partners—but in the morning he went meekly to the office just as usual. Should he try again, lowering his sights further, and look for something outside London, or even in another area of the law? The thought occurred to him, often, but somehow it never took root. He had no wish to do either. Staring at his face in the mirror in the morning as he shaved, he could see something had changed, as if some spark had faded from his eyes and he had adapted to match his failure. Nobody sacked him and so he remained at Blakeys, not by decision but from inertia, aware of the changing glances of others as his position in the firm became increasingly eccentric: a salaried partner who had become somehow stuck, like a caterpillar barred from the cocoon.

As if this were not provocation enough, there was also the dreadful business of the Pelhams' neighbors. When Peter and his family had first come to live on Wilmshurst Avenue, it had been far from fashionable, possessing a kind of flea-bitten gentility, with cars shrouded beneath plastic mackintoshes. The Pelhams' neighbors included a taxi driver, a madwoman with moss growing under her car, and someone who worked for the BBC. Peter and Harriet enjoyed thinking of themselves as a flagship of grandeur. Since then, though, the area had changed beyond all recognition. Dumpsters came and went as young arrivals set their money to work, violently improving their new properties. Now the High Street gleamed with croissanteries, the car mackintoshes and the madwoman's moss had long been displaced by Range Rovers, and it was the Pelhams who felt flea-bitten. Not that anyone was unkind to them—people always smiled and said hello on the street—and yet they felt themselves somehow looked down upon: they were rarely invited to the fashionable parties that they glimpsed through front windows, with marquees squashed into back gardens. At times Harriet grew quite angry.

"No wonder people think we're odd," she complained one evening as they loaded the dishwasher. "We must be the only people on the street who haven't built an extension."

For Peter there were more pressing concerns. He had accidentally scraped the car against a wall, denting the metalwork, and, fearing the shame of a bounced check, had put off having it repaired. Now two months had passed, the scrape still glowered at him reproachfully, and he had begun to make lighthearted remarks to neighbors. "Isn't it awful. I'm surprised we haven't been run out of the neighborhood for lowering the tone. Actually we've been meaning to get it done for ages, but we've both been so busy . . ." Money, money, everything was money, Peter would reflect during moments, which struck him from time to time, of disgust at the materialistic world in which he lived. There were also moments of sudden panic. From his childhood days Peter had always assumed that he was destined to be in some way remarkable. Now he was in his fifties, stumbling slowly toward the horror of his vanishing point, and this showed no sign of happening. He was utterly replaceable. How had this come to pass? It simply was not right.

And then, that bright spring evening, he found the black shopping bag beneath the slats of the bench. His only experience of drugs till then was a joint at a university party, which had made him violently sick. He was not even certain what substance this was. And yet, as he stood on the pavement in front of his house, listening to the drone of aircraft engines overhead, he knew precisely what he was holding in his hand. He was holding concentrated danger that, in one brief instant, could destroy every one of his fifty-three years of cautious, law-abiding life. He was holding something of vast, unknown value. Most of all he was holding a piece of chance, dropped from heaven. Peter had never thought of himself as lucky—he was the sort of person who never won lottery money or found a banknote on the ground—and if anything overcame his sense of fear that evening and lured him to the garage door it was the feeling that this windfall was something he was owed. As to what he might do with it, he had little clear idea. Not yet. What had carried him forward, more than anything, was an angry urge to hoard.

Even then, when his criminality was only a few seconds old and still easily reversible, there were worries. Harriet would be home soon. He knew this was something he could not explain to his wife. There was an old-fashioned Puritanism to Harriet that displayed itself most clearly as she sat over the Sunday papers, when she would comment with clipped approval on new prison sentences, especially those handed down to fallen professionals, from molester priests to embezzling college bursars. It was the pleasure of finding others far worse off than themselves. Peter knew she would never understand about the bag full of bags, which, for that matter, he barely understood himself. And yet he did not like the thought of keeping her in the dark. Their marriage had long ceased to contain the passion of the romantic films that she liked to watch, and yet in a curious way it was not such a bad marriage, based as it was on a kind of camaraderie of family management, and until now any falsehoods between them had been small ones. For a moment Peter hesitated, wondering if he should walk out of the garage and go to the police station after all. It was his anger that held him back. This was his redress. How dare anyone take it from him?

Oddly enough, in view of Peter's profession, the one thing that did not trouble him at all was guilt at breaking the law. He was frightened of being caught and punished, certainly, but he felt no guilt. Then again, perhaps this was precisely *because* of his profession. There had been a time when the law had formed a kind of personality in his mind, and was something he would hate to offend, like a respected schoolteacher or an angry God, but this had long passed. He had seen too many doubtful clients triumph and now regarded the law more as a kind of landscape in which to fight, using its thickets and hollows to catch out one's opponent. Who was right or wrong was merely one aspect of the struggle. What mattered was winning.

So, feeling a slight sweat break out on his neck, he switched off the cell phone and dropped it into the bag, which he hid behind an old storage heater. The rest of the evening passed surprisingly quietly. The children were away—Ginny at university, Theo at his school—and Peter and his wife ate leftover chicken and watched a documentary about the First World War. Staring at the blurred footage of trenches, Peter slipped between forgetting about the bag and suddenly remembering it again, and though it scared him, of course, it also filled him with a strange excitement. The next morning he was impatient to revisit his discovery, and telling Harriet that he needed to check the Mini's tax disk, he returned to the garage, where he crouched for some moments, squeezing the packets between his fingers, wondering what it was. Some substances were more valuable than others, and he was curious to know how much this was worth. At a whim he reached back into the bag, and his hand trembling slightly, he slipped the cell phone into his jacket pocket.

It was a quiet day at work with just a couple of meetings, and he spent most of his time researching a case of disputed planning permission for a parking lot. As he went through the facts, he could sense the cell phone in his pocket, transmitting possibilities. After an hour he surprised himself by suddenly taking it out and pressing the power button. Nothing happened. He returned to his work and had quite forgotten the thing when he was startled by the faint bleeping of "Speed, Bonny Boat."

"Larry?" This time it was a different voice, one that sounded well educated.

Peter hung up.

All that day he toyed with the idea of switching it on again, and several times he took the phone from his pocket and studied it for a moment or two. The next morning, finally, he pressed the power button. To his surprise it rang almost at once.

"Hi, Larry."

Again it was a different voice. "Actually it's not Larry," Peter began.

The line went dead.

Peter had had little clear idea of what he would have said, and yet he felt strangely annoyed that the caller had rung off. This time he did not switch off the phone. A call came half an hour later.

"Larry?"

Why not at least see what he wanted? "Larry's gone."

"Who are you?" The voice sounded wary.

Peter couldn't very well give his real name. He tried to think. "Jeremy." It was the name, he realized, of one of his firm's rising young stars.

The caller paused. "All right then, Jeremy, can you come over? It's sort of urgent."

Peter scribbled down the address on a piece of Blakeys letterhead.

"So when will you be round?"

Until now Peter felt safe in the fact that he had agreed to nothing. Now he hesitated. If anything decided him it was probably the address, which was in Chelsea: the sort of area where he would have liked to live. Why not, he wondered, a little breathless. Just this once? All his life he had lived correctly, and where had it got him? He was, he realized, bored with his existence, even with himself, and the thought of doing this warmed him, making him feel like somebody in a film. Besides, he couldn't believe it would be particularly dangerous. Never in all his life had he been stopped by the police: he was not the sort of person they stopped. "All right," he agreed. "I'll come over this evening. Around seven."

"I need quite a lot," explained the voice. "Forty Gs."

The phrasing baffled Peter for a moment. "Forty grams?" Peter had never been much good at the metric system.

Suspicion returned to the caller's voice. "This had better be okay."

"It will, don't worry."

Peter left work early that afternoon and took the tube and bus back to his house, going directly into the garage. How much was forty grams? The packets looked so small, and after a moment's indecision he slipped ten of them into his jacket pocket to be sure. That was when he heard the thump of the front door and the faint thud of footsteps from the house: Harriet was home early from her charity, which was bad luck as Peter had been intending to use her kitchen scales to measure out the quantity. So he closed the garage door quietly like a thief and walked to the High Street. The only scales he could find were in a trendy boutique—an Italian device in orange plastic with goofy eyes and splayed feet that looked better suited to weighing Parmesan cheese—and he discreetly weighed one of the bags as he sat on a bench overlooking the river, finding it was exactly ten grams. He was nervous about the exchange, but in the event this proved surprisingly easy. He took the tube to the address and rang the bell of a neat mews house, whose owner—young in his designer jeans and T-shirt—eyed Peter warily as he let him inside. "So what happened to Larry?"

What indeed? Peter's thoughts turned briefly to the retreating figure of the man who had bumped his arm. All he could remember about him was sneakers, a hint of paunch, and unwashed black hair. Peter assumed he was safely in jail. "He went off to the States."

Another frown. "He never said anything about that."

Peter cut short the discussion by handing over the four packets. He had been worrying about what price to charge, but fortunately this question solved itself.

"Usual rate?"

Peter nodded and accepted an envelope. As he walked back to the tube station his curiosity got the better of him, and he stopped at a telephone kiosk. Conveniently shielded by a screen of cards advertising prostitutes, he opened the envelope and, to his own amazement, counted out forty scarlet fifty-pound notes. He grinned all the way home. Two thousand pounds, and not a penny tax to pay. First thing tomorrow he would book the Volvo to be repaired.

By the next evening he had changed his mind about doing just one delivery, and he sold twenty grams to a woman in Battersea. Noticing the inflamed area between her nostrils, he concluded that the packets contained cocaine. So much the better, as he had never liked the idea of heroin, which seemed a druggie's drug: cocaine was so much classier. The next day, Friday, he bought a new charger cable for the cell phone as its battery was low, and that evening he made two more deliveries. One was to a youthfully gray-haired man in Putney who looked vaguely familiar, so Peter guessed he had seen him on television. The second was to a young couple in Roehampton who gave him a cup of tea.

"I'm glad you've taken over," the girl told him. "We never really liked Larry. And sometimes it was days before he'd bother to come over."

Sitting on the bus home, Peter basked in amazement. In three evenings he had accumulated over four thousand five hundred pounds. He had always assumed this world would be full of lowlife types, perhaps even deranged by the drugs they were taking, but so far his customers had been from much the same middling to wealthy London milieu as himself. He did not even feel as if he were doing anything very wrong. These were grown-up, educated people who should know their own minds, and he was giving them what they wanted. Where was the harm in that? He was even quite enjoying the sense of danger, and walking back along Wilmshurst Avenue, he felt more alive than he had in years.

That same evening disaster struck. He and Harriet were sitting watching a program about Australian animal life when she broke into a frown. "What's that noise?"

Just audible above the yelps of the sea lions was the faint yet unmistakable sound of "Speed, Bonny Boat." He had forgotten to switch off the cell phone. "That's mine," said Peter, as casually as he was able, and he reached for his jacket. Pressing the receive key, he heard the voice of his first customer, the man from Chelsea.

"Jeremy? I know it's rather late, but . . ."

Harriet was looking at him strangely. "That's not your phone."

Peter found himself caught awkwardly between two conversations. "I'm rather busy just now," he said into the cell phone. "Could you ring back tomorrow?"

"But tomorrow's no good. I've got some people coming over here tonight, and . . ."

Peter tried to think of words that would give nothing away. "I'm sorry," he said briefly, "but it's just not possible. Now look, I really have to go." He disconnected.

Harriet was staring at him. "What's going on, Peter?"

"It's just something to do with a case."

The trouble was that Harriet knew him far too well. "You're lying. You're so bad at it." Her voice went quiet. "Peter, are you having some kind of affair?"

Her accusation took him by surprise, and he felt somehow resentful that she could even imagine such a thing. Now he saw she was struggling not to cry, which he found shocking as Harriet never cried. His mind searched for some harmless explanation for the strange telephone but could find none. How on earth had he got himself into this?

"So you are," she concluded, her expression crumbling.

"No no, you don't understand," he insisted. Anything, even the truth, seemed better than if she believed he was betraying her, as that, he knew, would be the end of them, and he scrabbled for words. "I . . . found the phone on the common."

She frowned, unsure. "What d'you mean?"

It had all gone wrong, as wrong as it could, and he saw no way out now but to finish. "There was something else I found, too," he said hopelessly. He could not bring himself to explain, as words seemed to make it all worse. "I'd better show you." So he led her into the garage.

For a moment she stood staring at the bag full of bags, pale with anger. "You mean you've been . . ." She shook her head in disbelief. "I simply cannot believe you've done something so stupid."

He could not believe it himself. How on earth had this seemed a good idea? "Nobody saw me, I'm sure of it," he said feebly. "I'll get rid of all of it tomorrow. I'll throw it in the river. I'll even get rid of the money." In a rush to show his contrition he took the banknotes from where he had hidden them behind a rusting can of weed killer.

She glanced at the money with new disgust. "For goodness' sake, how much is there?"

"About four and a half thousand. I'll get rid of it all."

"What have you been doing, Peter? Did you sell another one like that?" She pointed scornfully at the shopping bag.

"Oh no." He picked out ten of the small packets. "More like that."

The garage fell into silence. Peter waited for her judgment, praying for some hint that she might, at least one day, be able to forgive him, yet Harriet was not a very forgiving person. They had been together for so long that he could not imagine life alone. The awful possibility occurred to him that she might even report him to the police. It did not seem very likely, and yet she could be so severe. All the while another part of him was hoping against hope that she might somehow let them keep the four thousand five hundred pounds. He had already booked the car to be repaired and wanted to have the window frames painted as they were flaking.

It was only after several long moments had passed that he realized, from the hard look on her face, she was not passing judgment after all, but was trying to calculate the total value of the bag.

FROM THAT MOMENT onward Harriet took charge of all arrangements. The next day was a Saturday, and she went out after breakfast, returning with a neat electronic weighing machine. "It says it's accurate to one gram. That should be enough." Next she moved the bag and the money to the cellar. "There's no room in that garage." Finally, impressing Peter with her thoroughness, she counted all of the small packages and checked their weight. "Some of these aren't correct at all," she announced disapprovingly. "I'm surprised you haven't had complaints."

Peter felt greatly relieved. Aside from the unpleasantness of lying to her, everything was so much easier now: he had a helper, and they could even use the car. They made their first delivery that same afternoon, to the customer in Chelsea, taking the Mini as it was better for parking. Harriet stayed in the driver's seat—"We don't want to get clamped"—and three minutes later Peter walked back from the mews house and handed her the envelope. She counted out the money beneath the dashboard.

"Let's get a Range Rover."

After that they drove to Kew, where Peter delivered twenty grams to a drawn-faced man in an undecorated flat, who hardly said a word during the transaction.

"I don't know much about any of this," said Harriet as they drove away, "but aren't these people buying rather a lot?"

Peter had been wondering too. "I think some of them must be selling it on. We're supplying other suppliers."

"That's a piece of luck. Otherwise it would take forever."

From there they went on to a smart house in Richmond, where the customer insisted on making the exchange through the half-closed front door. All that Peter saw of him was a glimpse of gray hair and hooded eyes. Harriet was quite affronted. "He didn't even let you in."

"And he only took five grams."

"Write down his number from the phone. I don't think we should bother with that one again."

On the way back Harriet parked by a clothing shop on the High Street. "Don't you think it's time you had a new jacket?"

A few moments later he had one. It was younger in style than what he would normally buy, yet today he somehow did feel younger. He wore it that evening when they went to Corrado's, where they had been only once before, for Ginny's eighteenth, when Peter had struggled hard not to show his anguish at the bill. This time he had no such worries: they ordered a particularly expensive wine and paid in cash. They were just about to go when one of their neighbors walked by. "I didn't know you came here."

"From time to time," said Peter, feeling oddly relaxed.

The neighbor smiled and was about to move on when he turned. "By the way, I've been meaning to say, we're having a little drinks party on Friday. Do come."

That night Peter and Harriet made love in a way they had not for years, with a kind of hunger, even a kind of wickedness. Perhaps it was the sense of danger, or of something illicit shared, but Peter could not remember feeling closer to her. The next day they went to the showroom and ordered a Range Rover. Harriet decided it was best to go with the purchase plan and pay from their bank account. "Otherwise it'll be too obvious. We'll pay for every-day things with the cash."

The trouble was that cash was flowing in so fast everyday costs could not begin to keep up. By the end of the next week, despite extensive spending, they had more than nine thousand pounds hidden in the wine box in the cellar. Harriet, who had more free time than Peter, did her best to think of purchases, and soon they had a new fridge, a new television, a new cherry tree in the garden, and a new computer. She looked into having an extension built.

"Are you sure we should be getting so many things all at once?" Peter worried. "The neighbors will notice."

"They'll just think we've come into some inheritance."

She was right. Their neighbors in Wilmshurst Avenue seemed to regard the Pelhams' rise to prosperity as being quite in the or-der of things, even viewing it with relief, as it meant the street was not sullied by a scraped Volvo or flaking window paint. In fact Pe-ter and Harriet found themselves more popular than they had been for a long time. Perhaps because of their new wealth, or sim-ply because they seemed more cheerful these days, the invitation they were extended at Corrado's led to others, until they began to feel almost like new arrivals, and had to turn down invitations as they got in the way of deliveries. At work, too, Peter noticed a change, and he found he was regarded with glances of greater re-spect by his superiors. He could only guess that this was a conse-quence of the utter disdain with which he now regarded Blakeys. How could he take it seriously when he earned ten or twenty times as much in a few evening hours as during his long, dreary office day?

"Been somewhere nice, Peter?"

"Actually no, I haven't been away."

"Really? Somehow you look like you've been on holiday."

Not that he would make equity partner—it was far too late for that—but he did find himself given a high-profile case to research.

A year before he would have been a little pleased; now he didn't care.

May and June slipped by. Work progressed on the extension, the shopping bag grew gradually emptier, and their list of clients grew, including several new ones who came through word of mouth. Peter found this rather satisfying as he felt it attested to his own reliability. Between their work and their deliveries, he and Harriet had never been so busy, and they had to resort to take-out food and a dog walker for Romulus. And yet for all their long hours, they had not felt so well in years. Peter loved the charged feeling in his blood when they drove out in the Mini each evening, and often they would celebrate their sales with lovemaking. Once, laughing at the very idea, they did it in the hallway on a bed of creased banknotes.

There were awkward moments too, of course. Peter hated it when a customer called them round and didn't have the money to pay. He firmly refused to give credit, and once or twice things got nasty. On several occasions their anonymity was threatened: Peter had to cancel several deliveries when he realized a new client's address was nearby his own house, and once he was forced to hang up in midconversation when he recognized a caller as an old acquaintance from university. Probably the worst moment, though, was at a dinner party he and Harriet went to, where conversation was monopolized by a woman recounting the grim details of her daughter's addiction, and her own struggles to have her attend a rehab clinic. The Pelhams sat quietly as the other dinner guests cooed their concern. When they left, Peter found himself feeling decidedly uneasy.

"That was rather dreadful," he remarked as they walked home.

He had underestimated Harriet's single-mindedness. "It certainly was. I'm amazed nobody changed the subject. I mean really."

"I meant it was a terrible story."

Harriet shrugged. "The girl should just have just known when to stop. It's no different from drinkers and alcoholics."

Peter frowned. "I don't know. And what about that woman in Hammersmith they were talking about who was found in her car?"

"What about her? If someone swallows a bottle of aspirin, you don't go blaming the chemist."

"But what if Ginny got mixed up in something like that? Or Theo?"

"Don't be ridiculous. They're both far too sensible."

Ginny and Theo were much in their thoughts as they would soon be back for the summer holidays. The prospect of their return put Peter and Harriet in a dilemma. Until then the children had returned only for the occasional weekend, which had been easily managed, but two months would be a different matter.

"Perhaps we should just tell the customers that we won't be making any more deliveries till September," suggested Peter.

"I don't think we can," considered Harriet, "as they'll go elsewhere and it'll be hard to get them back. Besides, I don't think this is such a problem. Ginny and even Theo will be out a good deal in the evenings, and we'll just tell them that we're busy ourselves these days. We can get one of those traveling boxes that you can lock for the cellar, just in case one of them goes down there."

Matters grew more complicated when Harriet's father, Joe, rang up to say he too was coming to stay. This was not a request but an announcement as Joe had helped them buy the house— helped them a good deal—and so had clearly defined visiting rights: the spare room was referred to as "grandfather's room." A retired country doctor, he came several times a year to catch up on old friends, to buy things he could not find in local shops, and to complain about London. Even now Harriet was not unduly troubled.

"He'll only be here a few days, and he goes to bed very early. It'll be fine."

Peter wondered if they had made the right decision when Ginny—the first to arrive—bombarded them with questions. "How come you've got all this new stuff?"

The briefest explanation seemed the best. "We just thought it was time to sort out the house. It's been getting into quite a state."

"But you always say we can't afford anything."

"Perhaps we've been overcautious."

Theo was less questioning. "Cool computer. Does it burn DVDs?"

Harriet's father was the one least impressed by their purchases. "I see you've got one of those dreadful cars. Awful tosh. Nobody in the country would touch one." But he went to bed early, just as Harriet had said, and for several days everything worked out surprisingly well. Ginny went to her summer job at the flower shop during the day and was out on most evenings, while even Theo was fairly busy. Joe was the only one who showed much curiosity about Harriet and Peter's busy evenings. "Regular gadabouts these days, aren't you," he observed disapprovingly. "Watch out for your livers, that's all I can say."

One of their nights out was genuine: a neighbor's marquee dinner, which Harriet was determined not to miss. They enjoyed the occasion though there was a price to pay afterward, and the next night saw them hurrying back and forth across London in the Mini to catch up with orders. The traffic was bad, and they were late by the time they finally parked near the last address, in Barons Court. The customer, who looked barely out of his teens, had a smugness that seemed faintly sinister, and he would have been struck off their list except that he bought so freely. Harriet joined Peter for the sale, offering a little comfort in numbers, though on this occasion Peter saw he need not have worried: turning a corner of the long corridor that sounded faintly of pipes, he saw the customer's door was slightly ajar and music was booming out.

"It looks like he's having a party."

The customer ushered them back into the hallway of the flat, where it was quieter. "Cool. I was getting worried you weren't going to make it."

"Twenty grams?" checked Peter. Harriet, efficient as ever, had already measured out the amount, and in a moment the packets and the money had been exchanged. Peter and Harriet were just turning to leave when something made them stop: a peal of laughter that rang out from the closed door beside them. It was, unmistakably, Ginny. Peter felt pulled in two directions. He was appalled, of course, by the thought of his daughter—his baby— being in a place like this. But to intervene . . . "Come on, let's just leave," he told Harriet, trying to take her arm.

She pushed him away with an angry look. "Let go of me."

The customer was looking puzzled. "What's up?"

Harriet was already reaching for the door, and so, with a dull sense of rising disaster like an itch, Peter followed her into what he saw was the kitchen, its table strewn with packets of crisps. For just a fraction of a second Peter saw Ginny before she saw them, leaning against a cupboard, her head thrown back and her eyes half closed in delight at whatever had made her laugh. Between her fingers was a long, neatly rolled joint. Then her smile fell away.

"Oh, God."

Peter peered round the room, and it was then that he saw Theo, his mouth hanging open in amazement. This grew worse and worse.

"You're both coming home this moment," said Harriet tersely.

The children stood up in shocked obedience, and for one brief instant Peter hoped Harriet might somehow get away with this, but then a defiant look came into Ginny's eyes. "What the hell are you doing here anyway? Have you been following me?"

Even now it might have been all right except for the customer, who broke into a strange laugh. "You mean these are your folks, Ginnsy? But they've just sold me twenty Gs of the best coke."

The room fell into a profound silence. The handful of other guests stared, and a girl with a navel ring let out a kind of giggle.

Theo frowned in new wonderment. Ginny was staring at her parents with the strangest look. "What's going on?"

Peter felt oddly quiet, the stillness of complete despair. Everything was ruined, without question, and yet even now, when it was far too late, his instinct was to try to keep things quiet. "Let's go home."

This time Ginny did not argue, and they tramped down the long, carpeted corridors in silence and crammed themselves into the Mini. "Now I understand how you got all that stuff," said Ginny, sounding almost as if she might cry. "I just don't believe this."

Peter tried to think of something to make things look better. There was nothing, nothing at all. "It was an accident. We found it on the common."

Harriet, as ever, was more aggressive. "At least we don't take the stuff."

Ginny was outraged. "I had a joint, Mum. I'd never touch coke."

"Oh?" said Harriet almost primly. "Then why was he buying it?"

"Toby? Toby would take anything."

It was then that the interior of the car was filled with the sound of "Speed, Bonny Boat." Peter, driving, reached into his pocket. "Yes?"

The voice was unfamiliar. "Jeremy? I need thirty grams. It's sort of urgent."

"This really isn't a good time."

"I can come to you," the voice offered. "Give me your address?"

"Wilmshurst Av——" Peter stopped himself. As if things weren't bad enough already, now he was telling some stranger where they lived. "Look, I can't help you." He rang off.

"Another customer?" asked Ginny acidly.

"I don't know how you could take Theo to a place like that," said Harriet in instant counterattack.

"He took me," said Ginny indignantly. "Toby's his friend, not mine."

Yet another blow. Theo had always been the good one, or so they thought. Peter drove slowly through suburban streets, not wanting to arrive.

"Is that true?" Harriet demanded.

Theo was undaunted, alarmingly so. "I want a new computer," he replied casually. "A really good laptop."

"What?"

"The thing I've got is ancient. Nobody at school has them anymore. And you got all that stuff for yourselves."

"You haven't answered my question."

They had reached Wilmshurst Avenue, and Peter was just opening the car door when he again heard "Speed, Bonny Boat."

"Yes?" he snapped.

"I rang just now."

"I told you," said Peter angrily. "I just can't—" Puzzlingly the line went dead, but even then Peter did not make the connection. Nor did he when, from the corner of his eye, he noticed a car creeping slowly toward them along the street. But he did, finally, when it drew to a halt just in front of theirs and three men clambered out, two bulging in their shirts. They looked so much like something out of a cheap film that for an instant, despite his rising fear, Peter almost wanted to laugh.

"I guessed you'd be somewhere round here," said the smallest of the three, "as that's where Larry got took."

"Who's this?" asked Ginny. Even Harriet looked uneasy. The family crisis was forgotten, at least for now.

"I don't know," said Peter, though he could guess. Oddly enough this possibility—that someone might come to reclaim the shopping bag—had hardly occurred to him until then, he had thought of it so much as something owed to him.

"Roy," the stranger introduced himself. "Shall we have our chat inside?"

Once they were off the street, they would be helpless in the face of . . . Of what? Peter wondered if he should kick up a fuss and try to attract attention from the other houses—their lights were on—in the hope that Roy might panic and leave them be. But even then he knew deep down that this was beyond him: even now he could not bear the thought of the neighbors witnessing their shame. Peter meekly turned the key, aware of a strange sense of unreality as he held open the door for Roy and his two helpers, with their faint odor of sweating muscle and their swollen shoulders that brushed against the doorframe.

"You don't look the part," observed Roy. "You look like you should be working in a bank. Nice house." Even in his compliments there was an audible menace.

Peter tried to appear equal to the situation, hardening his voice. "What d'you want?"

It was an unwise move, provoking Roy to show his power, and he grabbed Peter by the collar, then pushed him away so that he almost lost balance. "What d'you think I want, Four Eyes? A ticket to the ballet? Larry only paid the up front. You owe me twenty-five K."

Peter had never been brave, and he would comply with any demand—comply eagerly—if it meant there would be no trouble. For a moment he panicked himself with thoughts of injuries to faces, eyes, fingers. Twenty-five thousand? What if they did not have enough? For the last few weeks he and Harriet had been too busy to count up their takings, so he had no idea how much they had. Already he regretted spending so much on the new television, the fridge, and that damn cherry tree.

Harriet, to his shock, was on another tack entirely. "But that's our money. We earned it."

"Harriet, please," Peter tried to quiet her, amazed by her lack of instinct.

"You didn't earn it," Roy corrected her. "You nicked it."

"We're the ones who've been driving all round London making deliveries."

"So?"

The last thing that could have occurred to Peter at this moment was that something else could go wrong, but it did. A voice called out from the top of the stairs. "What on earth's going on?" Harriet's father was staring down at them, looking like a set of bones in pajamas.

"Dad's been selling coke," said Ginny simply.

He looked puzzled. "That awful brown drink?"

"Cocaine."

The old man's mouth opened in wonder, and he stared at Peter with a mixture of disgust and glee. "A druggie! My daughter's married to a druggie. I always knew there was something funny about you."

Peter hardly cared. What difference could this make? He might as well put up a sign by the door, Peter Pelham, Cocaine Vendor.

Roy, though, was losing patience. "I don't want to spoil the party, but can you give me my fucking money?"

"Who's that?" demanded Joe.

"I'm the debt collector, Grandpa. And if I don't get paid nice and quick, I'll start getting very annoyed."

The hall fell silent as even Joe sensed danger.

"It's here," said Peter, leading the way to the cellar. For some reason—a kind of redundant squeamishness—he disliked the idea of Ginny, Theo, and Harriet's father seeing what was down there, but he could hardly stop them, and soon the cellar was crowded with people, all watching as he opened the traveling box and removed the bag of bags—still a good third full—and then took out the Fortnum's hamper basket beneath, full of banknotes that Harriet had sorted neatly into different denominations. Peter rather assumed Roy would take it all, but no.

"Go on then, start counting."

It took so long. Every now and then Peter would glance round and see them all silently staring: Ginny, Theo, Harriet, her father, Roy, and his two muscled helpers. Was money that interesting? It seemed it was. As the minutes passed and Peter's murmured numbers climbed from five to ten, then into the teens and twenties, with still lots to go, he began to relax. There would be enough. More than enough, in fact: as he counted out the last note there was still a large heap remaining.

Roy scooped the money into a plastic bag. "I'll say good night then." He gave a faint laugh. "Just don't do it again."

They all marched back up the stairs, and Peter found himself seeing Roy and his two thugs to the door like so many dinner guests. Roy was about to step out into the street when he stopped. "Tell me, how long did it take you to make that stash?"

Peter eyed him suspiciously. What was he after now? "A couple of months."

"That's not bad, you know. Better than Larry any day, lazy little slug." He thought for a moment. "When you're finished with that lot, would you like another?"

Peter gave a kind of half laugh. "Definitely not."

SATURDAY MORNING BROKE quietly over the Pelham household. Peter woke with a shock, having dreamed that none of this had happened, and opening his eyes, he saw Harriet already dressed. "I'm going down," she told him, her face set. "I'm damned if I'm going to let her lecture me."

As Peter washed and shaved he found himself wondering if he should pack a bag. Did the police let you take one, or was he thinking of Nazis in wartime films? Creeping downstairs, like an intruder in his own house, he could hear Harriet's and Ginny's voices from the sitting room. Rather to his surprise, Ginny sounded frustrated, like a tennis player searching vainly for a smash shot. "What d'you mean, understand? You're the ones who were always going on about the evil of drugs."

Peter shuffled toward the kitchen, concentrating on the simple and comforting thought of breakfast, though he left the door ajar to hear. Harriet's voice was slow and calm, so he missed half her words, but he caught "lives haven't been easy," "your poor father," "money worries," and "your and Theo's education." Harriet finished with a triumphantly audible "I'm not saying everything we did was right, but we did it for you." Peter found himself impressed: she was almost making it seem like this was Ginny's fault, and it occurred to him that Harriet would make a damn good barrister. Far better than Ginny, whose voice was shrill and excitable, as she lost the battle for self-control.

"You're making yourself sound like Mother Teresa. You're a pair of drug pushers, for God's sake."

"Don't be absurd, Ginny, we never pushed anything. People rang us. It was all we could do to keep up." Harriet's voice was almost prim. "And we never touched it ourselves."

"Most people would say you should be in jail."

Peter shuddered slightly over the coffee machine.

"Sometimes," said Harriet serenely, "you have to take risks for the good of your family."

Ginny's voice rang out as she opened the door to the hall. "This is just obscene. It's like I don't know who you are." And with that she clumped up the stairs. He who holds the battlefield wins the victory, Peter thought to himself, but then the distressing realization came to him that he and Harriet had just thrown away any remaining influence they had over their daughter: never again would they be able to tell her off for being late or drunk or having the wrong boyfriend. The idea would have been more disturbing except that there were others that were far worse, such as the half dozen party guests who had been in Toby's kitchen. They were sure to recount what they had seen—it was not every day that you found your friends' mum and dad selling cocaine—and the story would travel. Not for the first time Peter spooked himself into thinking he heard a sudden knock at the door, but it was Joe, plodding down the stairs. This would be more trouble. Or would it? Peter was surprised to see he was carrying his suitcase.

"Harriet," he called out, sounding almost subdued. "I want you to take me to the station. I'm going home."

Peter assumed the crisis would rise to some final, terrible climax, but instead the rest of the day was quiet, as Ginny strode about the house in angry silence. Worse was to come. A couple of days after Toby's party—or "that night" as Peter and Harriet now referred to it—she appeared in the sitting room as they were watching the news. "Jean's asked me to go with her to church this Sunday, so I'll be out all morning."

Jean worked with her at the flower shop, but before now Ginny had talked of her disparagingly, describing her as "a real little God Squad," so there was no mistaking the significance of this announcement. Ginny—rebel Ginny, with her Green views and her radical-chic clothes—going to church? The idea appalled Peter. "Right you are," he answered lamely.

Theo struck the next day. Curiously enough, Peter had not been so worried about him until then, as he had seemed relatively unaffected, and his only protest had been to avoid family meals, which Peter suspected sprang more from convenience than principle, allowing him to play computer games in his room without interruption. Then Peter came home from work one evening and found his son slumped on the sofa smoking a cigarette.

"That's a very dirty habit" was all that Peter could think of saying.

"Is it, Dad?" Theo answered with a smirk.

The next day Peter found him smoking a long, neatly rolled joint. "Theo . . . ," Peter began.

Theo feigned wide-eyed curiosity. "Yes, Dad?"

"Can't you at least do that outside?" Peter left the room rather than witness his demand being ignored. The thought returned to him as he tramped purposelessly up the stairs, "He who holds the battlefield . . ."

It was that night that Peter finally decided to dispose of the bag of bags. They had given some thought as to methods (in the rubbish? But what if it burst in the trash can and someone noticed?) and had decided to fling it into the river: Harriet had spent hours in their bathroom carefully wiping clean all the packets with paper towels and detergent to remove any fingerprints. Was all of this his and Harriet's punishment, Peter wondered as he drove the Mini through the quiet suburban streets. No, even if matters calmed down he knew that nothing would ever be the same. Irreligious though he was, some part of him accepted the idea of universal retribution. And yet it was so unfair. Other people got away with all kinds of things. What about their neighbors with their million-pound annual bonuses and golden handshakes and share options: were they all so clean? Why couldn't he, Peter Pelham, win, just for once?

He parked close to the point where the towpath left the road and vanished behind trees. The moment could hardly have been better: a faint drizzle was falling, keeping people indoors, and the river was at high tide, ready to carry the bag away. Yet Peter did not hurry to take the bag from the trunk but remained in his seat. Something was changing in his thoughts, and his anger was shifting target, like a gun on its platform. He hated the bag of bags, certainly, but even more he was furious at how much it had cost them. What had they got out of all of this? Ten thousand?—he didn't even know the exact amount—plus an extension to the house and a few other trinkets. And for this they had thrown their lives into turmoil and lost the respect of their children. What made Peter angriest of all, though, was the thought that they had had to pay off Roy for what Peter still thought of as his windfall. For that matter they had paid that lowlife for all these remaining packets that he was now about to throw into the river. It was a thought that was hard to get past: he would be hurling away something he had bought, and at such a painful cost. It seemed so wasteful. Peter stared at the windshield, speckled with tiny dots of rain, and allowed his task of the evening to shimmer with uncertainty. What was the rush, he asked himself, already warming to the new line. Several days had passed, and there had been no police knocking at the door. Now he came to think of it, Toby's party guests were unlikely to tell drug anecdotes to anyone except other druggies. A seagull flew above the river, lit by the streetlights. Peter watched as the rain on the windshield merged into a blur, then turned the ignition key and, the bag of bags still in the trunk, drove home.

Opening the front door, he walked straight through the house, and taking a flashlight, he followed the circle of light to the greenhouse. The largest space was beside a sapling mulberry tree, and this was where he carefully buried the shopping bag with its packets and cell phone, scattering the excess soil on other flower beds. It was only when he had finished and began walking back toward the house that he saw Harriet's silhouette in the bathroom window, watching him. For a moment he froze. Would she be furious? But when he walked into the bedroom, he saw no accusation in her eyes.

"Will it be safe there, d'you think?" was all she asked.

Neither of them made any mention of the bag during the remainder of the summer. As the weeks passed, the children went from bad to worse. Theo began to come home drunk and seemed to take pleasure in leaving the dog ends of joints about the house: once Peter even found one stubbed out in the butter dish. On several occasions he or Harriet was goaded into protest, but to no effect, as Theo simply smirked. "That's good from you."

Ginny's evolution was marked by sudden appearances in the sitting room that seemed increasingly like ambushes. "Jean and I have decided to join Simon's discussion group," she announced one Sunday, wearing the frumpy clothes that she now preferred to radical chic. Simon, needless to say, was the priest. "Simon's so amazing, he makes the world seem a cleaner place," she told them a few days later with a disapproving glance. "Really, you should come. He said he'd like to see you." Peter wondered glumly what she had told him. A week later, with a look of solemn concern she declared, "Jean and I prayed for you this afternoon."

Harriet could barely contain her fury. "She's doing it deliberately." But even then she could see nothing—nothing at all—that they could do. It came as a great relief when September arrived and the children finally left for their autumn terms. It was Harriet who first raised the question of the bag of bags. "What now?"

Peter had given the matter thought. "We could try to sell it back to Roy, I suppose. His number should still be on the cell phone. And we've paid for it, after all." He had thought the suggestion quite radical, but once again he had underestimated Harriet.

"He'll hardly give us a penny, and I'm damned if I'm going to chuck it away for nothing after all we've been through."

"Then . . . ?" Peter found himself uneasy at the idea of resuming their deliveries, but he said nothing. It was ludicrous, but he felt a kind of playground reluctance to be seen as scared, especially by his wife. "Are you sure that's a good idea?"

"It didn't seem very dangerous before," Harriet insisted briskly. "And it would get rid of it."

That same night, walking briskly to disguise the sick feeling in his stomach, Peter went with her to the greenhouse, and they dug up the bag of bags. After almost two months of disconnection, it was not enough simply to recharge the cell phone, they had to renew contact themselves. Fortunately Harriet—efficient as ever—had listed customers' numbers and addresses in a ruled notebook. Peter made the calls and found himself coolly received. "I know exactly who you are. So you've finally decided to switch on your phone, have you?"

It did not take them very long to return to their routine of the spring. And yet nothing was quite the same. Rather than diminishing, Peter's uneasiness grew stronger, and he found himself increasingly plagued by panic. As he walked to a customer's door, he imagined a gang of police waiting just inside, while the sight of a police car—even speeding away in the opposite direction—was enough to make him break into a sweat, he began to have difficulty sleeping, and he became insistent on taking precautions, such as parking several streets away from a customer's door.

"What difference does it make?" complained Harriet. "You still have to go there. It just makes everything take longer."

"They might be taking down license plate numbers."

Rather to his own surprise, he found himself struck with attacks of conscience, which came upon him quite unexpectedly, when he was sitting at his desk at work, or brushing his teeth. Strangely enough, the face that troubled him at these times was never Ginny's, as he would have expected, but that of her church friend Jean, whom he had met only once very briefly at the door: a dumpy-looking girl with self-certain eyes. He could picture her precisely, shaking her large, round face in stolid disapproval. The only answer he could find for her stare was, rather lamely, that this would soon all be over: the bag of bags was steadily emptying. As weeks passed Peter became increasingly anxious to speed up the process, taking on almost any order, regardless of how late and tired this made Harriet and himself.

"The Cotswolds are just criminal these days," Harriet complained one rainy night when only a couple of dozen packets remained. "Thirty-five thousand won't get us a mortgage on a pigpen." She had sole charge of planning how they might spend their money—Peter found he was curiously indifferent—and had rung various country estate agents.

"Then perhaps we shouldn't get a house after all," said Peter warily, sensing what was coming. "We can always go off on weekend breaks to hotels."

Harriet lost her temper. "But I thought we were agreed that a place in the country is what this is all for. Besides, almost everybody else has had one for years." There was no missing the accusation in her voice, one that Peter had often heard in the days before the black bag of bags, suggesting that he had let her down, robbing her of the life she'd expected. "We can't stop now."

"For goodness' sake, Harriet," he complained, "we haven't even worked out how to get this money into our bank account and now you're saying we should get another bag."

"Have we had one bad moment since we started this? No, not one."

Peter said nothing, hating himself for his silence. But it was hard: she was so interminably fearless. Besides, she was right, they had had absolutely no trouble with their deliveries. And so, that same windy October night, they went to the greenhouse and dug up several bin liners of cash, then drove out to meet Roy and purchased their second bag of bags. Peter felt strangely numb as he drove back, listening to Harriet's complaints.

"He's just a lazy middleman. We pay him almost half our takings and he doesn't do a damn thing. He doesn't go anywhere or take any risks. If we could only go to the suppliers."

Peter shot her a disbelieving glance. "What? In Colombia or Bolivia or wherever it is?"

"Why not? That's where they grow this stuff, the cocoa plants, or whatever they're called. We should deal directly with them."

This time, though, even Harriet realized she had overreached herself, and she did not raise the subject again. Instead she became increasingly focused on their business efficiency. She bought an accounts book, just as if they were running a tobacconists' shop or a sandwich bar, and at the end of each week she carefully wrote down their takings before depositing them in the greenhouse in a fresh black bin bag, just as others would deposit their takings in the bank. As for Peter, the renewed supply of endless small packages seemed to fill him with an even greater sense of urgency, and on some evenings they did as many as eight or nine deliveries, returning at one in the morning. These days there were no thoughts of lovemaking on creased banknotes, as they were far too tired, and they went up to bed without a word.

It was in mid-November that Harriet's father rang. "I'm coming down for a few days."

It was bad news. As well as the inconvenience—they would have to cut down on their deliveries—Peter anticipated no end of scornful moralizing. But as they all sat in the kitchen with tea and biscuits, he was surprised to see how quiet Joe seemed. "I've rung quite a few times in the evening," he said at last, "but you always seem to be out."

Harriet shot him a warning look. "What if we are?"

A strange, insistent look came into Joe's eyes. "I could be very useful, you know."

Only now did Peter finally understand. If he hadn't felt so sick about everything, he might have laughed. He felt, if anything, a kind of satisfaction that Joe was, after all, no better than he himself. A few months was all it had taken for the remembrance of those crisp red and purple banknotes to ferment in his mind. Sure enough, Joe began listing his needs, in a curiously whining voice, as if he had been unfairly deprived. "And the house hasn't been decorated since before Julia died. I really can't live like that. For that matter, I need a new car, too. Something bigger, for the dogs."

Peter and Harriet discussed his offer as they lay in bed. Harriet was not keen. "He won't know what he's doing. He'll be a liability."

Peter, surprisingly, was enthusiastic, drawn by the thought of getting rid of the packets more quickly. "I think he could be very helpful," he considered through a yawn. "You can go out with him during the day when I'm at work. That way we might even get this next bag finished before Christmas."

First he would have to be trained. It was years since Joe had driven in London, which he might have to do if parking wardens appeared when he was minding the car. They decided he should sit in the back of the Mini for a few evenings. It was on the second of these that everything went wrong. Probably this was bound to occur eventually, as Peter and Harriet's drug dealing had now become a kind of headlong rush, tempting disaster. The end came on a black, rainy night in late November, when they were driving through Ealing in the Mini. It was proving a frustrating evening, as their first customer had had no money to pay, giving them a wasted journey. Now they had seven more deliveries to go and were already late, delayed by the traffic, which was heavy with the approach of Christmas.

"Can't you drive, you ninny?" Peter complained when the car in front stalled and made them miss a green light. When the light finally changed, he revved up the engine in annoyance and sped through the intersection. It was not so much that he saw the problem too late as that he never saw it at all, and as he slowed down at the next light he was aware of a thump against the side of the car.

"Oh, for God's sake," Harriet groaned. "It's a bloody cyclist."

Peter, exasperated by their delays, would probably have driven straight on, but this was impossible as the Mini was already stuck in the next queue of traffic. There was a sharp rap against the window, and when Peter wound it down he saw a surprisingly short figure draped in reflective yellow plastic.

"Can't you look where you're going?" The cyclist held up a slither of white plastic. "And you've broken my rear light. That cost me five ninety-nine."

Afterward Peter would often think of that face: a foolish-looking face, with small eyes and sticking-out ears: a face that one would never imagine might prove one's nemesis. Although, in truth, it was Peter himself who was the real cause of his own destruction. If only he had slept better during the previous weeks, he might have apologized for what was, after all, his fault. Instead he was overcome by a strange obstinacy. "You should have been looking."

"Silly oaf," agreed Joe.

It was Harriet, normally so oblivious, who saw clearly. "Why not just give him the money, Peter?"

Peter replied as if she had criticized him. "It was his fault."

By now the traffic ahead was beginning to move, and worried they might escape, the cyclist darted round the Mini and stood in front of the hood, blocking the way. "I'm not shifting till I get my five ninety-nine."

Car horns began to sound behind them, and Peter added to the din with his own, then leaned out of the window. "Can you please get out of the way?"

Even Joe was beginning to grow doubtful. "Perhaps we should just give him the money."

Harriet was more practical and fiddled in her purse. "I'm sure I have a ten in here."

Peter later wondered, not infrequently, what road his life might have followed if he had accepted their advice. Ten pounds? It seemed hard to believe he had refused when they were awash with cash. At the time, though, there had been no room for such logic, as his head was entirely filled with a kind of roaring din of irritation. All he could think of was that he was late, that customers were waiting, that the traffic was as bad as could be, and now this damnable midget with sticking-out ears was stopping him from moving. He turned the door handle and unwisely climbed out of the car. "Get out of the way."

The cyclist met his glare. "Five ninety-nine."

They were more easily matched than one might have thought. The cyclist was shorter, it was true, but he was young and fit, at least compared with Peter. The difficulty was that neither had any real comprehension of how to fight, and so they stood there, scowling and raising their hands as if they might push at each other.

Harriet had wound down her window. "Peter, for God's sake, there's a policeman coming."

Finally, Peter realized the danger. Yet fear can work in strange ways. Rather than try to defuse the situation with an apology and Harriet's ten-pound note, he instead became more impatient to end the matter, and he shoved at his enemy, pushing him clear of the hood. His success was short-lived, and as he marched back round the car, the cyclist darted after him, clutching his sleeve.

"No you don't, Grandpa."

By the time the policeman reached them, they were engaged in an amateurish tussle. Even at this late stage there was still an element of chance: it was inevitable that the policeman would try to prize them apart but not that his hand would push against—of all places—the front pocket of Peter's blazer. As he pressed Peter back, there was a faint popping sound, like a seaweed bubble bursting, and a white cloud appeared momentarily before Peter's eyes. He felt a soft coating on his face and involuntarily licked his lips, tasting a sharp, tangy flavor—it was the only taste of it he would ever know—and for just an instant he felt a strange glow of excited well-being.

The policeman was staring at him with a puzzled look. "What's that on your nose?"

Peter guessed he was doomed but he might at least limit the extent of the disaster, and so he made a pretense of losing his balance and fell against the car, murmuring into Harriet's window, "It was all me. You don't know anything."

NEIGHBORS AND OLD acquaintances of the Pelhams were intrigued, even quietly thrilled, by their sudden fall. Peter and Harriet had seemed so respectable, to the point of dreariness, that there was a kind of perfection about their arrest, which enriched the gray November weather. By summer it was impossible to get away from their story even if one had wanted to, as the trial was covered on television and in the papers every day. Inadvertently the Pelhams had become notorious: Peter's descent from dull propriety to drug pusher was so sheer that it instantly placed him in that pantheon of characters who float before the nation to be cheered or booed. For months the soft suburban air hummed with talk.

"Actually I did notice that they were always coming and going late at night, but I assumed they were just very sociable."

"And they had it all buried in their greenhouse . . ."

There were some who felt pity for Peter Pelham, whether from natural generosity or from a vague unease that something similar might one day happen to themselves. Others felt he had received nothing less than his just deserts. But was this really true? Yes, jail came as a terrible shock to Peter, and he hated the banging doors, the shared rooms, the simmering brutality, the lingering smell of urine and disinfectant. Also, finding himself in the same wing as Larry was particularly bad luck. Harriet's visits were strained, while he dreaded those by Ginny, who plagued him with her forgiveness. It was a relief to him that Theo never came.

And yet, as the weeks turned to months, Peter slowly began to adjust to his new life. He found he had protectors, who showed a certain admiration for somebody who had been given every privileged advantage and yet, just like themselves, had been unable to resist risking all. And so it was that Peter sometimes woke in the middle of the night to find himself filled with a glow of unexpected satisfaction. The fact was that he was famous. A newspaper wanted his story. He had received sack loads of letters from complete strangers, and though some were accusing, others were not, and a young woman from Scarborough had even invited him to spend the night with her in a hotel room. People he had never met thought of him as dangerously exciting. So in a way he had achieved what he had hungered for that bright spring evening when he first heard the beeping of "Speed, Bonny Boat." Peter Pelham was somebody.

MEANWHILE, MANY THOUSANDS
OF MILES AWAY . . .

3. Leaves

IT WAS NOT often that aircraft flew over the valley, especially so low and loud, and Julio ran out of the house to see. There were two of them—ordinary enough old planes with straight wings that looked like they might break off—but with them was a spectacular machine: a sleek, dark helicopter with tubes and pods stuck to its sides, so it almost seemed like something out of the future. Julio was so entranced by the sight of it speeding over the fields toward him that, ignoring his mother's shouts, he took no notice of the spray that began spilling out from beneath the two older planes, like mist, not until it was falling around him and he ran coughing into the house. That night a rash spread over his arms and neck that made him itch and itch, and he found it hard to breathe, as if his throat had grown mysteriously narrower. His mother sat with him, fretting with her crucifix, while even his younger sister, Isabella, watched him uneasily from over her pillow. By the next morning, though, Julio felt a little better, and he managed to eat some breakfast. His mother told him to rest, but it was boring lying there and before long he clambered out of the bed, eager to be free of its trap.

He found his father, mother, and sister in the bean field, wiping the plants' leaves with pieces of rag, which they dipped into the red plastic bucket from the kitchen. There was an intensity to the way Julio's father worked—a hunted stillness to his eyes—that was ominously familiar and that made Julio feel ashamed of his excitement at seeing the helicopter, as if he were somehow to blame. He took a rag from the bucket and joined the others in cleaning the leaves, smelling the chemical tang as he wiped. Hardly a word was spoken as they worked, and yet as hours passed, marked by regular changing of the bucket water from the stream, and they made their way gradually through the crop, and then to the cornfield beyond, he could feel the mood among them lightening, as they became revived by the exertion, and the satisfaction of completing their task.

"It was quite windy yesterday," said Julio's mother, ever the optimist, as they walked back to the house, their backs stiff from bending. "A lot of it must have blown away."

Even Julio's father seemed more hopeful. "Who knows?"

Julio was surprised to see Grandfather sitting on the veranda, waiting for them. He had been ill for some while, not with anything specific but from a series of minor complaints, following one after the other, until everyone had quietly begun to wonder. Now, though, he looked better than he had for some time, noisily tapping the floorboards with his stick. "I don't know why you bother," he said, stealing their smiles as they tramped up to him, "as it won't do any good."

Grandfather never had been one to trouble over saying the right thing. The hunted look returned to Julio's father's eyes, and his mother shot Grandfather a warning stare. "How d'you know?"

"I know."

But then, to Julio's surprise and relief, days passed and nothing happened. Julio's father went out each morning to inspect the bean and corn plants, which seemed to be thriving in the sunshine, and he came back nodding in satisfaction, especially toward Grandfather.

"It must have been because we cleaned the leaves," said Julio's mother excitedly over dinner one evening. "We beat them after all."

It was as if the devil had been listening. The next day when Isabella went to feed the chickens, she found them sprawled on the floor of the coop.

"Those Bogotano pigs," said Julio's father as they stood looking at the dead birds. "I'd throw them in a hole, every one of them. I'd feed them to ants." For all the violence of his words, his voice sounded flat.

"It's not the Bogotanos," said Grandfather, with a kind of sour triumph. "This is Gringos. D'you think the lousy Bogotanos would have a helicopter like that?"

They dug a small trench in the tiny kitchen garden, and it was then, as he helped his father scoop earth over the birds' carcasses, that Julio's anger began. They ate chicken only on special occasions and had been saving two for the next feast day, which fell in a few weeks. If they had known this was going to happen, they could have cooked and eaten them all. It was such a waste.

Two days later Julio woke and noticed the house, which should have been full of the usual noises of the start of the day—his father chopping wood, his mother banging pots as she prepared breakfast—seemed far too quiet. He found his mother, Isabella, and Grandfather sitting glumly on the veranda, watching as his father ambled round the bean field, poking at the plants with a stick. They were all wilting as if parched.

"They might get better again," said Julio's mother. "If it rains . . ."

Nobody said anything, and their silence was like an answer.

During the next days the corn plants turned brown and dried up, and then the beans, and also the plantains, the potatoes, and all the other vegetables in the small garden behind the house. The whole valley was just the same: three days ago it had been lush and green, and now it was dying, as if scorched by a great heat. The disaster was so sudden and so complete that he and his family hardly knew what to do with themselves. Their whole sense of time— their daily routine, the slow changes of the seasons—had always been through their crops: planting them, tending them as they grew, harvesting them, and then taking some to the market and feeding off the stored life of the rest, as the months passed and the next crop grew. Now they found themselves directionless, and they spent hours on the veranda, staring at the vanishing plants. Their neighbors were equally fixated and would drop by with the latest news—though it was all much the same—talking excitedly, almost as if something good had happened.

Gradually the disaster's novelty began to ebb and Julio's family was left only with the consequences. His mother retreated into prayers and constant nervous cleaning, while his father took to his bed—just as Julio had guessed he would—where he stared at the wall, refusing to speak. As for Julio himself, he went for long walks through the withering valley, as he found he could not bear to sit still. He hated those planes now, more than he had hated anything in all his life, and he hungered to fight them, kill them. As he walked an idea began to grow in his head, and he imagined himself going down to Guanavita to join the guerrillas. He was young, it was true, but he had heard of others who had joined at his age. Yes, people said bad things about them and what they had done, but people said bad things about everybody, while at least the guerrillas could fight. Suddenly he felt useless without a gun. Without a gun you had to put up with whatever people did to you. Not that he said anything to his family, not yet; he knew they would be angry.

Then, one afternoon when he came home from his walking, he found Grandfather looking at him expectantly. "At last. I thought you'd never turn up. I need a loan of your shoulder, boy. I've decided to go over and have a word with that neighbor of ours, Sánchez."

"Sánchez?" called out Julio's father—finally provoked into speech—from the bedroom. "And what good will that do?"

"If nothing else it'll make me feel better."

Julio rather agreed with his father that the visit was pointless, but he dutifully helped Grandfather over the field of wizened beans. His walks had not yet taken him in this direction, and when they were halfway across Sánchez's land, he was surprised to see a long swath of green: much of Sánchez's crop was still alive.

Grandfather gave a kind of laugh. "Isn't that perfect?"

Julio couldn't find it in himself to laugh too, and he helped Grandfather to Sánchez's door without a word. Even now Grandfather did not permit his anger to interfere with his manners.

"Good evening, Señor Sánchez."

Sánchez peered at them warily. "Good evening, Señor García. And Julio. Won't you come inside?"

"Thank you, no." Grandfather leaned on his stick. "I was just saying to Julio here how stupid those Gringos must feel, killing every plant in the valley except your coca, the very thing they came for." He glanced back at the green swath. "I expect you'll get a good price."

Sánchez had been expecting this, and his voice rose to meet the attack. "I didn't fly those planes, Señor García. And I'm hardly the only one round here who has a few coca plants. For that matter I've seen them in your own fields."

"Now there's nothing in our fields," said Grandfather slowly. "Nothing alive." He stood up from his stick. "Good evening, Señor Sánchez."

"Good evening to you, Señor García." The door banged shut.

Was that all? Julio had not been expecting much, but still he was taken aback: they might as well have stayed at home. He began helping Grandfather back but then found the old man was tugging him away to one side, behind Sánchez's house.

"Give me a hand, will you?" said Grandfather, prizing off the lid of Sánchez's water tank.

Curious, Julio helped lift it off and then watched in surprise as Grandfather undid his fly and began dribbling a stream of urine into the water.

"Come on, boy, we haven't got all day."

Julio had always been relatively well behaved, and he hesitated at this transgression, but if Grandfather commanded it . . . Just as he began he turned and saw Sánchez peering round the side of the house, his face stern with shock. Julio froze, but then, glancing at Grandfather, he saw that he was smiling back at the man, as if nothing remotely unusual were happening.

"Good evening again, Señor Sánchez," he remarked, still dribbling.

Sánchez opened his mouth as if to speak but then changed his mind and slunk out of sight.

"Didn't I say this would do me good?" said Grandfather as they made their way back. "A little revenge is healthy for the soul."

Julio realized he felt better, too. In fact the expedition to Sánchez's house proved a kind of turning point, and it was that same evening that Julio's family finally began to look the future in the eye.

"There's no point in staying here," said Grandfather, "as they'll just come and spray us again."

The discussion finally roused Julio's father from his bed, and he stood pale-faced in the doorway. "And just where are we supposed to go?"

"My cousin Alvaro said there's still good land to be had in the hills beyond his farm, up above Martires. We'd have to clear it, of course, which will be a lot of work, but it's better than starving."

Julio was shocked by the proposal. This simple house, with its two rooms and little veranda, its view of distant mountains, was the only place he had ever lived. How could they just leave? His father seemed equally doubtful. "Even if we manage to clear the land, it'll be at least a year before we have a crop to harvest. There's not much food left from last year, and our savings won't go far."

"Our cousins will help us out if we run into trouble," said Grandfather, though his voice sounded less sure than his words.

The thought of going was too huge to be swallowed in one bite, and the discussion petered out without a decision being made. In

the days that followed, though, as the valley grew ever more desolate and more neighbors packed up to leave, the idea gradually began to have an aura of inevitability, and when Grandfather
suggested it again, one morning over breakfast, nobody resisted. A
little sadly Julio accepted that he could not join the guerrillas, at
least for the moment, as he could hardly desert his family now.
They began preparations that same day, carefully going through
their possessions to decide what to take. Julio's father went into
town and talked to Salazar, who drove over in his pickup truck the
next Sunday and took all their furniture—the kitchen table and
chairs, the wooden plank beds, and the cupboard—to the market
at Chasim while Isabella walked the mule down. Unfortunately the
market was crowded with others from the valley selling similar
items, and so they had to settle for insultingly low prices, but at
least they got bargains on the machetes, the ax, and the double-
handled saw that they would need to clear the forest. That evening
they visited those neighbors who had not yet left, to say their good-
byes, and even Julio had a few glasses, so the next morning he woke
feeling bleary from the drink and stiff from sleeping on the floorboards. It was still dark when Salazar beeped his horn and they
heaved their possessions, packed into large cream-colored sacks,
into the pickup truck, but the sky was already turning a pale blue
when they unloaded it all at Chasim bus station.

"What've you got in there?" Julio's father asked Grandfather,
pointing at a sack he was carrying. "I don't remember that one."

There was a knowingness in Grandfather's look. "Just something we need."

Father was about to ask again, but then the bus was rumbling
into sight. It was already full, needless to say, so there was quite a
scramble to get aboard, while the luggage boy—sneering at their
country accents—insisted that there was not room on the roof for
all their things, and only after Grandfather kicked up a mighty fuss
did he let them take the rest inside. As they stood in the aisle,
wedged between their sacks, and the bus growled into life, Isabella

began to cry. "I don't like this place where we're going. I've never seen it."

Julio often found his younger sister exasperating, but now he felt for her. After all, that withered, brown valley—already vanished down the road behind them—was the only home either of them had known. "It'll be fine there," he told her, though of course he had no idea.

"It'll be more than fine," Grandfather added. "It's a wonderful place and much nicer than here. You'll meet Cousin Alvaro, who can whistle just like a bird so even the real birds get confused, and there's your cousin María, who makes the best meat stew in all Colombia. We'll be right in the forest so you'll see beautiful parrots and hummingbirds, as well as possums and sloth bears and bats and—"

"I don't like bats," interrupted Isabella. "I want to go home."

"This will be your home," Grandfather insisted with dogged cheerfulness. The bus was gaining speed now as it left the last of the town behind. "In fact it always has been your home in a way. Did you know that my great-grandfather lived nearby there, in Martires? He's your great-great-great-grandfather, José Luis García. He was the one who went into the forest with the Gringo who wanted to steal the trees." He smiled, letting the intriguing phrase hang in the air for a moment. "Did I ever tell you about him?"

Isabella sniffed, curious but not sure she wanted to give up her distress so easily. "No."

Julio always enjoyed Grandfather's stories, and the prospect of one seemed to soften the journey. "Go on, tell us," he urged, leaning back against a sack of corn.

"This all happened a long, long time ago, of course," Grandfather began, "long before airplanes or cars or radios. Though not everything was different even back then, and there were wars that never seemed to end, that were kept going by the usual crowd of dirty, thieving politicians." He spat carefully on the floor. "The Gringos hadn't invented cocaine yet, and they had to make themselves mad with whiskey and rum instead, but they still found reasons to come over here and make trouble. And one such Gringo was a fellow called Harman, who rode into Martires on a hot afternoon wearing a tall, black hat that Gringos used to wear in those days, like a pipe with a brim. Martires was a small town, and visitors were quite a curiosity, especially a rich one like this with his fine horses and his Gringo servant, and word soon spread that he was going up into the hills to collect flowers, and that he was hiring mule drivers."

"Flowers?" wondered Julio. "Did they really come all this way just to collect flowers?"

"Certainly they did," Grandfather insisted, a little annoyed at being questioned. "They'd come over to rob us of anything they could think of."

"I think it's nice that they wanted flowers," said Isabella, who had already forgotten her tears.

Grandfather rested his arm on a sack of pots and pans. "But I haven't told you about your great-great-great-grandfather. José Luis was a man of great talents. He was an excellent hunter who could ride and shoot as well as anybody in the region, and he was also well educated, having studied at a fine school, so he could write his letters as beautifully as the priests. Even great men, though, can have bad luck, and José Luis had plenty. First he lost his farm when the rain fell so hard that half a mountain of mud swept down the hill, and then, as if this were not already enough, he was robbed on the road by bandits, who left him with hardly a penny. He had been in Martires for some time looking for work but without success, and so he decided to go to this Harman. He didn't much like the man, who treated him like dirt, never troubling to notice that he was as educated as himself, but beggars can't be choosers and so José Luis took the job.

"Just a few days later they all set off, José Luis, two other mule drivers, twenty mules to carry all the food and tents and boxes for the flowers, and of course Harman, his Gringo servant, and their guide, who was from Piales, which is a dirty sort of town and full of thieves. Now your great-great-great-grandfather was not an especially suspicious man, but as the days went by he began to wonder about this expedition. Being well educated and a fine hunter, he knew about plants, and he could not help noticing that they had passed a good number of flowers, some of them very fine, yet Harman had showed not the slightest interest.

"The other thing that puzzled José Luis was the direction they were taking. He was familiar with these hills, you see, having traveled through them some years earlier to gather the bark of a particular kind of tree that cured people of malaria fever. Naturally this bark was highly prized and fetched a good price—José Luis had done quite well himself—and because of this there were strict laws against anyone taking the trees or their seeds out of the country. In spite of this, a number of Gringos had tried exactly that, greedy to make themselves rich by growing the trees in some rotten, faraway part of the world that they had managed to enslave, and never caring that this would leave our unlucky country even poorer than before. Fortunately not one of these Gringos had succeeded until now, as they had all been caught or had lost their ships on the long journey back. Your great-great-great-grandfather saw that they were traveling toward the very area where the trees were especially plentiful. He kept his suspicions to himself at first, biding his time, but sure enough, Harman made camp just a few hours' journey from where the trees grew, ordering the mule drivers to wait while he and his Gringo servant and the guide from Piales went off alone with three mules. It was three days before they returned, and when they did all the wooden boxes carried by the mules were locked.

"José Luis wasn't the kind of person who could keep a question quiet in his belly for long. 'What's in these boxes?' he said to Harman.

"Harman, who had hardly noticed him until then except to complain that he should go faster, gave him a scornful look. 'Flowers, of course. What d'you think?'

"Even now José Luis gave him the chance of being honest. 'Can I see? It'll help me with the mules if I know how fragile they are.'

"Now Harman looked at him suspiciously. 'I'm not accustomed to taking orders from mule drivers.'

"That was enough to confirm all of José Luis's suspicions. Your great-great-great-grandfather paid quite a price for his curiosity, though, and from that moment he found he was carefully watched. And so a kind of dance began, with nobody saying aloud what was happening. José Luis tried to recruit the other two mule drivers as his allies, but they only cared about being paid, and so there was nothing to do except wait until they reached Martires. As soon as they got back, José Luis would alert the mayor, who was an old friend of his, Harman would be arrested, and the seeds—which José Luis knew the boxes contained—could be confiscated. But then, when they were still a full day's journey from the town and—"

Grandfather stopped as the bus was braking sharply. Julio tugged himself from his reverie and, peering through the window, saw that the way was blocked by a battered car parked sideways across the road, behind which were standing a dozen men with rifles: a checkpoint. One of the guerrillas climbed aboard, impassively surveying the crowded space. "Everybody off."

Julio and his family exchanged looks. This was hardly unexpected, and yet for some reason it was something that none of them had really thought about. They were so vulnerable, as everything they owned in the world was on this bus. Julio, his thoughts turning to Grandfather's story and how José Luis had been robbed on the road—was that a bad sign?—wondered where his father had hidden their savings money. As he stepped down onto the road with the heavy sack of corn, his eyes strayed to the line of guerrillas. How good it would be to have a gun like that. He started to help get their possessions down from the roof, the luggage boy shimmying up and down the ladder beside him, looking nervous now, his urban sneer vanished. Everyone was made to line up with bags and sacks open in front of them, and Julio's thoughts turned to stories he had heard about what the guerrillas were said to have done to people they took off buses. And yet it was hard to believe that anything terrible might happen in this peaceful spot, among trees on a high hillside, where he could just see through the branches to a valley far below. It seemed an age as they waited for the officer to come to them. He stopped in front of Julio's father.

"Where are you going?"

"Martires." Father looked nervous, his eyes darting to the sack in front of Isabella. Was that where their savings were? One soldier reached into Mother's sack and took out a plastic plate, slipping it beneath his jacket, and the officer looked away as if he had not seen. Mother blinked in distress, and for a moment Julio wondered if he should do something, but he didn't, angry at himself for his feebleness. Everything was going wrong. Then Grandfather leaned forward over Mother's sack, resting his hands on it so that it was closed.

"We're from the valley above Chasim. All our crops were killed by those Gringo planes and their spray, so we have to find somewhere else to farm."

The officer stared at him for a moment, as if enjoying the weight of his own power. "Very well then. Back on the bus."

As they began trundling past him with their bags, Julio—trying not to smile too much at their escape—was surprised to see the man's face soften, just for a moment.

"Good luck."

Not everyone was so lucky. A couple of people were kept back—Julio tried not to think what for—and a woman moaned that they had taken her watch. As the bus engine stirred into life, Julio decided they had been lucky to lose only a plate. Grandfather seemed surprisingly untroubled by the whole incident, and he returned to his story almost as if nothing had happened. "So, one morning when they were still a full day's journey from Martires and they were packing up the camp, the Gringo Harman surprised your great-great-great-grandfather by walking over to him. 'Señor García, I feel there has been a great misunderstanding. Our guide tells me that you are a man of education, and I must apologize for not realizing this sooner, which I certainly would have if only my Spanish were better.' Then he smiled almost as if they were old friends. 'Let's be open and honest with one another. You believe that I have seeds to certain trees. I'm not saying you're right, but the fact is that if I did then I'd have a very good reason, one that you, as an educated man, would certainly understand. Those trees are disappearing. You know it yourself. Every year people take their bark, far too much, and more of them die. Can't you see that those trees are a possession of the world, a gift from God to preserve us from sickness, and to conserve them, even if elsewhere, is a service to all mankind?'

"José Luis smiled but remained unmoved, as in his experience when people talk of serving the world, they're never up to any good. 'Señor Harman, there are laws in this country,' he said simply. 'And these laws apply to everybody, even a foreigner like yourself, for every day that you choose to remain here. Tell me, as an educated man, if you had a fine clock in your house, wouldn't you prefer to see it fall and smash rather than have it stolen by thieves?'

"Harman scowled at this, especially at the word *thieves,* and he strode away. Soon afterward he called everyone together and, without looking your great-great-great-grandfather in the eye, he announced that the expedition would not be going back to Martires after all, as he wanted to spend a few more days looking for flowers. What was more, he had decided he had no further need of most of the mules, and the drivers would be paid off there and then. José Luis guessed his real intention, of course. Harman planned to make a dash for the Ecuadoran frontier, which was only two or three days' journey away, calculating that by the time José Luis got to Martires and roused the authorities he would be too far to be caught. José Luis was no policeman, and it was none of his business to go chasing after thieving Gringos, so he could simply have left him go, but your great-great-great-grandfather had a hatred of anything underhand, while he was also a strong patriot who loved his country dearly and could not stand by and see it robbed. So he decided to follow.

"This was not easy as the Gringo and his little party traveled quickly, but José Luis hurried after them, using his hunter's skills to follow their tracks along a deep, rainy valley, past waterfalls and rotting logs. On the first night he could do nothing, as Harman and the others clearly suspected they might have trouble and took turns guarding the boxes beside their tent. The second night was no better. On the third night, though, by which time they were just a few miles from the border, José Luis crept up to their camp by the light of the stars and saw that the guard—it was Harman himself—was fast asleep. José Luis crept up to the boxes. They were locked, of course, but locks can be picked.

"All at once there was a shout, and Harman was standing up, aiming his gun. 'Get away from those,' he ordered. In an instant the Gringo servant and the guide from Piales were clambering out of their tent, and your great-great-great-grandfather had three rifles aimed at his eyes. 'If so much as one single seed is missing,' Harman told him in his cold Gringo voice, 'you will not leave this place alive.' This was no joke either, as in the middle of nowhere three men with guns are their own country and their own law. José Luis watched anxiously as the Gringo servant opened first one box and then another. And, to Harman's evident surprise, every one of them was just as full as before."

Then Grandfather abruptly stopped talking and waited. This was a favorite technique of his, and it never failed to draw his listeners into filling the vacuum he had left.

"He changed the seeds for some other kind?" guessed Isabella.

"But how could he?" said Grandfather, shaking his head. "He

had no time to collect enough seeds to fill all those boxes. Besides, Harman would have seen the difference at once."

"He fought them?" said Julio, hopefully.

"With three rifles aimed at his eyes?" Grandfather leaned back on the sack. "No, there was no fight. In fact the Gringos let him go and he returned to Martires, where he went on to set up a ranch breeding horses and did very well. The ranch is still there, I've heard, probably owned by some rich, fat Bogotano."

Julio looked at him, puzzled. "And Harman?"

"He reached the Ecuadoran coast without any trouble and sailed all the way back to his cold, faraway country, where he wasted no time trying to find a buyer for his boxes, full of greed at the thought of the money he would make. But then something very strange happened. When he met the buyer and opened all the boxes to show him, there were no seeds."

"No seeds?" said Isabella, captivated by the mystery.

"He'd made holes?" wondered Julio.

"But the Gringos would have seen." Grandfather laughed. "Besides, I didn't say the boxes were empty. In fact they were full. Not with seeds but with beetles. Little white beetles, thousands of them, the same as you find on rotting logs, just as if a piece of damp bark had been shoved to the bottom of each one."

Julio felt confused. Usually Grandfather's stories were funny or heroic. This one was not quite either. "But wasn't this Harman right to try to save the trees?"

Grandfather frowned. "He came as a thief. He never once asked permission for what he was doing, or offered to pay. He insulted this country and its people."

"Did the Gringos ever get the seeds?"

Grandfather gave a dismissive wave of his hand. "That's another story."

They were stopping, drawing up beside a roadside café. As they stepped down from the bus, Julio saw that they all looked better than they had for some time, ever since the planes had come. They were on their way at last, halfway to their new home, whatever this might be like, their lives pointed forward not backward.

"Why don't you leave that on the bus?" asked Julio's father, pointing to Grandfather's sack.

"I'd rather take it with me."

"I can't believe anybody's going to steal it. What's in there anyway?"

Grandfather grinned and opened the sack wide. Inside was a bundle of green plant cuttings. "I thought we'd need something to grow on our new land. In fact, I took them from our old neighbor, Sánchez. He had enough to spare."

4. Weight

THE BUS JOLTED over a pothole, and Benny winced, wondering, not for the first time, how this journey—four days on bumpy northwest Chinese roads—had seemed a good idea. Not that the roads were the real problem, or even Benny's seat, which he found so uncomfortable: it was Benny himself. He simply was not built for this sort of space. Each morning he struggled down the aisle, scraping against the seats, and carefully squeezed himself into place. It could have been worse, as at least his neighbor—one of the Uygur locals, who always wore the same white Muslim skullcap—was small, though there was still so little room for him that he had to sit sidesaddle, his legs dangling into the aisle. The bus jolted again. Just because it was fat didn't mean it didn't feel, and Benny felt everything: the hard lump in the back of his seat, that stupid ashtray beneath the window, the sharp bit by his leg. Outside the window he glimpsed trees, houses, and a mosque: another oasis town. Perhaps they would stop for the night here? Benny's spirits began to rise—tomorrow was the last day of the trip, so if they stopped he'd almost be done—but then the bus speeded up, hurrying on into the desert.

Benny mentally cursed Carl, who had first told him about the journey. "You're on the old Silk Road, thousands of years old, and the places you stay in are old caravan stops. Even the buses travel in a group, like a kind of modern-day caravan. It's just great." That had been several weeks ago, on a quiet night at the drilling station. A dust storm was building up outside, there was no new film to watch on video, and Benny and three other oil workers had been sitting in the canteen, happy enough to pass some time listening to Carl's traveling tales. "And the landscape's spectacular, not just flat and boring like round here. There's red desert, snow mountains."

What had made Carl's account linger in Benny's thoughts? The journey's epic length? That was probably part of the appeal, as Benny had never done anything like it, not even in the United States, and just thinking about it made him feel a little heroic. Benny the adventurer for once, rather than just sensible, no-nonsense Benny the geologist, who did his job and earned his pay. The main reason, though, was Dana. It was she who had brought him to this forgotten corner of the world, after all. He still winced at the memory of that evening when he had come home from work to find her note on the kitchen table. "I'm sorry, Benny, but I just can't do this." She didn't say why. Just a few days later a colleague saw her in a parking lot hand in hand with some guy. And she had complained he was too suspicious of her. Too damn right he was suspicious. They hadn't even been married a year and he had been so crazy about her—he had even offered to help her start up her own hairdressing business—and then this. Benny had put his name down for the Xinjiang posting a few weeks later.

All he knew about the place—all he needed to know—was that it was a moonscape on the other side of the earth and there was a hardship bonus. In a way it had been just the thing he needed as at least here, in the emptiness of Chinese Central Asia, there was nothing to remind him of Dana. The routine of work had been soothing, too, and though guys on the drilling stations sometimes got cranky from boredom, they were mostly okay and respected Benny for knowing his job. He had even lost a little weight (not that it made much difference).

The only problem, in fact, was that his contract did not seem quite long enough. As the date to fly home grew nearer, he realized he was not really looking forward to going home to the empty condo in Dallas, where Dana would be in every room. Then Carl had sounded off about his Silk Road trip. Benny had never been much of one for playing tourist—he did enough traveling for work—but perhaps he should give it a try? It was not as if he were in any hurry to get home, and he would probably never come back to this part of the world . . .

Now the bus was climbing again, the engine whining as it made its way through a valley of jagged rocks. This really felt like the back of the end of nowhere, the last place anyone would ever live, but then, as if to contradict Benny's thoughts, a row of low, dusty buildings came into sight. Benny had just decided not to taunt himself with hopes that they might stop when he realized the bus was slowing down. Here? But what did it matter so long as he could get out of this damn seat? He squeezed himself triumphantly along the aisle and waited for his bag to be hauled down from the roof. What a place. It seemed to consist of little more than a couple of straggling streets of muddy-colored buildings, overshadowed by a huge slither of rock that pointed at the settlement like a shark's fin.

"From my map I think this is Sanchakou," said Frans, who had walked over from his bus. On the first evening of the journey Benny, Frans, and a Frenchman called Eric had gravitated to the same table of the crowded Uygur café, as if sensing what they had in common (middle age and misfortune). Benny had been pleased to discover some allies against the crowd of twenty-something backpackers—all thin as sticks—whom he found so irritating, with their interminable boasting chatter. Eric explained that he had worked in investments, "until they decided I was an asset they could dispose of," while Frans had been divorced just a couple of years previously, "and now she has the house, the kids, the dog, and I live in my small flat." Benny, in turn, told them about Dana.

The three of them followed the other passengers as they filed along the street toward the town's solitary, concrete hotel. The queue to check in was slow, and Benny had been standing there for some moments before he noticed the people ahead of him were all staring at something. A gap opened up between the bodies, and that was when he saw her, sitting at the desk, writing down passport numbers. Now he was staring too, as it was impossible to do anything else. She had dark eyes, jet-black hair, and there was a delicacy to her face, her neck, her wrists, a lightness to her smile as she glanced up at the next passenger. She did not look especially Uygur, certainly not Chinese, and she might have been from India or Greece or Arabia. Why not? Benny had heard people came from all over to travel the Silk Road. Somehow, in this terrible spot, she had made herself elegant: her hair was cut in a neat bob, and she wore a simple but tasteful necklace of pale stones, while her white blouse and jacket were spotless in a way that seemed almost magical in this dusty, stained room.

"Do you think she is a prostitute?" murmured Frans blankly. Eric shook his head with the air of one who knew about such things. Benny found he was annoyed at Frans's remark as he didn't like to think of her in that way. The queue crept forward until finally the three of them reached the desk and handed over their passports. Benny was too shy to say anything, but not Eric, and he picked up the book she had beside her. "Advanced English? But you should be learning French."

"English is better," she said simply, taking it back.

"So you can run away with some American? But you will be much better with a Frenchman. Even a gray-haired Frenchman like me."

She laughed, not at all shocked, and then she smiled, almost challengingly, first at Eric, then at Frans, and finally at Benny. It was a strange moment, as he felt her glance like a heat, making him catch his breath, and he grinned back, trying in vain to think of something to say.

Half an hour later, showered and changed, Benny walked down with Eric and Frans. He hoped he might find the girl at her desk—not for any clear reason, just to see her—but she was gone, and her place was taken by an old man with a long, curling beard. The three of them strode along the dusty street to the town's one café, where they ordered noodles in chili sauce, which seemed the only food to be found in this part of the world. "Here's to the last evening of this long journey," toasted Frans.

"I'll drink to that," agreed Benny.

"But I think I have something better," broke in Eric. "Here's to the dark-eyed beauty of the Sanchakou hotel." The image was hard to resist, and they laughed and clinked their glasses. "You know," Eric continued, "I don't think I've ever seen anyone who looked more like they wanted to escape. And why not, stuck in this terrible place. Yes, I think she would go with anyone who will marry her and take her away from Sanchakou."

Eric's words stayed with Benny as he lay on his flimsy metal bed, which scraped each time he turned over, and they were still with him when he woke. Would she be there by the desk? As if it mattered, he decided. And yet when he went down and she was not he felt irritated, as though he had been somehow cheated. It was better that way, he insisted to himself. He would only have stared and made a fool of himself. The departure was early, following—like everything official in Xinjiang—Beijing time, several zones to the east, and it was still quite dark. As he watched two bus workers load his bag onto the roof rack, shielding his eyes from the wind whipping up dust, he thought of the look she had given him, which had seemed to burn. Should he have stayed and talked to her? Too late now. He felt suddenly annoyed by the finality of it all: that he would never know what might have been. It was stupid to think like this, he told himself as he climbed aboard, but as he squeezed into his seat, the thought of her face gnawed at him. Soon everybody was seated and they were ready. Benny disliked the idea of the engine starting up and yet was somehow impatient for it too, as then he could stop taunting himself with this foolishness.

Nothing happened. A backpacker behind him began to snore.

Benny could see the first glow of dawn in the sky. How long had they been waiting? Half an hour? On previous days they had always left on time. If anything tipped him into decision, in a curious way it was this delay. Benny the geologist, vaguely religious Benny, was not one who usually contemplated great forces dictating his life, but as the minutes crept past he began to feel almost as if something were being intended for him: that each extra second was giving him another chance. Why else, on this very morning, was the bus so delayed? And hell, why shouldn't he have someone truly beautiful for once? Not even Dana had been beautiful: scrawny Dana with her puzzled, dissatisfied eyes. Just because he was forty-six and too heavy, did that mean he was somehow disbarred? He thought of her oval face, her shapely figure, which might all be his if he only had the guts to try. How could he let this slip away, this chance of a lifetime? Besides he would be doing good, rescuing her from this terrible place. He would give her everything she wanted. He would fulfill her dreams. He would love her. He felt he already did.

People were watching him, wondering why he was squeezing his way between the seats toward the door. "Sit down," called out the driver with a glare. "We go."

"I need my bag."

"Not now. We go."

Benny ignored him and strode down the stairs, catching his heel slightly on the last step. Frans, at the window of the bus opposite, was staring. "Benny," he called out through the window, "what's wrong? Are you sick?"

He laughed. "I'm fine. I'm staying here. I'm going to see that girl."

Frans's face broke into a deep, puzzled frown.

Glancing up, Benny saw that luck was on his side; the canvas cover on the roof rack had not yet been tied down. There was no sign of the luggage man, and all at once Benny was clambering up the ladder at the back of the bus, panting from the effort, amazed at himself. There were so many bags, but finally he spotted his own in the far corner and waded through to heave it free. Climbing back down, precariously gripping his bag with his free hand, he nearly collided with a tractor as it drew up below, its trailer full of sacks: the reason for the delay. Back on firm ground, his heroic act completed, Benny felt his bravado slipping away. He lingered in the road, watching as the men heaved sacks onto the roof racks and tied the cover. Even now he could still go back to his seat, which he could see, beckoning to him, empty. But he did not move. Finally the buses roared into life, and one by one they drew away, rows of curious faces staring out at him as they passed.

He stood for a moment by the road, which now seemed so desolate, and all at once he felt stupid, disastrously stupid. As if a girl like that could ever be interested in a guy like him. She would have been dreaming of a young backpacker, not an overweight, middle-aged fool. Now he would be stuck here till the next convoy of buses passed through, and if there wasn't a seat free he would probably have to stand the whole way. He felt reluctant to return to the hotel—she was bound to guess why he had stayed and would be aloof, even amused—but there was nowhere else to stay, so he began wheeling his bag back up the road, hoping someone else would be at the desk. But no, there she was, reading her English language book. She glanced up, eyes opening wide with surprise. "Why are you here?"

He could think of no reason, no excuse, as there was no possible explanation for stopping in Sanchakou. "To see you, I guess."

For just a moment she looked at him, uncertain. And then, to his amazement, her beautiful, perfect face broke into a smile. "How nice." She held out her hand, and he wasn't sure whether to shake it or kiss it. He chose caution and shook. "I'm Mina."

It was crazy, but Benny was almost tempted to propose there and then, standing at the hotel desk, though as yet he had exchanged only a handful of words with her. He wanted to take her away with him and make her his before something could go wrong. Instead he said, "Maybe we can meet later?"

She thought. "You would like to go for a walk? Come here this afternoon at three."

She must like me, he told himself, lying on a bed in the empty dormitory, or at least she must think she could. How strange this was. A day ago he had not known she existed, and now he felt like there was no space in his head for anything else. Was this crazy? Probably it was, and yet he had no desire to go back, as already his previous existence seemed faraway, and empty. His worry was that this would fall away to nothing, like some infuriating dream.

That afternoon they walked through the hot, dusty streets: Benny, Mina, and her younger sister, acting as chaperone. Benny could see people watching them from doorways and windows. The women looked mostly curious, but the men, especially the younger ones, stared at him with visible hostility. It was hardly surprising: a foreigner, not even a handsome foreigner, was threatening to make off with their local beauty. What on earth did he think he was doing? This question popped up from time to time, only to be trampled down by a glance at the girl by his side, by his longing for her, her face, her grace, her shape. How fine it was that she was walking with him, here for him. How wonderful it would be to kiss those lips, to possess her. Perhaps it was her beauty, perhaps it was the presence of the chaperone sister—Benny never did know how much English she understood—but their conversation was bland, and he found himself talking politely, almost like he would to a stranger on a plane, as he described his life in America, his job, his house and car. He mentioned Dana only once. Mina seemed pleased by his descriptions of the huge buildings, the vast roads, and yet she was never overawed, and he realized part of her beauty was her self-possession. Though he liked this in her, it also left him frustrated, as it was so hard to cut through. Only once or twice could he get her to break into a smile.

"No, really, you are cheating me, there are no people who leave a million dollars to cats and dogs?"

"It's true. In the States people will do anything." Each such moment was a victory to him. They were getting on great, just great.

When he asked about her family, she answered briefly, even tersely, listing various relatives. She was happier talking about the English language, asking what mistakes she made—she spoke well and there were not many—or the meaning of some word that puzzled her. When he asked her about her life in Sanchakou, she broke into a shrug. "You can see yourself." She waved an arm dismissively at the dusty street. "There is nothing here. Two streets, people with nothing to do, buses that come and go every day. Kashgar, that is a city, with fine buildings, a beautiful mosque, a famous market, but here there is nothing. Some people like it, as they feel safe knowing everybody they see, but not me. For me every hour here is wasted."

"You'd like to leave?"

"Of course." She lowered her voice. "And the Chinese treat us like animals. They take every good job for themselves, and each year more of them come here to live. They want to make us strangers in our own land. Once they put my brother in jail because he spat when a policeman walked near." Her face darkened. "We hate them."

"That's terrible," Benny agreed, sympathetic yet uneasy. He hoped she didn't want to get him involved in politics. "And you're Muslim?"

"Of course." Her eyes narrowed defensively. "People tell lies about Islam. It is a beautiful faith of peace and wisdom. Some people I know, Islam is their whole life, and they are the best people. But for me . . ." Her words trailed away for a moment. "I want to live, to know this world. It is my need. I cannot help it."

He nodded, reassured. "You're so right, Mina. You must follow your dreams. There's nothing more important."

An hour later the town was filled with the roar of the next convoy of buses. Benny slumped on his bed in the hotel, watching the new arrivals straggle in, and felt annoyed by the thought of her sitting at the hotel desk, exposed to their stares. What if one of them, some young, good-looking backpacker, decided to stay, as he had?

The next day he went for two walks with Mina and her sister. It was on the third morning that everything changed. The three of them had reached the edge of the town, near the huge, shark-fin rock, when Mina suddenly took his hand and, leaving her sister on the road, led the way behind an abandoned concrete building with red Chinese characters daubed on the walls. It was the first time Benny had been alone with her, and the intimacy of the moment took him by surprise, as they stood facing each other in the shade of the wall. The warm wind blew in gusts, making a nearby door creak. He had been waiting impatiently for this chance, and now that it was here—it was so stupid—he found he was overwhelmed, almost like he might cry. He was messing up everything. "I'm sorry, Mina," he said, feeling it all slipping away. "This is crazy, isn't it? You don't want to be with someone like me. Someone old and . . ."

For the first time she looked at him with a kind of warmth, or was it just pity? She silenced him by placing her finger on his lips, which made him shiver, as if somehow lost, and then she stepped forward and they kissed. He held himself back, restraining his own craving to take her in his arms, envelop her. Then she stepped away, watching him. He knew what she was waiting for.

"Mina, will you marry me? I love you. I'll give you everything you want. I'll take you away from here."

She looked at him, not surprised. "I must ask my father."

What did that mean? He hated this uncertainty—the thought that he might lose her after all—and that night he slept badly and ended up taking a sleeping tablet. When he woke, bleary from its effects, and went downstairs, he found Mina's sister sitting in the entrance hall. "Please come." He followed her under the burning sun as she led him through the town to one of the low, concrete houses. Walking inside, his eyes adjusting after the brightness, he found the room filled with a dozen people, all watching him with visible curiosity. A hard-looking man stepped forward from the rest, Mina just beside him.

"My father says welcome to our house."

There was a coolness to her as she spoke that left Benny troubled. Welcome to our house? Did that mean it was agreed? Surely he would not have been invited if it were otherwise, and yet he sensed an unsureness in the faces. Mina's father led the way through to a garden whose greenery took him by surprise after the dusty, dead streets. Vines with fat green grapes gave shade, beneath which was a long table heaped with dishes of meats, cheeses, tomatoes, fruit, and more. So this was what people really ate here: so much for noodles with chili sauce. Benny took his place next to Mina and her father, realizing he had no idea how things were done in this old-fashioned world. Should he make a formal request?

"Sir," he said to Mina's father, "I would like to ask for your daughter's hand in marriage."

He nodded as if this had already been said. "If you marry," Mina translated her father's words, "you will live in America?"

If you marry . . . Benny realized they were talking conditions, so he was right and this was far from decided. "Yes, in America."

The father nodded, satisfied. So far so good. "My father says that my two brothers may want to go to America someday. You will help them?"

Benny hesitated. The brothers were sitting across the table, both younger than Mina, both watching intently. At best this would be a nuisance. And at worst? "This is nothing to do with politics, right? They'd just want to live there?"

Mina's father nodded. "Of course. Just to live."

There seemed nothing to be done. "Sure, I'll do whatever I can."

The brothers looked pleased, but the discussion was not finished. "My father says that he will pay for the wedding, which is our tradition," Mina began, her head bowed, almost as if she were ashamed, "but he asks if there are some things you can provide which are hard for us to find."

Was this what it sounded like? Benny had paid a bribe or two in the past on research trips, and the phrasing seemed ominously similar. "These items, how much will they cost?"

Her father frowned in thought. Yes, this was about money: he could see it on the man's face. All of a sudden Benny felt a little sick. Mina looked far away, closed into herself as she translated the amount. With the strangest feeling, shocked and fascinated, Benny did the mathematics. Eight thousand three hundred dollars, give or take. That was a lot of money, especially here. This was so unreal. He could say no, he reminded himself, and could walk away from all of this. But somehow he knew he never would. He could have her, this beautiful girl, all for himself. Some small part of him was even a little pleased, as if paying money would make her all the more undisputably his. Then judgment returned and he struggled to retrieve his sense of doing right. Perhaps this was perfectly normal here? But Mina's face said otherwise. What did any of this matter anyway? All that was important was that he should be with Mina, that he would rescue her. He was her knight in shining armor. The phrase warmed him, carrying him through this ugly moment, on to practicalities. Could he raise that amount of money in a place like this? He had his credit cards.

"I guess that's okay," he heard himself say. He saw that the tension around the table had lifted now that a bargain had been struck. He sipped from a glass of tea and a little spilled on his shirt. He had just bought himself a wife. No, that wasn't it at all. He was fulfilling dreams, both his and hers. A knight in shining armor, a dream fulfiller. He just wanted to get out of this damn garden, crowded with strangers. Fortunately, it didn't take long to arrange the date. Mina's father understood that Benny could not stay for long, and it was fixed for nine days' time.

Mina walked Benny back to the hotel, this time without her sister as chaperone. Benny wanted to speak, to make a bridge to her, but somehow his thoughts were confused and it was she who broke the silence. "My father makes me ashamed," she said suddenly. "All he cares about is money, about being a big man in this town. But you must know that this is not me. All I want is to be your good wife, for you to be pleased with me."

His feeling toward her flooded back. She was innocent, just as he had always known she was. All at once he pulled her to him, not caring who saw, kissing her, first lightly, then harder, squeezing her tightly. She looked at him, pleased or startled, it was hard to tell. "Till later." She broke away from him and hurried back toward her home.

Benny spent most of the evening at the small telephone office near the hotel. It took him more than an hour to put through a call to his mother, and he soon wished he had not troubled. "Ben, you just can't do this. Think about it, you've only just met her, she's half your age, she's from another country, another religion. You don't know each other. You haven't a thing in common. Show some sense, Ben, this is not going to work."

"It's not going to be like that," he told her. "Ma, you don't understand, I've never been so happy in my life."

"You're leaping into this without thinking, like you always do. Haven't you learned anything from Dana? From Carrie? This will be the same all over again."

"You haven't even met her," he insisted, hating her voice. "She's so wonderful. You have no idea."

His sister, Jean, was more direct. "She's using you. She just wants a passport. This is the dumbest thing you've ever come up with, and that's saying something. Come home, Ben. Alone."

"I'm not asking your advice," he growled back. "I'm inviting you to my wedding." Neither of them was willing to make the journey, needless to say.

He had better luck with his supervisor. Ted Klein always had treated Benny pretty well. Then again, Klein was a lumbering, oversize man, much like Benny. He had even been divorced. "You sure about this, Benny?"

"I'm sure. She's so great. You should see her."

"Hell. Maybe I should pay a visit to Xinjiang myself," he joked. "And you're certain you can actually do this?"

"I rang the embassy. They said it wouldn't be easy, but they didn't say no."

"I guess we can spare you for a little while, seeing as you have a pretty damn good reason."

Benny wasn't looking forward to going to the small bank, just along from the hotel. Would they know what this was for? It seemed quite likely in a one-horse town like this. In the event the Chinese staff were only interested in his credit card, which was of a type they had not seen before. It took most of the day and a series of telephone calls, but finally Benny stood in front of the cashier, watching him count out thick wedges of renminbi banknotes.

Other arrangements proved surprisingly simple. Benny presented the money to Mina's father, and afterward the two of them went to a tiny, dark tailor's shop, where he was measured for a suit. Later Mina and her mother joined them, and they walked to a police office on the edge of the town, where Benny signed his name to a dozen documents while a homesick-looking Chinese official excitedly plied him with questions: Was it true that in America everyone had a car, if not two or three? Was it true that even children had cell phones? Mina walked Benny back to the hotel, and again they kissed. "Today I finished my work at the hotel," she told him. "After this you won't see me until the wedding."

"Why not?" he asked. Seven days away from her?

"It is our tradition."

In the small hours of that night, lying awake, listening to the backpackers' snores, Benny was suddenly certain that he had just been robbed of eight thousand three hundred dollars. How could

he have been so stupid? It was hard to believe Mina had been lying to him all along, as everything about her had rung true, and
yet . . . He got up early the next morning with the backpackers and
walked through town in the dawn light, wondering if he would
even remember the house. No, here it was. He thumped at the
door, expecting no answer, and was about to shout when it swung
open and Mina's father peered out, looking bleary like he had just
woken. In the room Benny could see some form of decorative paper stacked in heaps: just the sort of thing for a wedding. For once
he was glad of the language barrier. "I wanted to check that everything's okay," he said lamely.

The next days passed in a kind of limbo, and Benny spent most
of his time slumped on his bed, reading and rereading a paper-
back thriller about submarines that he had found on the floor, dis-
carded by some backpacker. Each afternoon another bus convoy
rolled in, filling the hotel with noise. Sometimes in the quiet of
night he woke in a panic, his fears oddly contradictory with one
another. Was this a disaster, like his mother and sister had said?
Should he leave on the next bus? What if she changed her mind
and he lost her after all? When he woke the next morning, the
backpackers gone and sunlight streaming through the dirty curtains, his fears seemed small and foolish, and his longing for Mina
was stronger than ever.

Finally the day arrived. Mina's father and brothers came to the
hotel with Benny's suit, which fitted so badly he could barely
squeeze his arms into the tight sleeves. As if that mattered. He
broke into a smile. Today he, Benny Gregg, would be married to
Mina, beautiful, slim, perfect Mina. It was the first time he truly
believed it would happen. The wedding was held in the spacious
garden of a house near Mina's, packed with what seemed most of
the town (aside from the Chinese), and as an occasion it left him
confused. His other weddings, to Carrie and Dana, had structure,
with vows, photographs, eating, and speeches, but this had none
that he could see: for hour after hour people ate and danced to the

Arabic-sounding band, and Benny was introduced to yet more strangers, smiling as best he could, knowing he would probably never see any of them again. Mina looked more beautiful than ever in her wedding robes, if nervous, while Benny's attempts to comfort her with a smile, a joke of "Hi there, Mrs. Gregg," did not seem to help. Her father, by contrast, was clearly enjoying himself, standing importantly in the center of the gathering, greeting all who came near.

It was dark when the moment finally arrived that Benny had been anticipating. The crowd cheered them both down the street to a nearby house, then the door shut, and suddenly they were quite alone in the quiet of a cleanly swept room. Everything seemed back to front. He was the one who had been married—twice—and yet he found himself shy, unnerved by her beauty. Never in his life had he been so close to a girl like this, even across a dinner table, or sitting on a plane. She sensed his nervousness, and it was she who started undressing, pulling off her clothes—almost brusquely—to reveal her perfect shape. Then his nervousness vanished. And what was he feeling as their bodies met? Hunger, of course: a craving to do this. Adoration and love, certainly. And also, somewhere in his mind, a faint sense of theft.

In the morning he found her awake, staring out through the window at an empty yard behind. "When do we go?" was the first thing she said.

They left the very next day. And so, a fortnight late and with a new bride by his side, Benny finally completed his journey to Kashgar. The other passengers, both Western and local, stared with curiosity as a large crowd escorted him and Mina to the bus. To Benny's annoyance, a backpacker leaned out of a window to take a picture. More aggravating still was the backpacker across the aisle, who gawped at Mina until Benny glared and made him look away. As the bus began moving and the crowd below waved good-bye, Mina started to cry.

"Are you all right?"

"Yes, all right," she insisted, and sure enough, once they were out of the town she wiped away her tears. "There," she said, briskly. "That is for my mother and my brothers. But not for Sanchakou." She looked at him with a kind of defiance. "Now I will be happy."

"Attagirl," said Benny, feeling strangely moved.

Not that it was so easy as that. They had to spend several weeks in Beijing, making endless visits to offices, Chinese and American. Of the two, Benny decided that the Americans were worse. The Chinese authorities seemed relatively unconcerned by the thought of losing some Uygur girl, while Benny's compatriots regarded them both suspiciously, as if they posed some kind of threat, to both national security and national morals. To Benny's anger, one official insulted Mina. "Just what kind of work did your wife do at this hotel?" he asked, lingering on the word *work,* but he backed off quickly enough. "It's just a standard question, Mr. Gregg."

Benny and Mina tried to lighten their stay with sightseeing, walking through the hazy furnace of the town to the Forbidden City, the Summer Palace, the Temple of Heaven, and taking a bus tour out to the Great Wall, but Mina refused to be impressed by this, her enemies' capital, while Benny was annoyed by the curious stares that they got from other tourists. Nights came as a relief, when he could possess her anew, and have her beauty to himself. Finally the time came when her documents were ready, and they made their way to the airport. As the plane lumbered into the air, Benny felt a tension lifting. He had rescued her, just like he had promised. Once they were home in Dallas, everything would be fine.

And for a time everything was. Benny loved the feeling of riding in the taxi along familiar highways with this exotic girl by his side. Even the chores of getting his life restarted—leasing a car, getting the condo together—seemed exciting with Mina there. She was intrigued by every detail, especially the machinery, from the timed garden sprinkler to the huge fridge with its spout to pour out ice cubes, and she gasped at the food store they visited, which was the size of an aircraft hangar. Even his car delighted her, with its air-conditioning and stereo.

"Can I learn driving?" she asked.

"Sure you can. I'll fix you up with some lessons."

He took her to some clothing stores, and all at once she was changed. She had looked good before, but now she looked American and her beauty seemed strikingly modern. Benny felt so good teaching her his world, riding in the sunshine with her at his side, and he grinned back at the stares they got, whether they were friendly, wondering, or plain suspicious. "Stare on," he said to himself. "This is Benny Gregg and his wife, Mina. You never imagined you'd see me with a girl like this, did you? But here I am."

He introduced her to his neighbors, the O'Sullivans, the Poznanskys, and Jeff across the road, who ran a sportswear shop in one of the malls, and they duly offered their congratulations. Benny ignored their doubtful glances, convinced he would soon change their minds. Even her meeting with his family was not the disaster he had feared. She cooked dinner at the condo, lamb and vegetables, which turned out really well, and Benny's mother and sister waited, making polite conversation, till Mina went to the kitchen and they could give their judgments.

"She's so beautiful," said Benny's mother, as if this were something tragic.

Jean, though, was more positive. "I like her. She's straight."

The next day Benny returned to work. Ted Klein insisted he bring Mina in for everyone to meet, and Benny fetched her in the late afternoon, enjoying the others' looks of amazement as they toured the corridors. "Bill, Jerry, this is my new wife, Mina."

As they left he could see she was looking a little sad. "Hey, what's up?"

"Sometimes I miss things, small things. It's hard when everything is new."

He tried to see things through her eyes. A town like this must be bewildering after Sanchakou, and he was surprised she was coping so well. "There's a Turkish restaurant near here. That's close to Uygur food, right?"

"I think." She looked unsure.

What was similar was the language, and even Mina seemed surprised by how easily she could communicate with the young Turkish waiter who served them. Benny watched as the two of them chatted away, smiling uneasily at his own exclusion, and interrupting to ask for translations.

"He says he has forty cousins in his hometown," she explained, laughing, "and thirty-nine of them want him to help get them to Dallas."

Work brought problems. Benny hated leaving her alone each morning, and the moment he walked out of the air-conditioning of the house into the heat of the garage he began to feel uneasy. By the time he reached the office, he was wondering what she was doing. He trusted her, of course, but she didn't know this country. What if something happened? He rang her once an hour. At first she laughed.

"I'm watching TV, Benny, learning English."

"Be careful what you watch. There's some gross stuff on there."

"If it's gross then I'll learn more. I don't know gross words."

After a few days she began to sound flat. "I think I must get a job. It's so quiet here. I want to do things here. Maybe I should ask at that Turkish restaurant."

He didn't like the idea at all. "What's the rush? You've only just arrived."

"But I should earn money."

"I'll have a think about it."

The next afternoon when he rang, he heard his own voice on the answering machine, and when he hurried home he found the house was empty. At first he was only frightened for her. Had some weirdo knocked on the door and lured her away? She would have no idea. Then, though, as the minutes turned to an hour, then another, concern turned to suspicion. What if she had left him, just like Dana? It seemed hardly likely, and yet the terrible fact of her absence made anything seem possible. This could have been her intention all along, from the very first moment he had walked back into the Sanchakou hotel: to use him and leave him. But leave him for whom? Unless she knew people here and had never told him? But no, he knew her better than that, surely? He was about to call 911 when the doorbell rang, and at the door were Mina and Jeff from across the road.

"I found this little lady walking over by the convenience store, looking lost as hell."

Benny's suspicions fell away. "Thanks, Jeff. I owe you one." Closing the door, he put his arms around her. "I was so worried. What happened?"

She was crying. "I thought I'd go for a walk, just to get out from the house, down to the mall to buy something for us to eat as a surprise, but it's so hard to find your way. All the houses look the same, and the streets are so long. I couldn't find the mall, and then I couldn't find my way back, till I thought I'd walk forever. The roads here are so empty, just cars, nobody walking."

"Mina, you've got to be careful," he told her, angry now from his fear. "You can't just go walking off like that. There are some bad areas in this town." What if Jeff hadn't seen her by the convenience store? She would still be out there, walking some street. "We've got to get you fixed up, Mina," he told her, businesslike now. "You need a cell so you can call me anytime. More than that, you need driving lessons. We'll probably have to get another car, too. Maybe you should even do some course—computers or something."

She brightened up at his words. "I'd like to know computers."

He did get her the cell phone, but the rest proved more difficult. They went to a driving school that was recommended by someone at work, but Benny didn't like the look of the instructor, with his rock-star ponytail and his eyes that lingered on Mina's face.

"I don't understand, do we go back?" she asked as they returned to the car.

"I want to check out another place to compare."

She frowned. "But I thought your friend said this one was best."

"I'm just not sure about their operation." He did go through the telephone book when they returned, staring at the listings of different schools, but that was all, and he didn't even look up the computer colleges. It was too soon, he told himself: he and Mina needed more time together, to learn to believe in each other, that was all. During the next few days, though, his belief wavered ever further. Everything was fine when they were together, but as soon as he was away he began to feel uneasy, and he dreaded the moment when he would be sent out to the field again. Even now he phoned her so frequently that it had become an office joke.

"Calling someone, Benny? Let me guess."

Her voice sounded less excited. "I hate this TV. They are so ugly, these programs."

"Maybe you should watch something else, Mina. I tell you what, I'll pick up a few videos from the rental store."

"Did you call the computer schools?"

"I wanted to ask some of the guys here in the IT section first."

"You said that before."

"I just haven't had a chance."

The moment he put the telephone down his anxieties began to return. Why was she so intent on a computer course anyway? He had been sure he would feel safe with her once they got back to his own country, but now he almost felt a nostalgia for their weeks of limbo in Beijing, when she had been dependent on him. Here he could feel the power of her looks all the time, turning heads wherever they went. It would be so easy for her . . . He couldn't face that all over again, coming home to find a note. He tried not to let himself panic but was weighed down by a sense of inevitability. It finally happened one Tuesday morning as he was about to go to work. He was late but not worried, as he had no early meetings, when he heard the doorbell ring. Mina was in the kitchen. Opening the door, he found Jeff standing there. "Hi, Benny."

Benny felt his surprise turning sour. "Hi, Jeff."

"I just wanted to make sure you guys are okay. If there's anything I can get you from the mall, let me know. I'm there every day, remember."

Was that surprise on Jeff's face, surprise at finding Benny still at the house? He had never much liked Jeff with his sportswear store, thinking he was so cool. He often had some girl hanging around, but none of them seemed to last. "Sure. If we need anything I'll let you know."

"Okay."

Benny half closed the door, then changed his mind. "Jeff, I don't like you calling round like this. Ring us up first next time, okay?"

Jeff looked stung. Or did he? "Hey, I was only trying to help."

Benny walked into the kitchen, where Mina was making tea. Turning, she saw his look. "What's wrong?"

"That was Jeff at the door. Has he been around before?"

She frowned. "Benny, stop this. I didn't ask him here."

Now he felt foolish. "Hey. I'm sorry. But he's a creep, okay? If he comes here again don't let him in."

"Of course."

The moment he was in the car, driving to work, his fears began to resurface. What if she was lying? But then how could she be? He'd rung her so often, and aside from that one time she had always been there. Unless Jeff had been there too. He was suddenly chilled by the thought of them lying naked in the bed—his bed—as she talked to him on the phone. The one time she had disappeared Jeff had brought her back. That could have been the start of it all. For all he knew they could have been at Jeff's place all that evening. Now he scolded himself for being suspicious, but the suspicion persisted. By the end of the day he had made up his mind, and on his way home he drove out to the security store, spending time examining various locks before he finally made his choice.

"That's a fine model," the salesman congratulated him, "the most child-safe on the market."

"Can you fit it tonight?"

A guy from the store followed Benny's car back through the long suburban streets. Mina watched as he screwed it to the door, looking huge and black above its predecessor. "What's this for?"

"I've been meaning to get a new one for ages," Benny told her. "I just want to know you're safe in here." He paid the locksmith and turned the key three times from the inside.

"Where's my key?"

"It just came with one."

"I don't believe you. You're locking me in here like I am in jail, all because someone came to the door this morning. You insult me." She stared at him. "I thought Sanchakou was terrible, but you know, I think this is worse." A strange look came into her eyes. "What does it take to make you trust me, Benny Gregg? What does it take? Do you want me to be ugly?"

When he woke the next morning, the bed beside him was empty. He touched it for a moment, feeling the faint warmth still there. He knew what had happened, and sure enough, when he searched through his jacket, his door key was gone, and a hundred dollars from his wallet. He sat down for a moment at the top of the stairs, suddenly robbed of breath. And she had lectured him about trust! An awful familiarity flowed through him as he walked through the silent house. He searched every room, but there was no sign of a note. Even Dana had left a note. Why did they have to do this to him? Anger renewed his sense of purpose. He wasn't going to let her get away with it. This time, for once, he would get even.

"Where is she?"

Jeff, standing in his door, looked confused for a second, but then a nasty smile appeared on his face. "So she's skipped? Sorry, Benno, I haven't a clue where she's taken her sweet little ass. If she's screwing around—and hell, who'd blame her?—the lucky guy ain't me. Go on, search the whole damn house for all I care. That bit of pussy ain't here, more's the shame."

Benny hated him, wanted to hit him, smash him, but still for all that he believed him: the surprise on his face was real. But if she wasn't here, then where? There was only one place he could think of, and so he climbed into the car and drove downtown. The Turkish restaurant was still closed when he got there, and he waited, angrily listening to the radio, until the young waiter appeared and began unlocking the door.

"Have you seen my wife? Tell me the truth!"

The waiter's eyes narrowed. "Don't yell at me. I don't know where your wife is. I'm sorry for you, fat man. Sorry but not surprised."

Benny drove back slowly, scouring the streets. She had to be out here somewhere. This made no sense. A hundred dollars wouldn't get her very far. Then a dark thought took him. What if the guy at the Beijing embassy had been right? And Frans too. He knew nothing about her life in Sanchakou, and all sorts of things could go on in a hotel. Benny almost wanted the worst now, to degrade her, so he could climb above his hurt, and he gave himself up to pure white anger. Selling herself, that's what she was doing, standing on some corner this very moment, like any cheap hooker, flaunting her body, selling her wares. The little slut, the dirty whore. Well, this piece of trash was going to get a surprise. He would call Immigration right now and tell them the whole sweet story. She only had status here as his wife. Dana might have got away with this, Carrie too, but this one was going to pay. This little miss would be back in Sanchakou before she knew what had hit her. See how she liked that.

Walking into the house, he opened the phone book in the sitting room and had just found the Immigration and Naturalization

Service entry when he heard a slight noise from the kitchen, the scrape of a chair leg. Benny froze. Should he run back out into the street? That was what people said—don't play the hero, don't take a chance—but then he hesitated. Surely they would have run off or held him up when they heard him come in. Unless? Curiosity got the better of him, and he stepped toward the kitchen, as soundlessly as he was able. Peering round the door, he saw Mina sitting at the kitchen table. In front of her were three huge bagged loaves of white bread and several packets of cheese.

"Where did you get to?" he asked, his anger beginning to ebb.

"To the mall. The grocery store." She sliced a thick piece of white, rubbery cheese and pasted it to a slab of bread.

"I don't understand. What are you doing?"

"What do you think?" She took a bite and began to chew, shooting him a strange look. "I am eating, Benny Gregg. Eating, eating, eating."

YOHANNES WORE RUBBER tire shoes and had a sky blue shawl wrapped around his head to protect himself against the strong Ethiopian sun as he climbed the hill to his village. He climbed purposefully, hurried by the news he brought, and did not stop at his own home but went directly to Mesulu's, calling out her name as he stepped into the yard. "I saw two of them just yesterday," he told her as she glanced round the door. "Two foreigners."

Her eyes widened with interest. He followed her into the hut, which was made from wooden staves, with gaps for ventilation, so thin strips of dazzling sunlight reached out toward them across the earth floor. A pan of water was coming to a boil on the log fire, and steam and smoke swirled into the air. "They were over on the ridge just by Gi'ich," Yohannes explained. "They were going slowly and it was already late afternoon, so they must have stayed somewhere near there last night. That means they'll probably be at Ch'enek tonight."

Mesulu had been waiting for this for some time. The rainy season had just ended, and it was about now that they usually started to come. There were uncertainties, of course. It was already midmorning, and it would be a struggle to reach Ch'enek before dark. Even if she got there it might prove a wasted journey, as Yohannes had admitted it was only his guess that the foreigners would stay there tonight. Still Mesulu had made up her mind. Her husband, who was behind the hut repairing the plow, agreed.

"Of course you must. Almaz can ride on the mule."

But Almaz, their daughter, did not like the idea. "I don't want to go," she told them. "I want to see the lambs."

These had been born the night before at a house farther up the hill and were the excitement of the village morning.

"You can see them when we get back," Mesulu told her.

"But they won't be new then. I want to see them now."

Mesulu and her husband had learned long ago that the only way to persuade Almaz of anything was with carrots. Sticks did not work. "You can see your cousins on the way."

Almaz was unimpressed. "I don't want to see my cousins. I want to see the lambs."

Her mother reached for something stronger. "Your uncle might give you a horse."

Almaz frowned, wondering. "D'you promise?"

"I can't promise. They're his horses. But if you behave well, then I think he will."

The frown slowly cleared. "All right then."

There was a bad moment when Mesulu and her husband helped Almaz onto the mule and she began suddenly coughing, but to their relief the fit passed almost as quickly as it had begun, and a few moments later mother and daughter were making their way down the hill. Mesulu could feel the air growing warmer and heavier as they descended, till finally they reached the stream. As they sat in the shade, letting the mule drink, the priest from Chinkwanit village walked into sight with his long, hooked staff, raising his fingers in blessing. It was a good sign, and Mesulu felt her spirits rise as they began the long climb up the other side of the valley. Several hours later, in the full heat of the afternoon, they reached Mesulu's brother's village. Mesulu had not paid a visit for some time, and her brother and sister-in-law were delighted by the surprise of her arrival, hurrying to prepare a meal of soft brown bread and fast-day vegetables, as their children excitedly plied Almaz with questions.

"Someone in the village here saw them," said Mesulu's brother, when she told him the reason for their journey. "There were two, a husband and wife." He gave a half smile. "Though from what people say you never know with foreigners."

Almaz had already finished her food and was tapping her fingers on the side of the tin plate expectantly.

"D'you want some more?" asked her aunt.

Mesulu remembered her promise. She turned to her brother. "I said you might give her a horse."

The cousins looked annoyed, as they wanted them for themselves. Their father, though, broke into a smile. "Of course," he said, and he led Mesulu and Almaz to the corner of the hut where he kept his carving tools. He had four that were finished, all different sizes, and Almaz at once pointed at the largest.

"Not that one," said Mesulu, annoyed by her daughter's greed.

"She can have whichever she wants," said her brother.

The words were kindly enough, but as he spoke them Mesulu saw something in his look that she did not like: a sorrow, even a pity. For just a moment she hated him. How dare he? Pity meant he already thought of them as doomed. "Have it then, Almaz."

Almaz snatched the horse, hugging it to her. "Can we go back home now?"

The request took Mesulu by surprise. "Of course not."

"Please, Ma." Almaz looked suddenly younger: small and scared. "I don't like those foreigners. They have strange faces."

Mesulu's brother tried to help. "They're nothing to be frightened of. They're people just the same as us. Now do what your mother says. She knows what's best."

Normally Almaz would have put up a fight, but to Mesulu's relief she seemed reluctant to argue in front of people she did not know well. She clutched her horse as they stepped back out into the glaring light.

"Come and visit on your way back," Mesulu's brother urged. "Stay the night."

"Of course," Mesulu agreed, her anger toward him already fading.

There was reassurance in movement, in progressing on their way, and as they plodded onward Mesulu's spirits began to rise. She remembered the priest's blessing by the river, warming herself with the thought. And they were making good time. From her brother's village the path climbed steadily for some way, and the air grew gently cooler and the land emptier and less farmed, until finally they reached a bare, sloping plateau of grassland, with stunted palm trees and giant lobelia that reached high above them like spears. The sun was getting low in the sky when they passed over a slight rise, and abruptly the ground fell steeply away before them, revealing a vast view of rocky hills like so many teeth, stretching away for what seemed a limitless distance, as if half of Africa were visible below them. It was a view that both Mesulu and her daughter had seen many times, but still they stopped for a moment to look. From here the path became narrower and more difficult, following the indented line of the ridge. They had gone only a short distance when Mesulu glimpsed a large group of baboons up ahead, gathered on a low hill, as if in conference.

Almaz's arm rose to point. "Look."

Mesulu nodded, trying not to seem alarmed. She had never liked these animals. Though she had never been harmed by them, she had heard too many stories of their sudden ferocity, and there was something about their eyes—so still and empty—that scared her. And there were so many here, like a whole village. Now she wished she had asked her husband to come. Surely he could have spared a couple of days from the farm. He should at least have offered to . . . The thought remained unfinished. Afterward she would decide that what happened next was the baboons' fault, that if she had not been worrying about them she would have seen how the path sloped awkwardly to one side as it skirted round a large rock. If she had noticed then she would certainly have stopped the mule and taken hold of his harness. By the time she realized the danger it was too late, the animal had felt itself slip and was rearing into the air in panic. In many ways they were lucky. Almaz held on somehow while Mesulu, whether by luck or by instinctive skill, managed to grab the flailing harness the first time. In a moment she had brought the mule back to earth, but by then Almaz had started coughing: a terrible fit that would not stop, not when Mesulu tugged them several yards farther on, where the path was wide and safe, or even when she lifted Almaz down to the ground, gripping her shoulders and shouting out her name, as her daughter spluttered and gasped for breath. Finally Almaz spat out a soft mush that fell scarlet onto the ground by her feet, and the fit was over. For a time the two of them sat by the side of the path, neither saying a word.

"Please, Ma," said Almaz at last, "can we go home?"

A large ant was making off with a piece of the red mush. Mesulu was close to surrender. She was tired and thirsty, and most of all, she was scared.

"We're almost there," she told Almaz with all the confidence she could muster. Oddly enough, it was as if this final effort of bravery unlocked a door. She coaxed Almaz back onto the mule, and then, just a few yards farther on, she saw that the baboons were farther from the path than she had thought, while they showed no signs of leaving their hilltop, watching them pass with only faint interest. A few minutes later she caught sight of Ch'enek and the strange, round house built from stone where the foreigners stayed. Better still, she saw the two foreigners themselves, lying below the building in the weakening sunshine: a man and a woman, just as her brother had said. She quickened her pace, straining to see if she could recognize their guide or mule drivers, who might help her talk to the strangers.

DAN AND LISA sat beneath the hut on a wide, flat rock that was still warm from the day's sun. Beneath them stretched the huge view that they had come all this way to see, spectacular at this dusk hour, an eagle wheeling high above them. Their thoughts, though, were elsewhere.

"I wish they wouldn't do that," said Dan glumly.

"You shouldn't have given her anything," Lisa told him.

"I had to. The little girl looked so terrible."

"If you hadn't given her anything, she might have taken her to a doctor."

They sat for a moment, neither of them much convinced by Lisa's claim.

"Besides," Lisa added, with greater honesty, "we might need those ourselves."

"I had to do something," said Dan doubtfully.

MESULU MADE HER way back down the hill, smiling as she walked, a plastic box of aspirin rattling in her hand. Almaz would take another one tomorrow, and each morning after that, just as the foreigners had told her. Already she was looking a little better, she was sure.

6. Metal

THE FLIGHT WAS an awkward length, too long to pass unnoticed but too short to let one properly relax, and Toby Chisholm had finished his newspaper by Greece, had lost all interest in the airline magazine by Egypt, and then waited for a film—it never came—until he was reduced to the safety leaflet, or peering down at the featureless, scorched beige beneath his window. It was a relief when he finally heard the thump of the landing gear on tarmac. Immigration and customs passed gratifyingly fast, and he was soon stepping out of the airport building and feeling the strong African sun on his skin. He climbed into the back of a battered Mercedes taxi, luggage and briefcase in the trunk, and watched without great interest as an avenue of palm trees flashed by. The thought did occur to him that the driver was going too fast, but he said nothing and then, of course, it was too late. They sped round a corner, and he caught a glimpse of a large crowd of people just ahead, far too close, some holding placards in the unreadable local script, and all facing the other way, toward a line of police beyond. The driver braked and swung the wheel, the car swerved, and Toby watched with a curious sense of unreality as a palm tree reared slowly toward the windshield.

It could have been a good deal worse. The driver had braked away most of the car's speed before it struck, though Toby was still hurled forward in a moment of noise and violence that was too much for his senses to comprehend. Afterward he found himself sprawled in the back, staring up through the window as the car horn blared. He began carefully testing his limbs, twitching ankles and wrists, reassuring himself that nothing was actually broken, though numerous bruises made themselves felt as he sat up, and touching his forehead, he saw a little blood on his finger. He pushed open the car door, and stumbling out onto the tarmac, the roar of the demonstration in his ears, he felt suddenly angry. How dare this happen? Somebody should have warned him. The cause of his trouble—the rioters, or protesters, or whatever they claimed themselves to be—were only a few dozen yards away, but fortunately they seemed uninterested in him, at least for now, as they were far too busy shouting at the police.

Toby took in the accident for the first time. The car looked faintly absurd with its front crumpled into the tree, the hood warped into the air like a spire. He pulled open the front door and peered at the driver, who was holding his head, which was bleeding, though not too much. Toby cast aside his annoyance at the man's driving too fast and tugged him from his seat, sitting him down on the road against a tree. The immediate urgencies dealt with, Toby's thoughts turned to wider questions. He had to contact the authorities, to get help, and he looked with frustration at the line of khaki-clad police standing unreachable beyond the demonstrators. Unless he went round? The crowd thinned at the edge of the road. This thought led him on to the question of his luggage and briefcase, both still in the car trunk, which had obstinately survived the impact: he tried the handle, but it was locked. He had just leaned into the front of the car and taken the ignition keys when a burst of shouting made him look up and he saw that the police had now launched a charge, sending rioters running toward him: it seemed the authorities were coming this way, in which case his problems would be solved. As the police drew near, Toby was about to shout out, but then something about them— the way they were moving?—made him think again, and instead he ducked down behind the taxi. He crouched there, peering over a rusting metal side mirror, and watched with disbelief as one of the police—a tall, lithe man with a drawn face, almost like material stretched over a mask—peeled away from the rest, raising his baton as he ran, and with a kind of elegance of timing, struck the taxi driver neatly across the chest, making a dull sound, like punching a cushion. The driver fell sideways to the ground. Toby was so shocked that he did not think but simply reacted, standing up from behind the car.

"Stop that," he shouted angrily. "How dare you!"

The policeman, who was about to hit the driver again, now glanced up, squinting in momentary confusion at Toby's foreignness, and then, so quickly that Toby had no time even to be surprised, let alone to defend himself, swung his baton and struck Toby on the neck, knocking him against the side of the taxi.

"You . . . ," said Toby feebly, but the policeman had already gone. For a moment Toby remained there, sprawled against the car, catching his breath and trying to digest what had happened, as much surprised as angry. His neck stung, and though he had suffered sharper pain before—his wisdom teeth—this seemed much worse somehow, not least because nobody had hit Toby Chisholm, even given him a slap, since his school playground days. His resentment began to froth up. Why hit me? I'm nothing to do with this, and besides I've just been in a car accident. It had all happened in a moment, and yet already, as he pushed himself free of the car, everything looked different. He glanced with disgust at the police, re-forming their line, and with empathy at the protesters, bruised just like he was. The main question, he reminded himself, was what to do now. Should he just run? But where? He had never been to this city before and had little idea where he was, while there were no cars or taxis to be seen. Something was in his hand, pressed into the skin of his palm by his own tension: the ignition keys, reminding him of his luggage and the briefcase. Everything seemed stuck in an awful kind of loop. As if in confirmation of this thought, he heard another roar of shouts and saw that protesters were again running toward him as the police readied themselves for another charge. Toby's first instinct was to run too, and he even took a couple of steps, but then stopped himself. What about the driver? Yes, he was a stranger who meant nothing to Toby aside from resentment at the man's poor driving, and yet Toby could hardly just leave him here to further violence. So, frowning with a kind of angry impatience, he tugged the man to his feet and began to drag him away—like helping a drunk—through the line of palm trees and toward a beckoning side street.

A few steps farther and everything changed: instead of the wide boulevard of the airport road, Toby found himself in a narrow, sloping street of wooden slum houses. He staggered down this with the driver, protesters hurrying past, and he was just beginning to wonder how far his strength would last when he noticed a man in a torn jacket excitedly beckoning toward the open door of a house. Toby hesitated, wary of exchanging his known danger for something entirely uncertain, but anything was better, surely, than remaining here on the open street to be batoned again. Following the man into the semidarkness of the house, the door rattling shut behind him, he found himself surrounded by a small crowd of staring people. Was he in danger, was he going to die, he wondered, feeling a curious lack of concern, his sense of alarm exhausted by the disasters that had already occurred. But no, he could see from their faces that these people were not angry but curious. The man in the torn jacket seemed to sense his unease and shooed the others back, helping Toby and the driver toward a kind of bench, made from a wooden plank on a platform of dried mud.

"He says his name is Mogas," explained the driver, who was now recovered enough to speak. "He says please be welcome to his poor house." There was something absurd about this polite exchange in the midst of a riot, and Toby fended off an urge to laugh. For some reason he found the others in the room were smiling at him now, as if in admiration. But why? The explanation came soon enough. "Thank you for helping me," said the driver. "I told them how the policeman hit you with his stick and you took me away from there. I hate them. They're not men. They're animals."

A phrase came into Toby's head—Toby Chisholm, the people's hero—and for a second time he almost laughed. He glanced around the room—not a house at all but a hut, with an earth floor and frail walls like garden fencing—and realized that never in all his work trips (and they had taken him to some out-of-the-way countries) had he been anywhere as poor as this. But at least he was safe here. How odd it was. These strangers, watching him, were the kind of people he usually saw only through a taxi window—barely saw at all—but now they felt like people he knew quite well. He could even guess their characters: Mogas had a kindly face, that one in the corner looked like he had a temper, while this one smiled with his mouth open, as if he would laugh at stupid jokes. Just for a moment Toby confused himself by imagining them all sitting comfortably in his favorite pub in the pretty English village where he lived.

A woman had brought a pot of water that she had boiled on the fire. "Mr. Mogas says his wife will clean your wounds," the driver explained. The cloth she held up was discouragingly gray, but he felt reluctant to refuse this kindness. "Tell him thank you."

"Mr. Mogas asks, What country are you from?"

For a moment Toby hesitated, uneasy. "Britain." His concern, though, was unnecessary as the answer was met with approving looks.

"Mr. Mogas asks, Please can you tell people in your country about the bad things that happen here? Two days ago government says prices for bread and gas must rise again, though our wages stay always the same. These days government think only to make themselves rich, to take our money and give nothing, and Mr. Mogas says, How can you have children when this happens?" To illustrate his point, Mogas ushered three of them forward. The youngest was small and still a little unsteady on his feet, while the oldest girl had clever eyes, cleverer than those of Toby's own daughter, Tina. Toby had always been proud of his worldliness, and on another day he would probably have regarded the scene warily, sensing himself being pushed, but now he felt strangely moved. What was it like trying to raise children in a place like this? Did they all live in this one room? Did they go to school? What happened when they got ill? Toby and Clary spent so much time worrying about their children's education, and the quality of the local hospital, and now their anxiousness seemed absurd.

"Very beautiful," said the driver, holding the photograph of Clary, Justin, and Tina in the garden. The sight of them sitting on the familiar bench on the deck in the soft, late afternoon English sunshine caused Toby a momentary rush of longing. "Please tell Mr. Mogas he has lovely children." It was odd, but all of a sudden Toby found himself wanting these strangers to think of him as their equal, as if to match the bruises they shared. "And tell him I'll tell people in my country about your troubles." Was this true? Anything seemed possible now. The smiles all around grew broader. Mogas's wife was holding out a plate of food—some kind of spongy bread next to a dark red sauce—and Toby would have accepted, but the driver was tapping him on the arm. "It's quiet outside now. I must go back to the car."

Toby glanced through a gap in the flimsy wall, and sure enough, it looked peaceful, with no sounds of trouble, just a couple of people strolling unhurriedly through the dusk. "I should be going, too." To his surprise, a part of him almost wanted to stay. With difficulty he fended off further insistence that he should eat and stood up. Everyone in the hut accompanied him as he walked stiffly up the hill. There was no sign of police on the airport road, or of the battle that had taken place. The car was just as before, hood crumpled into the palm tree, and though the driver tried the ignition, it was dead. "Is there something I can do?" offered Toby.

The driver smiled. "You have helped me enough." He took Toby's luggage from the trunk, and the others waded into the road, forcing a taxi to stop. In the back sat a pale-looking foreigner, glaring uneasily at the ragged crowd who had halted his journey, and it occurred to Toby that if his plane had been late this could have been him. Already the idea seemed impossible, as he felt like he was the opposite of this stranger in every way.

A few minutes later Toby walked into the foyer of his hotel. The desk staff, shocked by the sight of him, insisted on calling a doctor, who confirmed what Toby already knew—that nothing was broken—and put a dressing on the cut on his neck. Then Toby found himself in the quiet of his room, the door clicking shut as the porter left with his dollar, and all at once he realized his arms and shoulders were shaking. There was a note on the desk, and though it was short enough, it took three attempts before he read it and understood that it was from the embassy, telling him that his meeting had been postponed to the day after tomorrow. Should he ring them now, and give them a piece of his mind about what had happened? Instead he rang Clary.

"Oh, my God. Toby, are you all right?"

"Really, it was nothing, just a few bruises." He should tell her it all, about the policeman and his baton, about Mogas and the others, but somehow he could not, not just now. Already it seemed impossible that he had seen Clary just this morning, when she drove him through the English winter dark to the airport. "How was your day?"

Clary understood: she always did. There had been bad moments on other work trips, and nothing calmed him down more than to hear the small details of her life. "Let me see . . . Mum rang and said her cold's worse again. Justin rang and said he had almost scored a goal in the match against St. Anthony's but it hit the post and in the end they lost three to one . . ." Toby had so wanted to hear all of this, but now he found his thoughts drifting away. ". . . and the builders finally sent the quote for the swimming pool, though it seemed rather high. It stopped raining in the afternoon, and actually it was quite nice for a bit."

Afterward Toby sat for a time by the large hotel window, staring out at the faint, twinkling lights of the city below.

WHEN TOBY WOKE the next morning, something odd happened. Even before he opened his eyes he knew. It was hard to understand, as nothing had changed since last night except that he had slept, and yet everything felt different now, almost as if he had evolved into another person. He *knew*, without a shadow of doubt, that his life would never be the same. He would give up his job. He would change everything. Not just because of yesterday, either. He had been close to this for some time, he could see that now, and yesterday had simply nudged him on.

He wanted to tell someone, anyone, everyone. Most of all he wanted them all to go to hell: all of them at the office, with their bragging and competing and celebration booze-ups after a big sale. For that matter the ones at the embassies, too, with their smug smiles. He reached for the telephone, angry phrases ringing in his head, only to realize that the London office would not be open yet, or the embassy here. Should he ring Clary? He didn't want to wake her. He tried to imagine what she would think. She would be shocked, of course, but she would understand, he was sure, if not now then with time. The implications of his decision began to rise up before him, vast yet not so much so as to dent his determination. Yes, the children might have to change schools, and they might even have to move, but it would be well worth it in the end. Clary would be pleased because he, Toby, would be better, with no more dark moods or rages over small things. He *knew* he would be free of them.

He climbed out of bed, feeling lighter, then showered and dressed. He was about to put on a clean jacket when suddenly, at a whim, he changed his mind and picked up the one he had been wearing the day before, with its long, thin bloodstain across the collar, where the policeman had struck him with his baton. How extraordinary this was: he was living by symbols, almost as if this were a revolution, his own personal revolution. Or like falling in love. Walking down to the hotel foyer, he ignored the man at the desk—"Breakfast, sir?"—and strode out into the dazzling light. The city, with its hurrying crowds, its packed buses groaning by, seemed to match his racing thoughts. He had been to so many towns like this, but now he felt as if he had never really seen any of them, his eyes closed as he was whisked back and forth in airport taxis. It had taken Mogas and the others—even the brutal policeman—to make him see. This was not a beautiful city, all cracked tarmac and cheap concrete buildings, and yet in its own way it was extraordinary, with its views of distant brown mountains fading into dust. And what was more, he, Toby Chisholm, felt a part of this now, connected with the lives of the strangers striding by, in a way he never could have been before. He realized, surprised, that he had not felt so happy for years. He could even see his own happiness on strangers' faces as they grinned back, reflecting his smile.

All that day he walked, past street stalls and beggars, through the center and beyond, almost to the edge of the sprawling town. He stopped at a small, earth-floored local restaurant, where the customers watched in surprise as he sat down and pointed to the soggy, spicy food the others were eating. Their food would be his: it was another symbol. The sky was almost dark by the time he finally stumbled back into the hotel. The man at the desk gave him four telephone messages, one from the embassy and three from the office, and he took them with a nod, stepped into the elevator, and tore them into small pieces. As he walked into his room, he thought of ringing the office—it would still be open—but instead he lay down on the bed and almost at once fell into a deep sleep.

HE HAD NO idea what time it was when he woke, but from the quietness of the hotel he guessed it must be early in the morning. He was still wearing his clothes of the day before, and as he got up to undress he was aware that everything was slipping. His resolve was failing. He could feel it, as if his position as a person was shifting, sliding back from the high ground. He hurried back to bed, refusing to give up hope, determined that sleep would bring a change.

It did, too, but not the one he wanted. Dawn was breaking through the window when he woke again, and even before he opened his eyes he felt a kind of grayness: an anticipation of defeat. A thought came to him and would not go away. He could not let Clary and the children down, as they would never understand: how could they, when his whole existence for the last fifteen years had been to give them this life? He had insisted on it, in fact. Then another, more dispiriting notion came to him. None of this had ever been real, and deep down he had even known this himself: that was why he had never made the telephone calls.

Still he clung to hope. He wore his revolutionary jacket with its fading bloodstain to go down to breakfast, and walking into the dining room he looked with scorn at the people gathered there— the usual collection of journalists, salesmen, aid workers, and the odd spoiled tourist—as if they had nothing to do with him, Toby Chisholm. He picked up a Western newspaper, dated the day before, and hurriedly scanned the foreign pages, but no, there was no mention of the riot. He felt the tug of his disappointment, knowing he should not be surprised. He would never have noticed it himself if the plane had been late or early, or the taxi driver had not been driving too fast. All at once he was hungry, piling his plate high with bread, bacon, eggs, and sausages. Feeling slightly sick, he returned to his room and lay on the bed, and was surprised by a strange urge to cry, which he had not done since he was a child. He could feel his stomach tense as he began gently to shake and tears formed around his eyes. Tears for what? He hardly knew himself. They never came through.

After that he lay motionless on the bed for a long time, ignoring the ring of the telephone. Finally, just before ten, he slowly climbed to his feet, feeling blank. He showered, dried himself, and began dressing in front of the mirror. As he put on the white shirt and the spotless jacket, tied his red and blue diamond tie, and slipped his feet into his shining, polished shoes, old arguments came to him, but with a kind of halfheartedness that left him unmoved, like something memorized from long ago. *If it's not us then it'll only be someone else. What's more, it's better if it's us, as otherwise . . .* He dabbed clean the dressing on his neck and trimmed its fraying edge with nail scissors. Walking out of the hotel, he felt suddenly drained and wondered if he could do this after all, but then, as he sat in the taxi, his professional experience came back to him and a kind of automatic confidence bobbed into place. Of course he could do this: it was second nature to him. Sure enough, as he walked into the ministry building his stride became clipped and assured, and he could feel his smile was right: not ostentatious but winning.

"It has a good speed," he explained as he sat by the minister's desk, "of up to a hundred thirty kilometers per hour, which is faster than most vehicles in this class. The machine gun comes with a state-of-the-art night vision sight, and is of a very useful caliber, heavy enough to deal with all kinds of situations, while the main armament, the thirty-millimeter cannon, can pack a really good punch. It's presently in service in a good number of countries, including two of your neighbors, I have the full details here"—he flicked another document from his briefcase with a smile—"and was used very effectively by British forces during the last Gulf conflict. I think you'll find the price extremely competitive."

7. Taste

THE FUNERAL WAS not until noon, and so, smiling at her decision, Caroline made her way down through the house to the kitchen cupboard. Even before she opened the box with its elegant, old-fashioned lettering, she guessed what had happened from its lightness in her hand, and sure enough, when she peered inside she saw that a portion of the marrons glacés was gone. It was a week or more since she had last eaten any, while the removal was not excessive, perhaps a quarter of what had been there, and a less observant person might never have noticed. Caroline's expression hardened. There had been other times when she had suspected. She was almost certain about those Swiss chocolates, and the big tin of Italian amaretto biscuits that had emptied so suspiciously quickly. She had turned a blind eye so far, wearied by the very thought of the problem, but now as she stared at the looted box, she felt suddenly tight with anger. How dare this one small pleasure of hers be ruined? Her treat to brighten the day? Yes, there were still marrons left, but that was not the point, as the whole joy of them was spoiled. She knew who had done it, of course—there was only one possible culprit—but Caroline had a strong sense of mental orderliness and was determined to do this properly. So she turned to the cook, who was just round the corner chopping vegetables.

"Dina, have you by any chance used some of the marrons glacés? You know, those sugared chestnuts in the pretty red box?"

Dina, as Caroline had known she would, looked at her blankly, with no hint of alarm. "But no, Lady Farre, I don't touch them ever."

Caroline smiled. "That's what I thought." She climbed the narrow stairway quietly, almost like a huntress. Nadia was in the conference room, loudly humming one of her tunes, and Caroline squeezed her way round the long table toward her. "Nadia?" she asked, with a careful smile, "d'you by any chance know what's become of the marrons glacés? You know, those chestnut sweets? I think some have gone missing."

Nadia put down her dusting cloth and began what was unmistakably a performance. First she paused to think, then she frowned as if in disappointment at the thoughts that came, and finally she gave a slow, somber shake of her head. "No, I don't know what happens, Lady Farre. You are sure they are gone?"

"Quite sure."

Nadia frowned again, but then her face suddenly lit up with an answer. "Those men who fixed the water. Maybe they take it?"

"But that was much too long ago."

"You think?" Nadia opened her eyes wide in wonder. "Then really it is a big mystery."

Caroline walked up to her dressing room, annoyed with herself for not forcing the matter. And yet it was not so easy: if she had accused the girl outright, she would only have denied it, probably with tears. Caroline changed for the funeral, impatiently trying and discarding different arrangements of clothes, and her irritation worked away inside her like a bad seed, causing her to murmur aloud as she buttoned a blouse or reached for a broach. The sneaking, cheating impudence. How dare she insult her, Caroline, with her crude lies? She felt a sour yet exhilarating rush of dislike for the girl's noisy voice, her poor English, her cheap, showy clothes, her constant flirty smile—she even used it on Gerald's aged father—and her interminable humming of that salsa or tango or whatever it was. Brushing her hair in hard, angry strokes, Caroline surprised herself with lurid imaginings of retribution:

striking Nadia's head with a heavy glass paperweight, or choking her silly neck with the curtain cord. The poor taste of these thoughts cooled her feelings a little, but not greatly, and once dressed she strode purposefully into Gerald's study. As usual he was on the telephone.

"Just sack her," he told her when he finally finished. "Come to think of it, I'm sure some of my Gentleman's Relish has gone AWOL."

"But how can I? I haven't any proof."

Gerald rolled his eyes. "What's it matter? This isn't a court of law. Just tell her you don't like her bloody cleaning. You said the other day that she wasn't much good."

"I'm not going to just dismiss her like that."

"Don't then." Gerald gave an exasperated sigh. "Now I've got to get ready, as the car will be here. And, Caroline, can you do me a favor? The Baxters will be at this thing. I know you don't find them stimulating company"—sarcasm was creeping back into his voice—"but can you at least try to be civil? Ed's done really well on this African deal we're working on. It would be nice if you could help a little for once."

It was a curiosity of their house that, though it was full of rooms, somehow there seemed nowhere to sit. Caroline took her anger down the stairs, past Nadia's hateful humming, past Gerald's assistant, Angela, clacking on her computer in the office, and finally into the kitchen, only to be driven back up by Dina's preparations for dinner. The thought occurred to her, and not for the first time, that though this house was her property, with her name on a deed in some lawyer's files, it seemed more as if it belonged to all these people who filled its space—whom she and Gerald paid—while she, Caroline, felt almost like a hotel guest. She ended up perched on a chair in their son Marcus's bedroom—he was still up at Cambridge—until finally she was released by the sound of the doorbell. She and Gerald sat in silence as they were driven through a windy central London. The driver was slow to open their doors, and Gerald shot him a look, murmuring to Caroline, "And his cap's dirty. I might as well use some Brixton minicab firm."

The funeral was for a City colleague of Gerald's, whom Caroline was unsure if she had ever met, and yet she was aware that she should have been rather moved. The man had died relatively young, in his early fifties, and he had clearly been greatly loved, judging by his wife's and children's struggles to get through their addresses at the service. The eldest daughter was particularly affected as she recounted, in a dazed monotone, how her father had impetuously taken her to Scotland to help her recover from a broken relationship. And yet through it all Caroline found her mind kept wandering off, so she missed half of what was being said. She could not help it: all she could think of were the marrons glacés. It was so brazenly unforgivable. Ever since she had taken Nadia on, a year and a half ago, she had shown her nothing but kindness, asking Dr. Fothergill to look at her little daughter that time she had been so ill, and paying her wages for ten full days when her father had died and she had to fly back to Brazil. And in return . . . ? The little tart, stealing right from under her very nose.

Aside from the dead man's family, the reception was noisy and cheerful. Then again, in Caroline's experience these events often were, as guests excitedly caught up with people they had not seen for ages. She gulped down a glass of wine and was surprised for a moment by the sight of a young man chatting to some girl. He looked so much like Marcus. Or did he? He was probably just two or three years older than her son—people rose so fast in the City these days—and glancing more carefully she realized that the resemblance was less in his face than in his manner. The discovery was faintly bothering, as try as she might, she found she rather disliked this young man, with his smooth, throwaway smile and his showy way of leaning against the huge stone fireplace. The girl looked as if she did not much like him either. Was Marcus like that? Part of her still thought of him as a plump, needy infant of twenty years ago, hungry for her attention. What if she got one of those camcorders and set it up in the kitchen? She had heard of people using them to check on their nannies. But where could she put it? On one of the high cupboards, angled downward in some way? Nadia was no fool, and unless it was cleverly disguised she wouldn't touch a thing in the fridge. For a moment Caroline was faintly surprised by her own thinking: that she did not want to stop the thefts from happening so much as to catch the girl, and punish her in some way. She reached for another glass of wine, not caring that it was her third, and then found herself peering at a face, trying to divine its familiarity. "Julia?"

"Caroline."

It was the first good thing that had happened all day, and Caroline broke into a smile. "It must be so long."

Julia surprised her with her precision. "Eighteen years?"

"As much as that?" Even further back was their time together at secretarial college at Oxford, when they had strolled down narrow, echoing streets after closing time, talking loudly from sweet pub wine. "D'you ever see Debbie? Or that nice Dutch girl, Helena?"

"Not since then."

"And how's"—Caroline reached for a name and found it— "Freddy?"

"Decide for yourself." Julia nodded toward a figure some yards distant, whom Caroline failed to recognize in any way: plump, bald, and smiling too much as he held a canapé in each hand.

"He looks very well," said Caroline brightly. For a moment silence threatened. "So where are you living?"

It was the wrong question. There had been a faint wariness to Julia from the moment they had met—a resistance to Caroline's friendliness—and now she stiffened. "Teddington."

Caroline tried to think where it was—she had definitely seen the name, perhaps on some motorway exit sign—but all that came to her was a linked word. "Near the lock?"

Again Caroline had unwittingly said the wrong thing, and now a dogged look appeared on Julia's face. "Actually no." She looked away. "You're in Eaton Square."

It was a surprise, but not a great one. Gerald was often in the business pages these days, and Caroline had almost grown used to strangers and near strangers knowing details of her life. "Yes."

"That must be nice."

There was no missing the hard edge to Julia's voice, and Caroline felt a kind of impatience. How ludicrous this was, to fall out with this friend of years ago—a friend with whom she should be happily reminiscing about old times, or arranging to meet for lunch—and all because of houses and money. As if they mattered. She wanted to soothe away Julia's envy, to show that she had troubles too, to make everything right again, and taking a large gulp of wine, she began talking about—of all things—how Nadia had been stealing from the fridge. Even as she started she knew it was the wrong choice, and yet she could not stop herself, babbling ever more quickly as Julia's eyes narrowed.

"Trouble with the servants? How simply ghastly."

Caroline plowed on regardless. "I told Gerald, but he just doesn't understand."

Some form of verbal violence was inevitable, and Julia's eyes shone with a nasty gleam. "How is Gerald? Actually I'm surprised you're still together. Everyone assumed he was only interested in your money, and these days he's making such a ton of it himself."

Though Caroline had been steeling herself for something unpleasant, still she was taken aback, not so much by the words as by the depth of their mean-mindedness.

Julia, having stabbed, was looking to escape. "Really I should go and rescue Freddy."

Ripostes under pressure had never been Caroline's strong point, but this time she found one. "Have a safe journey back to Teddington," she said, stretching the name scornfully. It was hardly an inspired reply, and yet it worked, almost too well, and Julia's face crumpled.

Gerald was pushing his way through the melee. "I've just had a call from work. Something's come up over that damn weapons deal—bloody Africa—and I'll have to pop back for a few hours. Will you be all right getting yourself home?"

It was not a question. "I'll be fine."

Twenty minutes later, sitting in the back of the cab, her fingers drumming on her bag, Caroline felt unsure where her anger should point. It had to go somewhere as she could feel it pulsing round her, tightening her chest and clenching her hands. At Julia for being so foul? At herself for being so inept with her? At Gerald? Or . . . ? A thought came to her, sudden and captivating, and her eyes narrowing, she reached into her handbag for her address book and mobile phone.

"Hello?"

Caroline disconnected at once and then leaned forward to the driver's window. "Actually I've had a change of mind. I wonder if you could take me to . . ." She read out the address.

The driver glanced back in surprise. "You sure?"

They were soon leaving the high towers of the City behind them. In all her London years, Caroline had hardly been to the East End, and its remorseless ugliness took her a little by surprise: the disjointed landscape of small terraced houses and tower blocks, as if two cities had been awkwardly merged together. And it went on for so long. They seemed to be driving interminably, the cab meter clicking higher as they passed along yet another grim boulevard of chain stores and gas stations. Caroline's anger swept her through the miles, and it was only when they finally stopped that she began to wonder at what she was doing.

"That's the one," said the driver doubtfully.

They had stopped beside a muddy lawn, behind which stood a high, gray tower block. Caroline hesitated, but she could hardly turn back having come all this way—she would look such a fool— and so she opened the door. Hearing the cab drive away, suddenly self-conscious in her smart funeral clothes, she regretted not having made him stay. What if this wasn't even the right place? She might have written it down wrongly, or the driver could have made a mistake. A man walking a vicious-looking dog stared at her in surprise but, to her relief, walked on. And then, stepping into the dark entrance hall, she saw the familiar name on the list of flats. The elevator stank of urine and old beer, but she hardly cared as her anger had returned, filling her up with its heat; her hand gripped the rail. She stepped onto the landing, pressed the bell, and watched as the door opened and Nadia looked out in surprise.

"Lady Farre? But why . . . ?"

Caroline did not reply but pushed past her into the flat, passing brightly colored walls and a painting with palm trees, breathing in unfamiliar cooking smells. That room had music—the same moody tune that Nadia had been humming that morning—and so Caroline strode on to the next, only to find herself staring at a bed. Where was the damn kitchen? Turning, she found her way blocked by Nadia's little girl—Jeninha?—clapping her hands at the surprise of a visitor. Caroline stepped round her, ignoring Nadia's shouts.

"But, Lady Farre, please, I don't understand."

And here, at last, was the kitchen, with a huge bowl of strange red fruit on the table, and a pot of something cooking on the stove. Caroline tugged open the fridge door, and there, suddenly before her, was all the evidence she had sought, far more in fact than she had hoped for: a jar of Harvey Nichols choice Italian red peppers and another of black olive paste; a box of the Swiss chocolates; three Harrods jams, and two small pots of Gerald's Gentleman's Relish. And there on the top shelf, right before her eyes, wrapped in two napkins, were half a dozen marrons glacés.

Nadia looked alarmed. "Lady Farre, please listen to me . . ."

It was the moment of triumph that Caroline had been hungering for all day—she had her, noosed, caught, crushed—and yet now that it had finally come, something strange happened. Caroline tried to speak, but somehow she could think of no words, and she felt her lip begin to tremble. Full collapse followed almost at once, and to her great confusion, she felt her eyes fill with tears.

Oddly enough, Nadia did not seem entirely surprised. "Come and sit," she told her with new authority, leading Caroline into the living room, where she slumped on a long, comfortable sofa. Jeninha watched her with concerned eyes, and through the tears that would not stop, Caroline was puzzled to realize that she rather liked this flat with its bright walls and its rich cooking smell, all hidden away from the threatening ugliness outside. She even liked the music. Everything seemed upside down as, with a jolt, she finally grasped the crucial fact that she had failed to see for so long. She was envious of Nadia, and always had been. Why? Because she was so infuriatingly, incorrigibly cheerful. Because she never seemed to care what anybody else thought. Most of all because her life was so evidently her own, while Caroline's—and Gerald's— seemed like some dreary, uncomfortable display, to impress other people.

Nadia emerged from the kitchen carrying a tray with a bowl of the stew from the stove, as well as a glass of warming spirit and two marrons glacés. As Caroline ate the delicious, burning food, Nadia sat back on the sofa, watching her with undisguised curiosity, and Caroline wondered what on earth she could say.

"I'm not going back to all that," she suddenly announced, and even as she spoke the words, she knew that she never quite would.

8. Sound

COLIN GRIFFIN WAS happy with his life but less happy with this particular day, and as he walked home he glared slightly at the streetlamps with their yellow halos. He was proud of his job on the magazine, with its young atmosphere—people lounging at meetings in their casual street clothes—and he enjoyed the envious smiles of old university friends in more conventional jobs, but there were days, and this was one, when writing about the music industry could be infuriating. He had wasted half his afternoon trying to arrange an interview with a rising new band, being passed on from one telephone extension to another until, just when he thought everything was finally fixed, someone rang back and said that of course they could not do Wednesday as—didn't he know?—they were off to Bhutan to take in a Buddhist festival.

Colin had walked some yards along the lane where he lived when he heard footsteps echoing behind him. Without thinking he glanced over his shoulder and saw a man of about his own age, his dark-skinned face half shrouded in his fleece hood, so he looked like some kind of urban monk. Colin knew he had seen him somewhere before, though he had no idea where. In a pub, or club, or driving a minicab? Though the remembrance was elusive, tagged to it was a faint aura of distrust, and as if in confirmation of this, he saw that the man was glaring at him. Colin looked away. He was not especially prone to fear—he had rowed for his college at Cambridge, just two years back, and always assumed he could look after himself—but as he walked on, the footsteps clacking steadily behind him, he felt uneasy. He disliked this sensation of being seen without seeing, and made a conscious effort not to speed up and so betray his disquiet. If it came to a fight—as if it would?—would he know what to do? He had not punched anyone since he was fifteen. Finally he reached his door, shutting it behind him with a slight slam.

He had moved into the flat barely a month before, and until now he had never thought to worry about its location, as he had rather liked the lane's eccentric narrowness and absence of cars— he had laughed when the estate agent apologized about the lack of parking—while even the rattle of trains along the railway embankment opposite quite suited him, making him think of black-and-white films. Now, though, standing in the tiny hallway, hearing the footsteps tap unhurriedly past, he felt less sure. At the same time he also felt annoyed by his own reaction. Was he being absurd? Colin was no racist—he disliked people he met who were, and would tell them so—but he was also honest, and deep down, he knew he would have been less alarmed if the man walking behind him had been white.

It was a small enough incident, and his evening soon returned to the comfort of routine, as he strode back and forth through the small flat, with its showroom-new furniture and lingering smell of paint. He microwaved a Thai chicken meal from the supermarket, rang Phillipa, who was still away on her trip, then watched a dose of television and fell into his bed. He would soon have forgotten all about the footsteps except that, two nights later, he heard them again. This time he recognized their rhythm almost at once, though this did not stop him from glancing back over his shoulder. There he was, sure enough, half shrouded beneath his gray hood, and fixing Colin with the same angry-looking stare. Colin glanced away. Where could he have seen him? Working in the tube station? But they were all pretty friendly down there. At the music shop on the High Street? That didn't fit either.

He was closer behind him this time, the footsteps louder, and

Colin found the lane seemed somehow longer than usual and darker in the spaces between lampposts. As he approached his flat, key in hand, he found himself regretting that there was no front garden—all the houses opened straight onto the lane—and tried to calculate his pursuer's speed and nearness. Would he have time to unlock the door and close it behind him before he caught up? Probably it was foolish, but he did not at all like the thought of standing there, his back blind and exposed. Why take chances? He was reaching toward the lock when his disquiet won out, and almost involuntarily, he turned round to face the footsteps, clutching his keys in his fingers like brass knuckles. The moment that followed was strange, as the two of them faced each other, one walking and one standing still. Should he say something, Colin wondered. But what? He did not want to risk making this tension worse, but he was not going to look weak either, and so he met the other man's stare as he strode slowly past. Only when he had disappeared around the corner did Colin finally let himself into the flat, feeling his heart beating fast.

Later that evening Philippa came over. They had not seen each other for more than a week because of her work trip, and he had been looking forward to her visit all day. Ever since they had become a couple, several months back, their reunions had followed much the same pattern: the air would be filled with a pleasing tension as they drank their wine and cooked dinner. They would then eat on the sofa, often leaving their food unfinished as they lost themselves in the pleasure of releasing each other's bodies from belts and buttons and zippers, until the need grew too strong and they would carry their wineglasses to the bedroom. This time, though, nothing seemed quite right. Colin, worried after the footsteps business, watched for her anxiously through the window, and she had hardly walked in the door, carrying her neat overnight bag, when he began to recount what had happened.

She frowned. "How creepy."

He had been hungry to unburden himself of the story, but now it was done he wondered if he had been mistaken: the last thing he wanted was to scare her. "It's probably nothing."

She looked unconvinced. "God, I hope so. I've never liked that lane."

They ate dinner on the sofa, just as usual, and made love afterward, but without the simple spontaneity of other evenings, as if this one had been spoiled. Afterward, as they lay side by side in the dark, she again asked about the footsteps man. "Did he threaten you?"

Colin found it hard to explain. "Not exactly. But he gave me this really nasty look."

"Did he say anything?"

"No, that was the weird thing. I didn't either. And yet I could feel this anger coming from him, like real hatred."

"How awful."

When they parted the next morning, bleary and rushed as the tube train slowed for Philippa's station, she was vague as to when they should next meet. "Thursday? No, I'm pretty sure I've got some work thing."

"I'll meet you at the tube station and walk you down the lane."

"That's sweet." The train doors were opening. "Look, I'll give you a ring tomorrow."

It was not like her to prevaricate, and he hated the idea that she might be nervous about visiting his flat, as—though he had never told her so—he had really bought it for her. He had felt all wrong trying to woo her from the shared house where he had lived before, where tenants listened at their doors to hear if the bathroom was free. He had wanted somewhere where he could honor her and tempt her to him. Not that it had been easy finding a place. London prices were almost impossible these days, especially for someone barely two years out of university, earning a modest magazine salary, so even with help from his parents he'd had to search long and hard. What he found was not ideal—it was small, and not in one of the best areas—but still he had been proud. He was one of the first among his Cambridge friends to own a property and had felt wonderfully grown-up negotiating with mortgage companies and solicitors. He took time off work to decorate and order furniture, and as he made the rooms fresh and modern, all his thoughts had been of Philippa, how she would soon be kicking off her shoes and leaning back with a glass of wine on this sofa, or hanging her clothes in this wardrobe. She had seemed to like the flat, too, leaving a number of possessions on her first visit, as if to stake her claim. Now, as he stood in the crowded tube train, he worried that all his efforts might be in vain. Had he been stupid to scare her with the footsteps man? He so wanted them to be together, yet their relationship was still new and fragile, and there were so many things that could go wrong.

Friends at work tried to reassure him. "I'm sure it's all nothing," said Peter, one of the designers, "she'll see that."

"He was probably just some harmless nutter," agreed Dave, the restaurant critic. "If he was going to go for you he'd have done it."

"Just go home a bit earlier or later," advised Francie, the film editor, yawning as she waited on the phone. "You'll probably never set eyes on him again. London's like that."

The simplicity of her advice appealed to Colin, and he followed it that same evening, joining some others for an after-work drink. His lateness gave him a new confidence, and he was taken aback when, halfway along the lane, he heard the slow, unmistakable tap of footsteps behind him. So much for Francie's theory. Third time in a week? He could hardly believe this. At least his pursuer was farther behind this time, giving Colin ample time to unlock his door. He was just about to close it behind him when he stopped, the three pints in his belly giving him a new determination. How dare this stranger, whoever he was, spoil his life just when everything was going so well? He, Colin, would not stand for it. He left the door open a crack and peered out, waiting until the other had walked by, then stepped out into the lane.

It was a small enough change, following rather than followed, and yet what a difference it made. Colin almost grinned at the sight of his enemy's back, blind and vulnerable. Was that a slight nervousness in his walk? "So now you know what it feels like." Colin had half intended to say something—firm but polite—to try to warn him off and settle this, but now he found he rather liked this turning the tables, stalking his stalker. Besides, it would even things up if he could see where the man lived and so take away his threatening anonymity. Colin's brave new plans, though, proved short-lived. The other man had barely reached the far end of the lane when he stopped and turned. Fixing Colin with that familiar angry stare, he half pulled something from his jacket pocket, and just for an instant, Colin glimpsed a pale gleam of metal.

Until that moment, worrying though matters had been, Colin had half assumed that everything would turn out to be harmless. This suggested otherwise. Colin froze, took several careful steps backward, then turned and walked quickly away. He heard no footsteps following him, thank God, and once he passed his own flat—he did not stop—and risked a glance back, he was relieved to see that his enemy had gone. Colin's new sense of danger made him practical, and he hurried on down the lane and into the light and bustle of the High Street. He had no hesitation as to what he must do.

"You're quite sure this was a knife?"

Not for the first time Colin found everything seemed to make less sense when he tried to describe it with words. "I didn't see it that clearly, but what else would it have been? It was metal. He'd hardly go threatening me with a teaspoon."

The duty officer at the police station frowned. "And you say you know this man?"

"I've seen him before, I'm sure I have, but I just can't remember where. Believe me, I've tried."

"D'you have his address?"

"That's what I was hoping to find out when he flashed the knife at me."

The policeman folded his arms. "You're not making things very easy for us, Mr. Griffin. You're not even certain he had a weapon. We can't very well go arresting people for giving out dirty looks. Of course if another incident occurs, or you find out where he lives, then you should let us know . . ."

He had stopped. "Is that it?"

"What else d'you suggest we do?"

The question made Colin see the absurdity of his position. What was he asking for? A bodyguard? They'll be interested enough when I've been stabbed to death, he thought grimly as he stepped out of the police station. This time there was no sign of his stalker on the way back, and he walked the lane in silence. He found a message on the answering machine from Philippa and was about to ring back but then changed his mind, guessing he would only alarm her more: better to wait till tomorrow, when he was calmer. Lying in bed, unable to sleep, he wondered if he'd got everything out of proportion. As the policeman had said, he wasn't even certain he had seen a weapon. Fear could do strange things, especially in a large, anonymous place like London, where it felt as if anything might happen. The fact was that in all of his twenty-four years Colin had never had to face real danger. He had been brought up in the safe tranquillity of a small town, and until now his most life-threatening moments had probably been cycling home tipsy from student parties. Was he losing his sense of judgment?

It was as if someone had been listening to his thoughts. Just a few moments later he became aware of that unmistakable clack of footsteps outside. He froze as they grew steadily nearer, slowed down, and then stopped altogether. He must be just outside. As moments passed, Colin's imagination whirred with guesses. A brick through the window? Something through the mailbox? Urine, a dog turd? Or gas poured in and lit? He tensed himself, ready to jump up from the bed. But then the footsteps tapped slowly away.

Of all the incidents so far, this should have been the least significant, with no contact, let alone confrontation, and yet, for some reason, it was the one that left Colin most disturbed. He hardly slept that night, lying in bed, tensely listening for footsteps. He heard them, too, panicking him afresh, until he realized they were different, with innocent rhythms.

The next morning, as he stood blearily in the crowded tube car, one alarming thought led to another. What if this man were dangerously insane? It seemed beyond coincidence, after all, that he had followed him three times in a week. Had he been waiting for him somewhere, perhaps at the tube station? Had their earlier meeting, which Colin could not recall in spite of all his trying, sparked some kind of deluded, obsessional hatred? This would fit in with his own remembered feeling of distrust. Colin wondered if he should rent out the flat for a time and find a room for himself in some other part of London. But that was absurd. He had just finished making the place his home. He was not going to be chased off now. Instead he made a telephone call. Most of his university friends were embarked on careers in journalism, television, the law, or the City, but there was one who had followed a more novel course and was managing a band. Colin had arranged a number of mentions for him in the magazine, so he owed him.

"You sure about this, Col? It all sounds a bit wild."

"Believe me, I'm sure."

"Let me think . . . There's a bouncer at one of the clubs we play. He's a bit of a nightmare, but I think he knows about this sort of stuff, at least he's always saying he does. If you're really set on this . . ."

Colin met him that same evening: a shaven-headed man who

spoke each sentence with a kind of prophet's intensity. "You know what happens if you carry one of these?" He planted a knife between them on the table with a light clack, then waited until Colin obliged him with a shrug of defeat. "You get stabbed."

Colin distrusted the bouncer's moralizing, which sat poorly with his evident fascination with weapons. "I'm not going to fight anyone. I just want to scare the guy off."

"That's what they all say, and they're all wrong." The bouncer gave a theatrical shake of his head. "A blade can start a fight all by itself. It's next to useless at stopping another blade, so it forces you to go for the other bloke. You still want to know how to handle one?"

Colin's lesson was over in an hour, and afterward he stopped at a kitchen shop. He hesitated by the chopping knives, feeling that all of this was utterly unlike himself, but then fear made up his mind. He felt uneasy on the tube—what if he was stopped by the police?—but later, as he approached the lane, the feel of the blade in his pocket was reassuring.

That night Philippa rang, and without quite intending to, Colin told her everything. He simply did not have it in him to keep her in the dark. She was furious, of course. "I just can't believe this. It's so wrong and stupid."

"I had to do something."

"Not this. Anything but this. It won't make you safer, it'll get you killed. Promise you'll throw it away, please."

"That's all I want to do, believe me, but I have to have something or I won't stand a chance."

Resentful of his stubbornness, Philippa was reluctant even to meet, and only after some argument did she finally agree to Sunday afternoon, so punishing him with the loss of Friday and Saturday. "And leave your precious knife at home." When Sunday came, he found himself in a dilemma. She had insisted they meet on neutral territory, in the center of town, and had made it quite clear that she would not go back to his flat afterward. Few weekends had passed without their spending a night together, and yet Colin had no wish to inflame her anger by making a false presumption, and in the end he threw a few overnight things into a small backpack that did not look too obvious.

Nothing that day went right, as if in reflection of the tension between them. They had agreed to see a new art show, but the queue was ominously long, and after waiting for an hour they gave up. Afterward Philippa set off for the nearest tube station without either inviting him to go with her or telling him not to—using vagueness to wrong-foot him—and he found himself straggling after her. They hardly spoke a word on the train back to her shared house, and as they walked toward her door, he felt a panic that their relationship was about to end. Hoping it might help if he drew back, he made an excuse. "I probably ought to get back. I've got a lot on tomorrow."

To his disquiet, she made no effort to dissuade him. "Really? That's a shame."

They kissed uncertainly on the doorstep, like a couple on their first date.

Walking back into his lane, he felt it would be just his luck if he were attacked that night, when—at Philippa's insistence—he had left the knife at home. Then she would understand, he thought bitterly. A part of him almost wished it, just to prove himself right. But there were no footsteps.

The next morning he woke in slightly better spirits, helped by the weak November sunshine filtering past his curtains. Perhaps everything would be well with Philippa after all, he told himself, as he hurried to shower and eat a little tea and toast. Pulling on a jacket, he stepped out into the light, slamming the door behind him, and there, impossibly, just a few yards away, walking toward him from the near end of the lane, was his stalker. Colin froze. He always came in the evening, never the morning. Had he been waiting for him all night? Now Colin regretted having shut the door without looking first. Was that perhaps the sort of small error that cost you your life? He put his hand in his fleece pocket, not sure if this was for defense or reassurance, but found neither as, of course, the knife was not there: he had never imagined he might need it now and so had put it in the inside pocket, whose zipper was always hard to open. As his foe walked toward him with that familiar angry stare, Colin was aware of a strange tingling sensation across his chest, as if in anticipation of being cut. This was bad, very bad. He had to be ready and struggled to unzip the inside pocket, which to his own surprise he managed the first time. Now he was scrabbling to pull out the knife, slightly cutting his thumb. Not a second too late, either, as his enemy had his ready in his hand. Here we are, thought Colin, not sure where the words had come from, aware of a sense of unreality—a kind of refusal—at what was happening: that he, Colin Griffin, who had never got into trouble in his life, was now embarked on a knife fight just outside his front door. He tensed, trying to overcome his own deadening sense of fear. Be practical, this is no moment to lose it. If somebody is going to get stabbed, then make sure it's not you. He tried to remember the bouncer's moves, but all he could think of were his words, "a blade is next to useless at stopping another blade," and so he stepped round, crabwise, as if in a kind of dance, his arms outstretched and ready, jabbing at the air, wondering if this was how it was done. And that was when his enemy shouted out.

"Get away from me."

Ever since the whole strange business had begun, these were the first words that Colin had actually heard his stalker speak, and he found himself confused in two ways. First he was surprised that his enemy was warning him back, as if it were he, Colin, who was the aggressor, which made no sense. The greater surprise, though, was not what he said but how he said it: his voice did not have the low London whir Colin expected but a singsong public school drawl.

Residual anger made Colin shout back. "You get away from me."

Now it was the other's turn to look shocked, and his glare changed to a confused frown. They lowered their knives, and for a moment they stood there, adjusting. Colin's foe looked uneasy. "I thought you were some skinhead out to murder me."

"I thought you were some kind of psycho. Why did you stare at me like that?"

"You were the one who was staring."

Hearing the other's voice had unlocked something, and Colin found himself thinking of a room with large, sunny windows, and a crowd of people sitting on cushions on the floor. The realization caught him unawares. "Were you at one of Sarah Cressington's tea parties?"

The other's eyes were wide. "Oh, my God. You're that friend of Peter Stapleton and Mike Hilary-Smith."

It was almost funny now, but not quite. "And you're Rick . . ."

"Rick Daunda."

Colin remembered it all now: how he had watched uneasily as Rick chatted animatedly to Emma Symes, who had been his great passion during that winter term. So that was where his feeling of distrust had come from. "But why have you been following me like this?"

"I haven't been following anyone. I'm setting up a studio round the corner for my painting, and this is the only way I can get there from my place. Then you started giving me these murderous looks every time I went past."

That was the end of Colin's knife-carrying days. He and Rick Daunda became friends, as neighbors who have much in common usually do, though there was a guarded quality to their friendship even then, as if the fear they had inspired in each other could not quite clear. Philippa proved forgiving, and moved into the flat early in the spring. And so Colin's London life, of which he had been so proud, was fully restored. Or almost fully. Occasionally he would come awake in the middle of the night, breathing fast, having dreamed he was standing outside his door in that weak November sunshine, knife in hand, ready to cut or be cut. And then he would wonder what might have happened if Rick had not thought to shout out when he did.

9. Sunlight

SOME ITALIAN DAYS are persistently charming, almost as if by
a kind of prearranged intent. Malcolm and Melinda woke in
Urbino to the sound of Sunday church bells and breakfasted on
cornetti still warm from the bakery. Melinda paid, as always. Afterward they drove northwest into empty hills, their spirits raised by
the late March sunshine, though they responded to the morning
in different ways: Malcolm was cheerfully sardonic, making fune-
real jokes about the local driving, as if unwilling to submit without a struggle, whereas Melinda submitted eagerly, wide-eyed with
the romance of the moment. "Look at that little ruined tower way
up there. It's so beau-ooo-tiful."

They had only one task that day, to visit a monastery famous
for its liqueurs, and they dawdled along the endlessly winding
roads. It was pure chance that they reached the small town of San
Bernardino just as cars were hurrying to park in front of the main
restaurant. "Shall we give it a try?" said Malcolm, aiming tentatively at the last space.

"The Rosetta," said Melinda. "What a lovely name. Yes, let's."

As a joke they ordered what their dictionary told them was
ravioli filled with nettle, only to find it was delicious. By his second mouthful of goat casserole, Malcolm had reached his verdict.
"This one's going in for sure. Actually, I'd say it's our best meal
so far."

Melinda closed her eyes in wonder. "No question."

Malcolm felt good about himself in a way that rarely happened, and when the waiter arrived with the bill, he sat back in his chair and mentioned, almost casually, that he was writing a travel piece and intended to praise the restaurant. It was a fine moment. The waiter, once he had deciphered Malcolm's strange mix of English and Italian, became warmly enthusiastic—"Scrittore? Vero?"—and called over the cook and the cashier to join in the excitement. Even Melinda played her part, casting Malcolm admiring glances, and in the end they were given free desserts and grappa.

"I wonder if there's anything to see in the town?" said Malcolm importantly as they stepped into the street. There was nothing, at least nothing that would suit his article—a piece for a suburban London newspaper titled "Marche: Tuscany Without Tourists"—and yet, in spite of after-lunch weariness, they both found themselves entranced. San Bernardino could have been the setting of an Italian film: the gang of old men playing dominoes in the tiny park; the two female traffic wardens—were they really twins?—with long black curls frothing out from beneath their caps; the amateur jazz concert in the main square. Malcolm and Melinda lingered over coffee before setting out on the road once more. It was luck or mischance—depending on one's point of view—that led them to the house. Malcolm had brought the most detailed map obtainable, but somehow there seemed to be more roads than he expected and they were soon lost. Not that either of them was too troubled, as the view was spectacular, with layer upon layer of rounded hills fading into a smudged blue distance.

"The sun's over there, so we must be going west," decided Malcolm, as they stopped beneath a straggly tree.

Melinda was squinting at a wooden sign a few yards ahead. "Doesn't that mean 'for sale'?"

The arrow pointed not at a building but at a track. The success of his lunch had left Malcolm with a taste for the impulsive, and he dropped the map into the backseat. "Why don't we take a look?"

Normally Melinda would have tugged back at this assertiveness, but not today. "Why not?" Two hundred yards later they parked beneath a square house which faced the same view they had seen from the road.

"Hmm," said Malcolm, climbing out of the car.

"Amazing," agreed Melinda. For some moments they pottered excitedly about the building, trying and failing to see in through the shuttered windows, or surprising themselves afresh with the view.

"Isn't it fantastic?"

"Really fantastic."

On the surface their responses seemed much the same, but this was deceptive. Melinda's enthusiasm was comparatively straightforward, being dreamily acquisitive, as she imagined herself lying among the spring flowers of the lawn, as their owner, or saw herself cooking goat casserole, stirring the scented mixture in a large copper pot, watched by a pack of grateful guests: her London friends, or her daughter from her marriage to Rick. Malcolm's enthusiasm, by contrast, was one of ambition. Probably it was his flattering lunch that was responsible, filling him with temporary confidence, or his delight at being far away from his English life, but when he first climbed out of the car and looked at the house, something strange happened, and in that brief instant he had a vision of a book he could write, almost as if he could see it, held out to him like a life preserver.

The idea was simple enough, if presumptuous: it would be the story of his and Melinda's adventures living here and remaking this beautiful house (it looked like it needed some work). Ideas can deflate away to nothing, but as he strode round the building, smelling the grass or tapping a patch of brittle plaster, his excitement rose and rose. He would forget the novel, at least for now. He had the new book's style so clearly in his head, having seen it just an hour ago in San Bernardino: it would be light and picturesque, affectionate toward the local people yet also enjoying their almost laughable quaintness. True, there had been other books like this before now, but what did that matter? His would be better, he had no doubt that it would. Besides, some of those other books had sold awfully well. This could be the making of him, he was sure.

It was something he needed so badly, and the very thought of it reawoke in him a faint yet painful craving. It had not always been so. When he and Melinda had first met, he had been full of confidence in his writing, having just had a short story accepted by a magazine and being on the point of starting work on his first novel. In a way the tone of their affair had been set by this self-belief, and also, of course, the age gap between them (he was thirty-one, while she was forty). So, in spite of her wealth, it was Melinda who slipped into the role of the needy one, and soon after they met she began coaxing him to move into her well-groomed house in Camden (she refused ever to visit his South London shared flat). After just a few weeks he did so, piling his cardboard boxes in a corner beneath one of her Buddhist paintings. He felt strange living there at first, especially when her daughter was home from boarding school for holidays, or when his friends paid a visit or—worse still—his parents, who disapproved. But he soon adjusted: comfort is never hard to grow used to, and he liked having his own study, while Melinda was good about leaving him in peace to work. Did he love her? Perhaps in a way he did. He liked her company, both by day and by night. Besides, it was not as if he were looking for anything else: his eyes were fixed not on marriage or children but on his career. He did not try to play stepfather to the daughter—which was probably just as well—and they kept a workable distance from each other. After a few months he let Melinda persuade him to quit his day job at the computer superstore ("It takes up so much of your writing time, Malkie, and it's not as if you need it"), and his dependence was complete. He was not bothered. What did it matter if he was a kept man, or a "toy boy" as his parents once complained? All his dignity would be restored once he finished his novel.

Unfortunately he never did. Years went by, and the book continued to slip and slide from his grasp. The maddening thing was he could never quite see what was wrong. Everything felt fine when he was deeply absorbed, but as soon as he stood back, distracted by a few days' break, or even an absorbing program on television, it all seemed to fall to nothing: characters he had thought intriguing and complex became somehow indistinguishable from one another (changing their names, which he did repeatedly, never seemed to help). Likewise, plot lines that had felt ingenious suddenly appeared lacking in any sense of surprise, as if the whole story might be the background to something else more eventful. A number of times he tried to abandon the whole project, only to be pulled back, like a cart dragged into the same muddy ruts it has got stuck in ten dozen times before. How could he give it up when he had already invested so much time? Besides, what else could he write, seeing as he never seemed to think of any other ideas? So he worked on, accumulating first chapters—he never quite got started on a second—of wide variety, one opening with Lucinda dancing passionately in a 1932 Berlin nightclub, another beginning with poor Hermann breathing his penniless last breath in the chill wind of 1979 New York, a third starting with Leonora (previously Lucinda) weeping tight-lipped in her Stepney home at the news that Gerhardt (Hermann) has been reported missing in action from the Afrika Korps. The novel did not grow so much as spread, as pages of handwritten notes and printed openings piled up in his study, on shelves, in drawers, on the floor at his feet.

As the weeks turned to months, then to a year, he became worried that Melinda would be disappointed in him, until he realized, a little uneasily, that she seemed quite content with the state of affairs, and rather than berate him she began to look for ways to make his failure more palatable (and so more permanent). When he was at a particularly low ebb, she persuaded him to come with her on a holiday to Spanish Galicia—at her expense, naturally—

and arranged for him to write a short travel article for a London real-estate magazine run by one of her many friends. The pay was pitiful, but he found he quite enjoyed doing the piece: it was so nice to get to the end. Others followed and a few food articles too, though he never broke into the big-paying league of magazines and Sunday papers. As a consequence his commissions depended, in effect, on Melinda's willingness to take him on holiday, which was not very often, and even in a good year he earned a fraction of what he had at the computer store. Melinda never asked him to contribute to household expenses, insisting on paying for everything they did together—"That's your money, Malkie, spend it on something fun"—and though he was relieved, her generosity also added to his sense of humiliation: his earnings felt like pocket money, and he spent them like a teenager, on CDs or a new computer that, as he hoped, might help him with his novel.

He did make attempts at escape. On occasion he would break into sudden, indefensible bursts of anger, only to find Melinda wearily forgiving. Once or twice he looked at places to live, but they seemed so dingy, and expensive too. Sometimes he flipped through the newspapers for jobs, but the sight of them gave him a vague sense of defeat and sent him hurrying back to his writing (what if Petra joined the mime troupe instead of Denise? In a way that would be even more tragic . . .). As time passed he realized the power balance between himself and Melinda was beginning to change. He looked older, with white strands in his thinning hair, and noticed that other people seemed less surprised by the sight of them together—almost as if he were catching up—and perhaps because of this he sensed she was growing more assertive toward him and less concerned to please. Eventually his urges to escape became matched by moments of fear, especially in the middle of the night. What if something went wrong between them? She was still attractive, after all, young and shapely for her years, and there had been a few moments when she made him wonder. He was almost forty and did not even have a place of his own to live. If she wanted she could fling him out tomorrow. Marriage—had she accepted—would have been an answer, but somehow this never really occurred to him: though years slipped by, he doggedly continued to regard his situation as temporary. Until this afternoon, when he found himself looking at the house above San Bernardino, filled with sudden confidence. How glorious it would be to have a huge, bookshop-busting success: to be important and needed and rich. To be safe. None of this could happen, of course, unless Melinda bought the house. Part of the unwritten constitution of their relationship was that he should never push—all the more so these days—and Malcolm trod carefully. "I'd love to see what it looks like inside."

To his surprise, this was all that was needed, and Melinda gave a wide-eyed smile of agreement. "I'm sure I saw a telephone number on the sign."

So they abandoned the search for the liqueur monastery and turned back to San Bernardino. When they viewed the interior of the house the next morning, Malcolm was relieved to see it had a charming rustic style, with a huge if crumbling fireplace in the sitting room and red terra-cotta floor tiles (mostly cracked) in the kitchen. "Guests certainly wouldn't be a problem," murmured Melinda as they looked at the fourth bedroom. Their exchanges were hushed, as if speaking too loudly might raise the price. In the event this proved rather higher than they expected, though it was far from unreasonable. There would also be the cost of repairs, of course, and with this in mind the estate agent had brought along a local builder, who frowned unhappily each time he was required to give an opinion. "For the roof he says it does not look so bad, with just small works, and the same for the walls on the outside," the estate agent translated, "though these may be worse when he looks carefully. If he must guess . . ."

Malcolm totted up figures in his notebook as Melinda took a picture of the For Sale sign. Afterward, sitting at an outside table of the Rosetta restaurant, the two of them hardly noticed their lunch. "It's still very good value compared to England," said Malcolm.

Melinda, fortunately, seemed undaunted by the numbers. "I could sell the house in Dorset as I hardly go there anymore, and that would probably cover the actual building, and perhaps some of the repairs, too. Worst comes to the worst, I can always sell a few shares."

They had just ordered pannacotta with red currants when Malcolm saw a Vespa pull up carrying, implausibly, two men, a small boy, and a dog, all of whom glanced toward him and Melinda. A moment later they approached their table.

"Please forgive us for the disturbance," the passenger translated for the driver. "Here is San Bernardino builder Giorgio Petroni, who is very expert and not expensive. He has heard you are interested in the house near Collegrigia." After half an hour of discussions, it was clear that his estimates were lower than the other builder's.

"I liked him," decided Melinda after they had gone. "He had a nice face."

"I liked him too," agreed Malcolm, thinking of how the overloaded Vespa would make a perfect character introduction.

Later that same afternoon, Melinda put in an offer. Everything took time, and Malcolm found the next few months tense, in spite of the fact that nothing went wrong: the sale of the house in Dorset went through easily, and his fears that they might be swindled by some Marche local proved groundless. Twice they had to fly out to present their documents and sign others: their first taste of Italian bureaucracy. The estate agent seemed untroubled when they said they wanted Giorgio to do the repair work rather than the builder he had introduced. "As you like."

Malcolm's progress with his book idea was less smooth. Even during his brief, promising days of eight years before, he had never found an agent, though he had spoken to three on the telephone. When he tried these again he found that one had left the book world and opened a cheese shop, the second was "full," and only after Malcolm resorted to something close to pleading did the third reluctantly agree to let him send a manuscript, which he insisted must be finished. Malcolm found it hard being alone with his dream, and he soon told Melinda about it, if in an edited form that left out his hunger for success. Her response annoyed him. "What a lovely idea. Even if it doesn't get published—and I'm sure it will—it'll be so nice to have a record of everything that happens."

His optimism revived a little in September, when they drove down to Marche in the Volvo with select necessities and the house finally became theirs. The handover ceremony, held at the office of their San Bernardino lawyer, was both formal and noisily confusing, attended by the previous owner of the house—an aristocratic-looking figure with a splendid cavalry officer mustache—as well as the estate agent and several people Malcolm never quite managed to identify. Afterward, now joined by wives, children, and Giorgio the builder, everybody went for a noisy lunch at the Rosetta—Melinda took pictures—and as carafes of wine were drunk, increasingly warm toasts were made, wishing the new house owners every good fortune. Afterward in their hotel room, Malcolm took notes.

The next day Melinda gave Giorgio his check for building materials and the first half of his fee, and work began almost at once. Melinda rented a small flat in the town—cheaper and more comfortable than the hotel—and they drove up to the house each day to see how everything was progressing. To Malcolm's delight, Giorgio and his workers proved just the eccentric characters he had hoped for. There was the implacably grumpy old man in a gray cap—he never took it off—who drove a tiny three-wheeler van with a huge dog perched in the cab beside him; the young cousin of Giorgio's who would flick back his hair, as if fancying himself a film star; the huge one who seemed to do almost all the work, tearing out cracked roof tiles by the dozen while the others languidly passed up replacements. Giorgio seemed to spend his time smoking or talking on his cell phone, and the only moment of the day when he seemed truly concentrated was at lunch, when he and the others gathered around a battered table and opened tins of food their women had prepared for them, which gave off aromas that—as Malcolm wrote in his notes—would have been the envy of London's finest chefs.

Yet somehow the work progressed at a reasonable pace. It also grew more repetitive—the replacing of roof tiles, the scraping away of old wall plaster—and Malcolm found that his notes were growing steadily briefer. October came and the weather turned autumnal—Malcolm had had no idea Italy could be so rainy— and, as they discovered the ineffectiveness of their rented flat's heating, Melinda became restless. "It's rather boring just hanging around here," she said one evening as they sat, once again, in the Rosetta restaurant, where they had tried everything on the menu except the tripe. "I can't believe we really need to stand over Giorgio every day. Perhaps we should go back to London, just for a little while."

Malcolm, though he tried to persuade her to stay, also found it dull—you couldn't even go to see a film, as everything in the town's tiny cinema was dubbed into Italian—and eventually, in late October, they both flew home. Malcolm had intended to stay for no more than two or three weeks, but then something changed his plans: to his surprise he found he was writing, really writing. Finally, after eight long years of barrenness, his study came into its own, and each morning he sat down at his desk with a full mug of tea and set to work. It felt so different from his novel, which even when it had been going better had had a kind of heaviness about it—a feeling of vague impossibility—almost like trying to push all the water to one end of a bath. Now he woke in the morning freshly astonished to find that he was going forward, and quickly, too. Within a month he had completed a first chapter, "A Sign by the Roadside." By Christmas he had finished a second, "The Paper

Labyrinth," and in mid-January a third, "Cominciamo!" In a reckless moment he walked through the windy drizzle, and ignoring the instructions of his potential agent to send a completed manuscript, he dropped them into a mailbox. Two days later he and Melinda flew back to Marche, and as the plane descended over a Po valley lost in fog, Malcolm vowed that this time he would stay.

They struck disaster almost at once. Even as they walked toward the house, they could see something was wrong. "What have they done to the windows?" said Melinda. The frames, which had been of tasteful if decaying wood, were now ugly metal. Worse followed when they walked into the sitting room, where the huge worker was replastering what had been the graceful, arched fireplace. It had been squared off with what looked ominously like blocks. Worst of all, though, was the kitchen: in place of the red terra-cotta tiles, the floor was now covered with icy, gleaming white marble, and the walls were lined with plastic-looking cupboards. In the center of the room, his beaming smile already fading at the sight of them, was Giorgio.

"It's ruined," said Melinda. "It's all ruined." Furiously she itemized her complaints via the cell phone to the English-speaking cousin. "But we said quite clearly that we wanted everything to be just the same as it was before." She held the phone to her and Malcolm's ears as the cousin translated Giorgio's answers.

"He says those old tiles are very hard to find these days while marble is much more strong and modern and he has just the same in his own kitchen." As for the cupboards, it seemed the local carpenter was away visiting his son in Australia, while these were "good cupboards, from IKEA, and Paolo drove all the way to Bologna especially." Metal window frames lasted longer, and they had had to make the fireplace square as there was nobody in San Bernardino who could do that sort of work anymore.

"But this isn't what we agreed," Melinda insisted. "I'm sorry, but he has to change it all. There's nothing else for it."

Giorgio's eyes hardened.

"My cousin says that is quite impossible. The work he has done is very good."

"But it's not what we want. He's ruined the whole house."

"You were not here, so he must make decisions, while this work is very beautiful and much better than the way it was before."

Malcolm listened with a rising sense of alarm. He was concerned for the house, of course, but much more he was worried about his book. This did not fit at all. Giorgio had let him down, failing to be what he had promised from the moment of his arrival on the Vespa: a charming local eccentric with a kind of rural good taste. How dare he? Normally Malcolm would never have dreamt of interfering in a dispute over Melinda's property, but as he glanced angrily at the glaring IKEA cupboards, an Italian word came to him—from the opera, or some book he had read?—and, as the argument between Melinda and Giorgio began to stall, it grew irresistible to him, like throwing a snowball at a statue. "Ladro," he called out. "Ladro! You rotten thief!"

The half-restored kitchen fell suddenly silent. Giorgio threw Malcolm a slow, burning stare and then turned and marched from the room.

"That was clever," said Melinda as they stood listening to the workers pack up their tools.

Malcolm's mistake, as he realized with a sinking heart, had been twofold: not only had he insulted Giorgio and so hardened the dispute over the repairs but he had also broken a cardinal rule of his relationship with Melinda. As they drove back to San Bernardino, she made her displeasure clear. "It's just common sense. It never helps to insult people." Malcolm, on the defensive, was pushed into uncharacteristic assertiveness. "I'll sort it all out, Melinda. Really I will."

His attempts to do so quickly revealed the full extent of their predicament. When they visited the lawyer who had arranged the sale, he looked at them in faint amazement. "You have no contract for this work? But you must. If there is no contract, then there is nothing you can do." This, at least, was not Malcolm's fault—it was Melinda who had accepted Giorgio's smiling insistence that written quotes were not the way business was conducted in Marche—but this hardly seemed to lessen Malcolm's culpability in her eyes. Afterward he swallowed his pride and rang Giorgio's cousin. It was a discouraging conversation.

"Of course he will not. You have insulted him, as a workman and also as a man. I am sorry, but you have made this trouble and it is yours."

"If I apologized," offered Malcolm tentatively, "d'you think he might at least redo the kitchen?"

The cousin almost laughed. "But why? It is already done very well."

In the end Malcolm did apologize, but not to the cousin. As they sat at the café in the main square, he took the one course left open to him and pleaded for Melinda's forgiveness. "It was stupid, I know. I'm sorry. I was just so angry, and now I've messed everything up."

It was the right thing to do and Melinda softened at once. Then again, she had been more annoyed by his display of autonomy than by the problems it had caused. "Don't worry, Malkie. I'll ring my solicitor in London tomorrow and perhaps he'll know what to do." Order between them was restored, and in celebration of this peace they went, once again, to the Rosetta restaurant for dinner. It was there, in fact, that they found an unexpected answer to their problems. The restaurant was quiet on this winter Tuesday evening, but soon after they sat down they saw the estate agent walk in through the door. He listened patiently as they recounted their troubles, shaking his head. "But you must not blame Giorgio too much," he told them. "Probably he really did think he was being kindly to build things in that way. I've seen his house, and it's all like that. Actually a lot of houses here are. People here don't like that old-fashioned style anymore, they want rooms to be clean and bright and modern, and IKEA is very popular. I have some of it myself. But still he was wrong to stop the work, even if you did call him a bad name."

"Is there anything we can do?" asked Melinda.

The estate agent looked at her carefully, as if weighing his sympathy. "Well . . . Maybe there is one thing. Though if I tell you, you must agree never—and I mean never—to tell anyone of this conversation. San Bernardino is a small town to live in."

"Certainly not," Melinda murmured.

In a lowered voice, he told them how Giorgio was very fearful of the revenue department, as they had ruined his brother a few years earlier over his taxes. He even suggested that this—and not any desire to cheat—could have been the reason for Giorgio's reluctance to have a written contract, as then no evidence of the work would exist. "He's frightened of them, but he still hates paying taxes. Certainly he won't have declared any money he took from you. If you have some proof that you paid him . . . ? Giorgio is not an educated man, so even a small thing might be enough."

This was easier said than done, as Malcolm and Melinda soon realized. The estate agent shook his head when they described the banker's check they had used to pay Giorgio, which it seemed was all but untraceable. "Only in Italy," Malcolm remarked glumly. Afterward, when they went back to the flat and Melinda went through all their paperwork, they found Giorgio had not given them a single receipt of any kind. Only later, as he lay awake fretting, did Malcolm see a possible answer.

"It's worth a try," Melinda agreed.

The meeting took place two days later at the house. Giorgio looked aloof as he got out of the car with his cousin, but this changed when Melinda handed him the official-looking folder addressed to an Officer Rossi of the Urbino revenue department. Inside was an enlargement of Melinda's photograph of Giorgio in the main square of San Bernardino, her check in his hand (it had come out well, and it was almost possible to make out the writing). There were also pictures of Giorgio and the others working on the repairs, and finally a signed statement by Melinda detailing precisely what she had paid. Giorgio's face turned pale.

"I thought I'd put it in the post this afternoon," she said coolly. "Or I could ring." Theatrically she held up her cell phone. "I have Officer Rossi's number right here."

Work resumed the very next day. Melinda soon grew bored again and returned to England, but Malcolm stayed on this time, visiting the house each day despite Giorgio's cold looks. Each evening he took what notes he could. Nothing was quite as he wished, and yet he still felt optimistic that he would see a way of retrieving the situation once the house was finished: what mattered was that the work was going ahead. In fact it was proceeding very well. Giorgio seemed determined to finish as quickly as possible, and as February and March passed and the sun grew gradually warmer, the metal window frames were replaced by wood, red terra-cotta tiles spread across the kitchen floor, and the carpenter built neat fitted cupboards. Even the sitting-room fireplace was restored to an approximation of its predecessor. In late April, Melinda flew back to choose furniture, and by June, as the air began to grow heavy with the first summer heat, the work was almost complete and they moved in from the San Bernardino flat. Later that month Giorgio sent the man in the gray cap to ask for payment of the second and final part of his fee, and though there was still a little work to be done—a bedroom to be painted and a bathroom to be tiled—Melinda felt that it was churlish to make him wait. This time Giorgio insisted on payment in cash, and Melinda did not take her camera. Payment gave the house a sense of completion. "I'll have to start ringing my friends," said Melinda. "They'll be queuing up."

Then, a couple of days later, something unexpected happened. Malcolm and Melinda were enjoying a lunch of salad, prosciutto, and beans when the telephone rang and Malcolm heard the voice of his would-be agent. "Thank goodness. I've tried your London place a hundred times. I finally got some kind of cleaner."

His news was not good. It was revolutionary. Not only had he read and liked the three chapters but he had sent them to several publishers. "I should have waited and got your say-so, I know, but you just weren't around, and I never thought they'd all get back to me so quickly. Before I knew it everything turned into a bit of an auction. Nothing's agreed, naturally, but I think you'll be rather pleased." Malcolm listened with a kind of amazed numbness as he heard the final bid.

Melinda said all the right things, but he could not help but notice a thinness to her smile. This time, for once, he made no attempt to win her round. Why should he? She would just have to get used to this. While they sat in the Rosetta restaurant—supposedly celebrating—there was a certain glee in his voice as he again went over each detail of his telephone call to the agent, or talked about the trip he would be making to meet his new editor. By the end of the evening, Melinda barely concealed her annoyance. "Actually I think I'll stay here," she told him coolly. "I don't really feel like traveling just now."

For the first time since they had been together, she did not offer to pay for his flight. As if he cared, seeing as he could easily afford it himself now. Shortly afterward, watched by the old man in the gray cap, who had come to paint the last bedroom, Malcolm slung his bag into the Volvo and Melinda drove him to Rimini airport. Five days later he was back. Melinda was there to meet him and no longer seemed annoyed, just a little distant, throwing him the occasional sardonic glance as he recounted his tour of his publisher's office, his lunch, his editor's ideas for the jacket cover. Only when they were almost at San Bernardino did he finally ask, "Did anything happen here?"

"They finished the bathroom. Paolo, the one who looks like an actor, did the tiles."

If he had been less wrapped up in his own news, he might have noticed the way—a slight emphasis—with which she spoke. "So it's all done?"

"Certainly is."

Malcolm's first concern was how to approach the remainder of the book. He had made only faint, lighthearted mention to his agent and editor of the trouble he and Melinda had had with Giorgio, not wanting to risk jeopardizing the deal before it was agreed, while he was sure he would find a way forward. Now this optimism would be put to the test. The next morning he spent an hour sitting fruitlessly in his new study, until he decided walls were not suited to the broad thinking he needed and he drove to San Bernardino, so he could sit with his new fountain pen—a real English author in Italy—at the café on the main square.

His first intimation that something might be wrong came when he walked up to the bar and saw the old man in the gray cap in the corner, grinning and nudging someone at his side. Malcolm paid them no attention and took a seat outside, facing toward the small, trickling fountain. He had sat there for an hour, feeling the heat and achieving little beyond a couple of pages of meandering, uninspired notes, when looking up, he saw Giorgio and the one who looked like an actor standing in the shade nearby, watching him and smiling in a way he did not much like. Before he could look away, he glimpsed Giorgio make some kind of sign with his finger. Annoyed, Malcolm sat out a few minutes—to show he was not being chased off—and then chucked coins on the table for the coffee and strode away. As he neared the car, he noticed there was a piece of paper beneath one of the windshield wipers. A parking ticket? He'd always thought you didn't need to pay on this street. Frowning, he unfolded a handwritten note.

Malcolm look by the wheel near your foot

Unsure whether to be amused or worried, Malcolm did so and found a brown Jiffy bag propped against the tire. Standing in the hot June sunshine, he tore it open, and his fingers felt something soft and silky. He pulled out black material, faintly smudged with white marks, and it was a moment or two before he recognized it, in this strange context, as Melinda's underwear. The note was in the same unpracticed handwriting as the one from the windshield.

Actually your wife was a little pleasure for me, Malcolm, even though she is old, and i like to touch the small brown pimple spot just beside her cunt hair before i permit to give her my good fucking. From her shouts each time i do it to her i think she very grateful to get me as her fucking man and not ugly Malcolm with his small old penis. Everyone in San Bernardino will laugh to hear of old Englishwoman Melinda who is so tired of her ugly husband and so hungry for her fuck that she will pull any man in to her dirty bed.

He drove away in the wrong gear, and from the corner of his eye he was sure he glimpsed someone smile. The questions that roared through his head on the short journey back were answered almost the very moment he walked into the kitchen and found Melinda eating salad and mozzarella. She glanced up, read his look—read it largely correctly—and answered with a defiant one of her own. So it was true, and what was more, she had wanted him to know. To punish him for his new independence? To scare him in a way that might replace the lost control of her wealth? Her expression quickly changed, though, when she opened the Jiffy bag. "That little shit. How dare he?"

There was surprisingly little else to be said. Malcolm felt somehow less annoyed by her betrayal than by her stupidity at letting herself be used. Was there any point in casting blame? He did anyway. In some incomprehensible way she also seemed annoyed with him—for pushing her to this?—and after a brief, vicious exchange they crept about the newly decorated house in silence, avoiding each other. By the next day Melinda had made up her mind. "We've got to get out of here, Malkie," she told him in her soothing voice. "This place isn't good for us anymore. Let's just jump on a plane and get the hell out. Go back to London right now."

Her suggestion involved, among other things, the surrender of his book and all its hopes. "No, I'm staying here."

He drove her to the airport the next day. She hardly spoke during the car journey, tight-lipped at this further rebellion. "I might just sell the damn place," she threatened him as she queued to check in.

He drove back by a different road, avoiding San Bernardino, and walked into the empty building. For a week he traipsed from room to room, feeling beaten and directionless. There seemed no answer. Giorgio had robbed him after all. But then, one morning as he showered, he suddenly saw the way, just as clearly as he had on that March afternoon a year and a half before, when he had first come to this place. Within an hour he was at his desk, his jaw set almost grimly, and he began to write.

TWO YEARS LATER, applause ringing out around him, Malcolm stepped down from the stage at his first writers' festival. Melinda bobbed up to his side—her new role of literary partner seemed to suit her well—and they made their way over to a small but enthusiastic hubbub (it would soon be far larger) by the signing table.

"My favorite was Giorgio, he's so funny and wise . . ."

"The grumpy old man in the gray cap who says telephones are the work of the devil . . ."

"When you and Melinda help Giorgio make wine from the clementines . . ."

"The way everything's so wonderfully traditional . . ."

"When Pietro gets so lazy that his mother has to get the priest to kick him out of bed . . ."

"Giorgio's lovely daughter who sings to the birds . . ."

"When the snow makes the roof fall in and everyone comes from miles around to help . . ."

"When you're all alone and ill and Giorgio and his wife bring you the special wine that cures you . . ."

"Near the end when the grumpy old man in the gray cap makes you that beautiful wooden statue . . ."

"When you catch the builder who thinks he's a film star in the back of his tiny little Fiat with both the traffic officer twins . . ."

"The celebration when everything's finished, with the banquet in the garden and the priest who makes the fireworks display . . ."

"It made me feel so good inside . . ."

"I can't wait to see the film."

"And now I hear it's going to be translated into Italian . . ."

"It sounds so wonderful there. I'm amazed you can tear yourself away."

This last comment was the only one Malcolm found awkward, and he replied with a benign but vague smile. The house, needless to say, had been sold long before.

10. Seasons

ROBBO FELT SELF-CONSCIOUS walking into the Angel Inn. Everyone looked different—scruffier, more slumped—and he knew he must look different to them. One glance round the room and he saw his friends were already there, sitting beneath the black of an autumn window, by an early season Father Christmas with a flickering red hat. The four of them had never been formal, anything but, and Robbo was surprised to see they had not touched their pints but had waited, the foam fading.

"There he is," said Mikie.

Robbo took his place beside them, and they raised four glasses into the air.

"Here's to you, Robbo," said Dale. "You come home safe, now."

"Don't you worry about me," said Robbo almost dismissively, flattered by the honor being paid him but reluctant to show himself too pleased. As they thumped their glasses down on the table, there was a silence—the awkwardness of people who knew one another well but had not met together for some while—and their pints were soon finished.

"I'll get this one," offered Robbo.

"No you don't," insisted Dave Natson, or Nutter. "You're not paying a penny. Tonight's on us. No arguments."

Mikie and Dale nodded agreement, and Robbo saw he might as well accept gracefully. "All right, then. And ta, eh?" Sitting back, he recognized a girl who came in, who had worked one of the cash registers at Tesco when he was stacking shelves. How long ago that seemed now. Quite a nice looker she was too, in a Goth sort of way. Without meaning to, he caught her eye, but then, to his annoyance, she frowned and glanced away.

Dale carefully placed four fresh pints on the table. "Here's to the Gnome Boys."

"The Gnome Boys," they chanted in unison, and for the first time that evening they looked truly relaxed. The name had come into being several years earlier on a mild May evening. Someone at school whose parents were away for a funeral had held a party, and—parties being a rarity—it had been a cause of some excitement, only to prove disappointing. There was not enough to drink and the girls were few and standoffish, so even Nutter—who usually did well in that department—had got nowhere. It was largely chance that Robbo, Mikie, Dale, and Nutter all gave up hope and left at the same time. Rightfully they should have gone home, but something made them restless—their disappointment, or the evening itself, which was the first of the year that felt like spring, with a glimmer of light in the sky even at this hour—and so they made their way down to the High Street. They stopped outside the DIY store, thwarted, as ever, by the small town's limitations.

"I suppose we could go and see Kev," offered Mikie. His brother Kevin was that rare thing, someone of their generation who was not living with his parents, as several months ago he had moved in with his girlfriend.

"Jackie'll love that," said Nutter scornfully. "Four of us thumping on the door at eleven thirty at night pissed out of our heads."

Nobody had a better idea, though, and so they began trudging up the hill. They were halfway there when Dale stopped by a front garden. "Look at those gnomes. Stupid bloody things, aren't they?"

Any diversion was welcome, and they all stopped. Dale was right that they were absurd objects when you troubled to notice, with their silly hats and plastic paunches. The garden had a dozen or more, one fishing in a tiny pond, another playing the cymbals.

"Hang on," said Dale, warming to his discovery, "there's a girl one." He opened the gate and stepped into the garden.

"Come out of there, Dale," said Nutter, who in spite of his name, was the most cautious of the four.

"I'm just trying to cheer them up, poor miserable buggers," Dale insisted, putting the girl gnome on the wall with a male one and leaning them together.

"That's enough of that," said Robbo, feigning disapproval.

"Leave 'em be, won't you? They're getting more fun than I've had tonight, I can tell you."

It would have gone no further if not for Mikie. "I heard there's some group, over in France I think it is, call themselves the Gnome Liberation Front. They took hundreds of the things, thousands, and put them all in a wood, saying they were setting them free."

"Free the gnomes," called out Dale, and there was a moment of silence as the idea sank in. Part of its appeal was that it would give them a project for the evening, but most of all it offered the lure of transgression: with a few pints in the belly, the idea of misbehaving in this stultifyingly small, correct town was irresistible.

"The castle," said Robbo, "that's where they should live."

So the four of them went to work, scurrying back and forth with surprising energy along the empty streets, until they had emptied almost every front garden in the town, and the lawn in front of the castle was lined with dozens of gnomes—large and small, with fishing rods, musical instruments, garden implements—all staring soberly toward the parking lot below.

"Free the gnomes," the four of them called out together, before meandering back to their homes.

They had been seen, of course. Robbo had noticed a curtain or two twitch and so was expecting a little trouble, but he was taken aback by the strength of the reaction. It was not helped by the story being taken up by the local paper, which made a good deal of the fact that many of the gnome owners were elderly and had a picture of a sad-looking couple struggling up to the castle to re-trieve their property. First the four of them were hauled away to the police station and threatened with criminal charges—though these came to nothing—and then they were called before Mr. Stephens, the headmaster, who said they were lucky not to be ex-pelled. After that it was the turn of their parents—Dale got quite a thumping from his dad—and finally the rest of the town had its chance, and they found themselves met with disapproving glances and tut-tutting whenever they ventured out. It was this treatment, in fact, that turned them into the Gnome Boys. They had been friends before, of course, but only as part of a larger, straggling generation, while now they stuck together, so they might at least suffer in company, and in the process they fused into a group. And a group they remained even when, with passing months, their crime was forgiven and came to be regarded with a certain amused affection in the town. A group they were still on that au-tumn night when they gathered in the Angel Inn for Robbo's send-off.

It was months since they had all met together, and there was a lot of news to catch up on. Nutter had the most to tell, and the sec-ond and third pints were his. "We're going to have it in the church by the market," he explained, "and the reception'll be in the castle. You remember Linda, Mel's friend who's so good with the violin? She said she'll play for us, and Mel's aunt Jean will sing."

Nutter's description of his wedding plans was accepted for a good while, but eventually his enthusiasm was too much. "I hope it doesn't rain," said Mikie darkly.

Dale attacked from another direction. "I don't know why you're in such a rush, Nutter. I'm not hurrying into any church, I can tell you. I'm going to have some fun first. Sow a few wild oats."

Nutter met his look. "If you can find a field that's willing."

Dale scowled as the others laughed.

Robbo had never much taken to Nutter's Mel, with her self-important looks and her talk of becoming a fashion designer, but tonight he felt mellow about the whole business. Why shouldn't they have a nice wedding? It all felt somehow far away.

The fourth and fifth pints were Dale's. "She's nothing flash and she's certainly not new but she's a nice little runner. I've driven her all over, down to Cardiff and across to Aberystwyth, and she hasn't given trouble once. We're goin' in June when it hardly gets dark up there."

Nutter waited for his moment. "You know what they say about Japanese cars, mind? They're all right for seven years and then everything goes at once and you're left with a car key and a big chunk of scrap metal."

Dale was unbowed. "A lot of tosh, that is. No, she'll get us to John o' Groat's, no trouble."

Up until then Robbo had kept aloof from the skirmishing, reluctant to step down from his special status of the evening, but the thought of Dale's brother driving was too tempting to resist. "I wouldn't be too sure with Rick at the wheel."

Mikie let out a deep laugh. "Too damn right. I was there the time he hit that No Parking sign. I wouldn't trust Rick as far as Tesco's, let alone John o' bloody Groat's."

"I don't know why I bother," complained Dale, who usually came off worst from these encounters, and he got up to buy the next round. Robbo glanced around the room. It was strange, he must have been here a hundred times but he had never noticed that picture of a coach and horses driving through a crowded street, or the one by the bar of sailing ships in a battle. Then again, he'd never felt the need to notice: why should he when he knew he'd soon be back?

The sixth pint was Mikie's. Like Robbo—and unlike Dale and Nutter—Mikie had left the town, off to college in Cardiff. "I'm still all for the environment, course I am," he explained, "but there's no job there. The way I see it I can do more to help if I go in for something else—something more practical—and that's why I've changed to media studies."

Mikie the brain: he always had done well, going on to do A levels when the other three had had enough. His news was received more warily than Dale's or Nutter's.

"So you're going to be a journalist," said Dale, pronouncing the -*list* of *journalist* in a funny voice, just to show he was not awed.

"Actually I was thinking more of television."

Now he had to be brought down. "Television?" said Nutter, seeing his chance. "An ugly mug like yours would break the bloody camera."

Mikie took it with a grin. "Better mine than yours, Nutter. You'd wreck the whole damn studio."

"The whole of Cardiff," added Dale in a doomy sort of voice, to finish off the exchange.

One glass was empty, the others were three quarters done, and the prospect of another round was looming. Robbo was about to offer—not that he'd be allowed, but he should offer—when a voice shouted out from behind him. "Think you're tough, do you? I'll show you tough."

It was Harry Owen, who worked at the gas station and who often got nasty when he'd had a bellyful. With the drink inside him Robbo felt an anger rise from nowhere, and he would have met Harry's challenge but Nutter and Mikie jumped up to block him. "No you don't, Robbo," murmured Nutter. "Not tonight."

Already Harry was staggering away, his burning eyes searching for some other target. Dale called over to his mates by the bar. "Keep an eye on him, can't you? He should be on a leash, that one."

The incident was minor enough, but somehow it decided the question of the next round and the four of them filed out into the breezy autumn night. "Chip shop?" suggested Mikie.

"Why not?" agreed Robbo, who still held sway over the evening. A few moments later they were standing by the locked gates of the market, holding open parcels of chips and pies, the paper rustling in the wind.

"So when are you off?" asked Nutter.

"Next week, that's when they say," said Robbo. Even now it was hard to believe.

"I suppose it'll be hot down there?"

"They said it shouldn't be too bad."

Their meal finished, they began making their way through residential streets. Dale stopped by a front garden with two gnomes. "Stupid-looking things, aren't they."

The other three laughed.

"I don't believe it," said Dale. "It's another girl one." He pushed open the garden gate, and in a moment he had them balanced on the garden wall.

"To the castle," said Mikie, but they all knew he was not serious and Dale carefully replaced the gnomes. Soon afterward they reached the corner where they would go their separate ways. For a moment there was a silence, but then Mikie snapped to a drunken salute and Dale and Nutter jumped to do the same, though Dale's was all wrong so it looked like he was chopping at the side of his nose. Robbo saluted back, correctly.

"You watch out for yourself, all right?" said Nutter.

"They don't like it up 'em," added Dale, trying to lighten the moment with the familiar television catchphrase.

"Bring us back a gnome, eh?" added Mikie. "An Arabic gnome."

"Right you are."

Robbo went home feeling subdued. As he walked up the stairs, his foot slipped with a thump, telling him he was drunker than he had realized. On the landing he saw light glimmer from beneath his parents' bedroom door: on another occasion his dad would have come out to give him a good yelling. But not tonight.

He let his head crash onto the pillow, and his eyes rested for a moment on a poster on the wall opposite: a fantasy planet with buildings on stilts and three moons lined up one behind the other. It had been up for ages, and was probably there on the night of gnomes. Below the poster were his CDs and a model aircraft he had built. He closed his eyes for a moment, feeling the room spin, and pictured his uniform waiting for him at the barracks, clean and ready. A thought flitted through his mind, but it was hard to grab, like a fly. Then he caught it, and for the first time he realized that he felt angry, even envious. Mikie, Dale, Nutter: in different ways they all had their next months mapped out with hopes and plans. For him the approaching months were a mystery: a dark blank. Then his anxiousness began creeping back.

11. N u m b e r s

JIM HARVEY WAS the sort of person for whom small details were important in making or unmaking his sense of contentment, and for most of that April Wednesday the small details were satisfactory. Glancing out of the bedroom window, he saw there was no frost, which meant last night's weather forecast was accurate and the clothes Marcy had hung out for him were correct. Marcy's ironing sometimes suffered lapses, but today his shirt was neat and creaseless. Their son, Carl, had not indulged in one of his late-night chocolate drink binges, and there was ample milk for Jim's cereal. Lauren, their older daughter, was not lost in one of her teenage moods which Jim had to get Marcy to explain. The car started first time. Stan at the security gate waved Jim by without making a fuss about checking his pass. The cleaner had not re-arranged his desk. Analyses were in for a couple of the drone's wind tunnel tests—the modified tailplane and the new placement of the payload—and they both looked good, so Frank, the project manager, was pleased. The line at the canteen was short, and they had Jim's favorite submarine sandwich, with ham, cheese, and tomato. The coffee machine did not spurt and mess up his cup. The parking lot, which was a little cramped, was half empty when he left, so he did not have to maneuver to get out of his spot. There was no slow train passing at the rail crossing, and he drove straight across.

Things only started going wrong when he got back home. As he walked through the door, he noticed there were no cooking smells:

Marcy finished work at the library early on Wednesdays, and he always came home to find her preparing dinner (usually ribs). He called out her name twice, heard a murmured reply, and finally found her in the living room, sitting with her back to the silent, flickering television. For just a moment the thought came to him that some intruder had got in and she had been hurt.

"What's going on?"

She would not look up. "It's my brother. I got a call from Susie. Bill's sick, in the hospital."

They all drove up to see Bill that weekend. The five-hour journey was subdued. Marcy dabbed away tears, and Lauren did too—she had always been close to her uncle. Even Carl was quiet, playing computer games on his console, and Jim kept the stereo on to mask the hush. As they reached the city limits of Bill's town, Jim became aware of a familiar feeling of irritation, which he realized was because of his brother-in-law. It was awkward to think of now that Bill was so sick, but Jim had never much liked him, or understood why everyone else seemed to think so much of him. Especially women: Jim was often annoyed by the way that Marcy—quiet, sensible Marcy—grew excited when her brother came to visit. It was not like he was a rock star (he ran a kitchen and bathroom business), yet people treated him almost like he was on MTV every night.

"Just try and act normal, okay?" Marcy instructed the children, twisting round in her seat to glance at Lauren. "Try not to get upset, as that's not going to help your uncle just now."

In the hospital ward Bill's wife, Susie, and their two kids looked as if they had been listening to Marcy's advice, and Susie had an aura of desperate, everyday cheerfulness. "The nurses have all been just great." Bill himself looked a little pale but otherwise seemed surprisingly composed—much more so than his family—with his usual smile and joking manner. "But you don't want to know about the food. Believe me, you'd eat better in the army." The way he lounged back in his bed it was easy to imagine he was still wearing his blue jeans and cowboy boots rather than a hospital robe.

"I'm out of here then," Jim joked feebly. They stayed for an hour, and he was surprised by how little there was to say.

On the way back Jim found himself talking optimistically, trying to steer Marcy away from getting more upset. "He looked good. Besides it's not like they know anything for sure." His efforts had little effect, needless to say, and during the days that followed, Jim was taken aback by the change in his wife. Ever since they had been married she had been so dependable, quietly arranging his life, and he was alarmed to see her unable to get out of bed in the morning, calling in sick to the library, or sitting blankly in the living room with her back to the TV. At first he tried to ignore what was happening, hoping she would recover, but if anything she seemed to grow worse, as if some part of her had switched off, like a computer program that had been corrupted. She would not even ring Susie to find out the latest news.

"I don't feel up to it just now. I'll call her sometime later."

Jim felt at sea. Marcy was everything to him, and all he wanted was for her to be fine again, but how? Should he soothe her with words? He tried, only to find himself talking about Bill's illness, and so upsetting her afresh: it was the scientist in him, always seeking the most relevant analysis of the facts, which in this case led straight to Bill's cancer. So he retreated into coping, trying not to mind as the details of his life slipped into chaos, though he found it hard not to get distressed by the dust on the stereo (Jim hated dust) or when he reached into the fridge and found no milk. Mornings were especially fretful as his clothes were rarely ironed, and on one occasion he had to go to work in a check shirt because nothing else was clean. Lauren did her best to help, bustling importantly about the house, or bickering at Carl for not doing his part, and she made a particular effort with meals, though these still proved fraught: in the past they had always eaten at seven sharp, but now Jim sometimes found himself waiting beyond eight. One evening he was served bread and jam. Bread and jam for dinner? The person who had always helped him to understand the troubling mystery of other people was Marcy, and he could hardly ask her how to make sense of her own self. Should he take her to a doctor, or a psychiatrist? The very names alarmed him, inspiring a fear—irrational, he knew—that they might somehow steal her away from him. One night he tried to talk to her. "I'm really worried about you, Marcy. You've got to snap out of this, for the kids."

For a moment her eyes showed new life, as if she were waking from a daze. "I don't believe this. Bill's my brother and you're telling me not to mind what's happening?"

"That's not what I meant."

She looked at him almost with a kind of hatred. "You don't care about me. You just want someone to look after you. You never did care, not really. You wouldn't even take me to Paris, the one thing I really wanted."

Jim pulled back from her on the bed, profoundly confused. What did Paris have to do with Bill? That had been years ago, and no, he had not liked the thought of going somewhere where they spoke a strange language he would not understand. In the end they had driven up to Canada, though he had not much liked that either, as the money was different and they used kilometers on the road signs.

After that he stopped trying to find an answer and instead took refuge in his work. Here at least everything was reassuringly in order, and he felt calmed by the faint whir of the computers and the familiar view of the parking lot, where his car sat waiting in its spot. At home everything might be going backward, drifting into a frightening place he did not comprehend, but at work there was progress, as the team designed this clever, beautiful machine. A good machine, too, that would make the world a safer place as it circled the globe. Jim was proud to be at the heart of its creation. Technically his role was computer analysis, but he was the best mathematician on the team and others would often come to him when they hit a snag. It was an arrangement that had the full approval of Frank, the project manager, and Jim himself enjoyed being the resident expert. Numbers never felt like work to him. Ever since he could remember he had always loved playing games with them, and sometimes he stayed late at his desk, as the office grew empty and quiet, and checked calculations that were not quite necessary, just for the pure pleasure of following the patterns the numbers made. Numbers were never confusing like people. Do a calculation a thousand times and it would come out the same. Numbers were always honest and always right if only you knew how to let them speak.

Susie rang three weeks after their visit, to tell them that Bill had had his next operation and was back home from the hospital. Though she did not say as much, Jim guessed from her voice that the operation had not gone well, and as they drove up that next Saturday he dreaded the effect this would have on Marcy. It was illogical, but he wished they were not staying over at Bill and Susie's, almost as if Bill's misfortune were somehow toxic, and Marcy should be exposed to it for as short a time as possible. In the event, though, nothing went as Jim had expected. Walking into Bill and Susie's spacious living room, Jim was surprised by Bill's appearance. It was not that he was changed physically—he looked thinner than before, but not greatly—it was his clothes. Gone were the blue jeans and cowboy boots, the country-and-western shirt, and in their place was an unfamiliar plainness: gray slacks, pale blue shirt, and laceless black shoes. Even his hair was trimmed short, and Jim found himself thinking that Bill looked almost like a preacher. The comparison was more apt than he knew.

"Susie and me have something to tell you," said Bill, watching his guests with a knowing smile. "We've gone through quite a change. These last weeks have been hard, for sure, but they've brought us something really special. We've been blessed by Jesus' love."

Susie beamed strangely. Jim was surprised, as Bill had never been a churchgoer. Quite the opposite in fact, and he had sometimes joked about money-hungry TV evangelists. His change, though, seemed real.

"Jesus and me are going to fight this together," he said with quiet determination, "and we're going to win." Afterward he led them all in prayer. For all his surprise Jim was happy with the transformation, if only for Marcy's sake: in her own quiet way she had always been devout, and already she looked lightened by her brother's announcement. For that matter Jim, too, felt relieved and a little less weighed down by the whole awful business. Driving back the next day, everyone was more cheerful than they had been for weeks.

"I really think he can beat this thing," Marcy said as they drove back onto the highway after filling up at a gas station.

"Sure he can," agreed Lauren.

"He looked really good," chipped in Jim, wanting to be part of this new mood. And if things were not exactly back to normal during the next few weeks, they were much better than before. Marcy missed only the occasional day from work at the library, and it was now rare for Jim to find her by the TV crying. Even the details of his old life began to return, and he found his shirts ironed and his dinner ready at seven. Marcy paid regular visits to her brother, and the whole family went a couple of times in the summer. By then Bill had finished his treatment, and though he looked older from his hair loss, he seemed better otherwise, and had even put back a little weight. "We're winning," he told Jim one night when they both drove out through an August thunderstorm to collect a take-out meal. "Jesus and me and the doctors are taking out those little gray fuckers. We're frying every last one of them."

Jim was taken aback by this sudden, angry confidence from a man he had never really liked, and for a moment he was unsure how to respond. "You get 'em, Bill," he said, finally filling the silence. "You get 'em."

Autumn came and went. Work on the drone project continued apace. All hell broke loose when a request came in for a feasibility study into enlarging the fuel tanks to extend the aircraft's range, which in turn entailed innumerable new calculations, but while others on the team complained, Jim quietly enjoyed having something to get his teeth into. "You're doing a great job," said Frank one day after Christmas. "When this machine's finally done, I think they should call it Jim's Baby."

It was in the spring that Jim began to wonder about Bill. Until then he had rung at least once a week, his sentences cheerfully peppered with phrases like "God willing" or "with Jesus on my side," but in February he stopped calling. When Marcy phoned him to arrange her next visit, Susie put her off. "He's just had the flu and he's feeling pretty tired right now."

"Flu can really knock you out," said Marcy afterward, and though her voice was calm, Jim noticed her face had the same taut look as when Bill was first sick.

"It sure can," Jim agreed. Perhaps that was all it was, just a bad flu. Marcy called a few more times and took what comfort she could from Susie's varying excuses, until one hot day in late June, Susie rang in tears.

"I think you'd better get over here."

They drove up that next Saturday, direct to the hospital. By some quirk of chance that allowed Jim's thoughts to find momentary refuge in estimating the odds of probability, Bill was in exactly the same bed as he had been the year before. Nothing else, though, was the same, and Jim found it hard to think of this person lying in the bed in front of him as Bill. He looked short—there had been nothing short about Bill—and tightened, so his thinned limbs made the bedsheet seem sharp and pointed. Almost the worst thing, though, was the change to Bill's manner. All his fight, his resolution, and his religious talk were gone, and in their place was a kind of awful carefulness. He hardly talked about anything except his pain.

"Actually it's a little better since they upped the dose last night," he reported in a whisper, watching them with scared, dreamy eyes. "It's the one low down on the left that I really feel, especially when I move. The one on the right isn't too bad today . . ."

Susie did not look upset so much as lost, as if some part of her had shut down. For some reason Jim found himself thinking of the red, open-top sports car that Bill used to drive, that had been some European make. Bill and Susie had been to Europe several times for holidays. For a moment Jim found it hard to understand why he had disliked him for all these years. How could you dislike this wreckage of a man? It was difficult to stay there by the bed—everything was too strong—but Jim assumed this was what they were doing, and he was surprised when Marcy picked up her jacket. "I'm kind of hungry. Maybe we should go find a sandwich or something."

"I wouldn't eat here," said Bill in that flat whisper. "It's worse than in the army."

Jim grinned as he knew his laugh would come out wrong. It was not often that he felt a sense of self-sacrifice, but as they stood in the elevator he knew what must happen. It would not be easy to do without Marcy for the next days or weeks, or however long it might be, but he would have to manage. "I guess you'll be staying."

Marcy, to his confusion, looked almost angry. "I don't know. I just don't know."

They went back after lunch, but then, after less than an hour, Marcy began edging away from the bed. "I guess we'd better start getting back."

Susie looked let down. "You can stay at the house. It's no problem."

"No, we should really get back."

Bill was her brother, and Jim said nothing. As they backed away from the bed, he knew his smile looked false, while Marcy's face was a mask of cheerfulness, as if she were trying to convince everyone that this parting was nothing final at all. Only Lauren and Carl looked true, watching Bill with a kind of sad puzzlement. Bill's dreamy eyes burned back, knowing everything.

Lauren protested as they rode the elevator down. "What's going on? Why aren't we staying?"

Marcy was almost shouting. "Don't ask me to watch him like this. I just can't do it."

Jim had a feeling that something terrible would happen when they got back, but oddly enough, nothing did, at least not at first. True, Marcy looked bad, but she did not collapse in on herself like before, in fact she became filled with a kind of unlikely energy, and Jim often woke to find her already up. She did not miss a day at the library and worked busily around the house in the evenings, her face set. Jim found all his shirts expertly ironed, and his socks were so flat it was as if they had been put under a steamroller. The fridge and larder were always full to bursting, and sometimes he heard the vacuum cleaner droning after midnight. For the first time he felt uneasy that all the small details of his life were so perfectly in place.

Then one Tuesday Jim came home from work to discover Marcy was not there. His first response was simple confusion. Marcy was always home when he got back. He tried her cell phone, but it was switched off. By eight he, Lauren, and Carl were in a panic, and he started making phone calls, first to Susie, then to the police, and finally to all the local hospitals, without any result. By now his fears were roaming freely. A road accident that had somehow escaped notice? She sometimes went to the shopping mall by the back road, which could be really quiet. A mugging? A carjacking? Or—almost the most frightening thought of all—what if she had harmed herself? It seemed hard to believe, as Marcy had never been that kind, but she had been so upset lately that Jim no longer felt sure of anything. This had always been his worst fear: to be left alone, without her to guide him through the world.

He and the kids were still waiting up when, at midnight, they heard her key in the lock. Jim was furious. "Thank God. Where the hell have you been?"

Her expression was flat and strangely unrepentant. "Just out."

"What d'you mean 'out'?"

Lauren was angrier than he was. "We called the cops and everything."

"Well you shouldn't have." Marcy was obstinate in the face of Jim's hunger for the comfort of details. "I was driving around. What's it matter where? I just had to get out for a while."

Two nights later she vanished again. Then on Saturday afternoon she said she needed to get some groceries and still had not returned that evening.

"Is Mom going crazy?" asked Carl in his matter-of-fact voice as they sat in the living room, waiting up once again.

Was she? "She's just upset." Jim got no sleep that night, lying alone in the bed. By now he was troubled less by the thought of accidents than by a general unspecified fear, and though he tried to soothe himself with imaginings of her driving slowly through the empty city streets, or lying awake—just like him—in some motel room, somehow none of these seemed quite convincing. She finally breezed in on Sunday afternoon, carrying bags of groceries, as if the previous twenty-four hours had never occurred. "I was just out, that's all."

"But you've been gone all night. Where did you stay?"

"What's it matter?"

"What's going on? Don't you like being here with your family?"

"Of course I do."

That evening as they lay in bed a question surfaced in Jim's thoughts. "Marcy, are you seeing someone?" It was not a real question as he knew the answer—Marcy would never cheat on him, she was not that kind—and what he sought was reassurance: a way to break through her wall.

"I guess."

He assumed he had misheard. "What's that?"

"I guess."

He looked at her, still not believing. "But . . . Who?"

"Nobody you know. Some guy who comes into the library."

Finally, belatedly, he felt the betrayal. "Marcy, how could you?"

She rolled away from him. "It just happened, okay? Why don't you just throw me out? Nobody'd blame you."

Should he? People in movies would. At the very least he should make a scene. Oddly enough, this was the very last thing he wanted to do, as he feared that then everything might be more fixed and irreversible. If he could pretend this wasn't quite happening, then maybe it would go away. What he wanted, so much that he could almost touch it, was for his life to be just like it had been before. And so he did nothing at all.

He was determined the children should not find out, but they did, almost at once. When he came home the next evening there was no sign of Marcy, but Lauren was waiting for him in the living room with Carl. "The weirdest thing happened today." Lauren looked at Jim intently. "I was walking out of the school with my friends when I saw this car go by, and there, sitting in the front with some guy, was Mom."

Outside the school? It was almost as if Marcy had wanted her to know. Jim saw his expression reflected in his children's eyes: their rising shock of understanding. There seemed no point in denying it. Jim found himself grimly curious. "What did the guy look like?"

"I don't know. He looked a little like Bill." She frowned at him, exasperated. "Jesus, Dad. Aren't you angry?"

He wasn't. He just felt tired, very tired.

Marcy came home later that evening. By then Jim was in his

study checking his e-mail and he heard Lauren go into the hall to confront her. "So you're back? I saw you driving around today with that guy."

Jim half expected Marcy to crumble, but instead she met Lauren head-on. "Just leave me alone. This is none of your business."

Jim couldn't listen to any more, and he crept quietly upstairs. He had just reached the landing when he saw that Carl was behind him, doing the same.

The next day something confusing happened to Jim. He found he could not work. It was almost as if his numbers had turned against him, and when he tried to penetrate a calculation, his thoughts bounced away like stones off a wall. It was baffling. He'd had worrying times before now, of course, but nothing had ever affected his concentration. Now when another member of the team came to him with a problem, he found himself making excuses. "Hell, actually I don't think I can right now as I'm just working on something for Mike." He knew he should tell Frank about what was happening, but instead he said nothing and just kept quiet, aware that he was putting himself more in the wrong.

Soon afterward something even more disquieting began to happen. Jim found he was affected by sudden, grotesque imaginings, almost like clips from the horror movies he used to dread school friends dragging him to see. What was more, these seemed to be set off by, of all things, the drone project. They came quite without warning: he might be glancing at the new design for the placement of the wing cannons when, in graphic detail, he would find himself picturing a rib cage being cut open with a pair of bolt cutters. He would be reading an e-mail on the rocket payload and would find himself imagining a head of human hair burning away to nothing. Or he would be trying to estimate the recoil from the wing armament—those numbers, slipping away from his grasp—when he would see bullets, not metal like ordinary bullets but dull and gray, the way Bill had described the things growing inside him. Bill: he was the real cause of all this, Jim realized that same afternoon as he stood in line at the canteen. And, though Jim knew it was wrong to hate someone who was dying, he hated him more than he had ever hated anyone. It had not been enough to drive Marcy half crazy with grief and to wreck their marriage. No, now Bill was out to ruin Jim's work as well. He was determined to spread his dying as far afield as he was able, and to infect the drone—the one thing that still seemed clean and good—with the horror of his own decay. "Can't you let me alone?" Jim found himself murmuring by the coffee machine. "Just leave me be?"

Jim assumed that his life would reach some kind of final collapse now that all its keystones had been removed, but rather to his surprise, time continued to slip by, almost as if nothing unusual were happening. Nobody on the team seemed to notice that he couldn't work properly, and he guessed he was living off his past reliability. He woke, he had breakfast, he went to work, he came home. Sometimes, when he was distracted—by sleep, or just watching TV—he forgot that Marcy was having an affair, and so it would come to him all over again, freshly unbelievable. He hated leaving her alone in the house and would delay going in the morning, so he was often one of the last in the lot at work and would have to maneuver back and forth to park. Sometimes, to his relief, Marcy was there when he came home, sometimes she was not. Unexpectedly, she continued to manage the house, cleaning his shirts and keeping the fridge stocked, though now he hardly cared. As he lay beside her at night, he was disgusted by the thought of her body, which had been squeezed and enjoyed by another man's hands, and yet he wanted her, too, more hungrily than he had for years. Sometimes he tried to touch her, but she would turn away, rolling into a ball like she was cold.

"Leave me alone."

A curiosity of this time was that Jim found there was no place where he felt comfortable—not at home, not at work, not anywhere—and in a way it was this that inspired his final crisis. One lunchtime he drove away from work, taken by a sudden urge to eat doughnuts. Somehow he never did get to the doughnut shop, and instead he found himself wandering in one of the city's largest stores. As he meandered through the endless aisles, his eye was caught by a cheap spinning top made of tin, just like one he had had as a child. "Made in China, probably," he murmured, and looking at it on the shelf, he wanted it, almost like it was something he was owed. So he slipped it into his jacket pocket. Afterward he felt he had known what would happen, and sure enough, a security guard stopped him in the car lot. When Jim wouldn't answer his questions—wouldn't speak at all—the police were called. One of them looked through Jim's wallet and found his security pass, and half an hour later Frank was sitting beside him.

"Tell me everything."

Jim guessed he was quite ruined, but still it felt good to get everything off his chest. Frank was interested in the Marcy business, of course, but it was Jim's problems at work that really caught his attention, and he frowned unhappily as Jim described his lurid imaginings about the project. "This is bad, Jim. I wish you'd come to me sooner." He shook his head. "But I want to help you. You're important for this project, and I want you to be important for other projects in the future."

Did that mean he wasn't ruined after all?

"This is how it's going to be. The store is going to forget all about what happened today. You're going to take a few days off to rest. Take a walk in the park, watch some TV. And then I want you to see someone who can clear up what's going on in your head. He'll probably want to see Marcy, too. He's helped people on the team before, and believe me he knows what he's doing."

A shrink. Did that mean Jim was going crazy? Most of all, though, he felt relieved. Now he was somebody else's problem. He drove home, to rest, just like he had been told.

In the event, though, this did not prove so easy. Walking into the living room, he found Marcy sitting with her back to the TV.

It was the first time since they had visited Bill in the hospital that he had seen her cry. "Susie rang."

The funeral was set for early the next week. Frank agreed that Jim should go—"Who knows, maybe it'll help"—and they traveled up early in the morning along empty roads. As Jim drove, Marcy slumped back in the seat beside him, expressionless, he wondered how things would get worse. Though it was hard to think how they might get worse now, as everything had already gone wrong. As they reached the city limits of Bill's town, Carl broke the silence. "Mom, Dad, you've got to sort this out. You've got to talk to each other." The suddenness and feeling of his remark—from Carl, of all people, who usually talked only about computers—took them by surprise.

Half an hour later they were at the funeral. Jim felt strangely peaceful sitting in the church, with all those people, quietly listening. The reception, too, could have been far worse. Susie and the kids looked terrible, of course, and the daughter shot Marcy an angry stare, but they also seemed somehow relieved. Jim and his family stayed over at their home that night, and as he and Marcy lay side by side in the spare room, beneath a picture of a horse and plow and a wide, empty sky, Marcy rolled over to face him.

"I won't ever see him again. Okay?" She looked at him, defiant. "But there's one thing I want you to promise. Don't ask me why it happened." Now her toughness was slipping away. "You know, I didn't even really like him. Can you believe that? It was like it was something I just had to do, almost like I needed to screw everything up and make everyone hate me. Can you understand that?"

Jim could not, not at all. He found he was shaking, both relieved and angrier than he had ever felt toward her. He touched her cheek with his finger. She cried as they made love.

And so Jim's life, which had seemed quite beyond repair, slowly began to come back together. Marcy was as good as her word, and though Jim's mistrust of her never entirely vanished, it was easily outweighed by his relief at having her back. Lauren and Carl displayed a lingering disillusionment toward their parents, Lauren especially, and yet somehow they went on, a family still. The details of Jim's life fell back into place, and he clung to them as never before. Even his work returned to him, and surprisingly quickly too, so he hardly needed the therapy that Frank had arranged. He found he could concentrate once again, and though it took a little longer to free himself of his random, nightmarish imaginings, with time the project returned to being what it had before: something important and good, a wonder of intelligent technology, a challenge of numbers. Frank was so pleased with Jim's recovery that he picked him for a special honor. And so on a warm July day, just two years after Bill's funeral, Jim took a group of military guests through the drone's specifications—its speed, its formidable range, its varied payload options, its advanced remote-control system, the precision of its weaponry—while all the while the machine itself soared and banked through the blue sky above them, full of graceful intent.

12. White

THERE WAS SOMETHING about the sound of the footsteps climbing the stairs—their slowness?—that made Yunis guess the moment had arrived. He glanced up from the Koran, which he had been reading all morning—murmuring the familiar phrases—and sure enough, the door opened and Hussein walked into the room carrying the harness. Yunis found himself staring at it, strangely fascinated. Hussein placed it carefully on the table, beside it the jeans jacket, T-shirt, and a pair of fawn jeans: *their* clothes.

"Are you ready, friend?" Hussein gave him a questioning look.

To his own surprise Yunis felt quite ready. In fact he felt more than ready: he felt serene. Today all would be perfect: today God would lead him forward to make everything white. He put on the jeans and was relieved to find that he did not even flinch when Hussein tied the harness around his shoulders. It was lighter than Yunis had expected, and he decided that the feel of it pressing around his chest was comforting, like an embrace. Hussein threaded the cord so it hung down behind the jeans pocket, which had been cut away.

"Don't touch that," he warned Yunis, "not until the moment is come." He held out the T-shirt and jeans jacket, but something made Yunis wave his hand in refusal.

"Later." This was his day, after all, and he could do just as he wanted. So he walked down shirtless, with the harness showing for all to see. It was the culminating moment of his time here. The other three—Thaher, Abdul, and Salah—had been lost in discussion round the dining table, but now they looked up in silence. How different it had been when Yunis first came a month ago and they had been aloof toward the new arrival. Matters had not been helped, of course, by what had happened with Yunis's family. Now, though, all of that seemed far away, and Yunis felt high above the others, untouchable in his serenity. He put on the T-shirt and jeans jacket and accepted their emotional farewells.

"Good-bye, friend." Abdul, the joker of the group, was now as serious as could be.

"Good-bye, friend," echoed Salah.

Even Thaher—plain, pure Thaher, who never laughed—bowed his head, as if acknowledging that he, Yunis, was his superior. "Good-bye, friend."

Hussein insisted that he would drive him himself. Normally he preferred to keep a distance from the operations. "No, really, it is my honor."

During the previous days Yunis had imagined and reimagined each stage of this day, willing it all to go well, and now, as he stepped through the door, everything felt as if it were going by too quickly, almost as if it were not happening properly after all. As if it mattered, he told himself, concerned not to puncture his serenity, but then, walking to the car, he slipped slightly on a stone. It was a small enough thing, but he felt annoyed, knowing the others were watching: he hated the thought that they might think him nervous.

"I'm so proud of you, Yunis, my old friend, my friend of all these long years," said Hussein as he drove, his eyes faintly glowing. "Today you are doing something beautiful. Today, God willing, you will make history."

Yunis smiled, but he felt distracted. Strange things had started to happen: he could feel his breath coming too fast, as if he had been running, and—worse—his hands were trembling, so he curled his fingers into fists to stop this showing. All in all he felt relieved when the journey was over and they drew to a halt on a dusty track by an olive grove. Hussein opened the trunk and pulled out the long traditional shawl and headdress, and also a wooden staff. "Perhaps I should go through the details one last time, just to be sure."

"Of course." Yunis smiled, putting on the shawl, though all he wanted was to be gone. He had heard the instructions so many times he knew them by heart, while he could feel his arms and elbows were beginning to shake.

"Walk in this direction and keep the sun always on your left. Always on your left, remember? That is most important. After three kilometers you will reach an old stone sheep pen, and you must go to the right of this. Soon after that you will see the watchtower. It's quite far, so don't be worried, Yunis—God will lead you through—but walk slowly and stiffly and lean on your staff so God will make them see an old farmer and not you. The town is just beyond the watchtower. Be careful when you throw away the clothes as that will make them suspicious. The bus to Tel Aviv stops by a line of trees, and you have a ticket in your jacket pocket. Make sure you get off before the last stop as that is where they will be watching. After then it is for you to decide. God will guide you. A café or a restaurant, you will know." He gave Yunis an embrace. "I am so proud of you, my brother. Today you will do something for all the world to see. Today you will be rewarded with the beauty of paradise."

Yunis turned and began walking through the olive grove, dust rising up from each footstep. He had been so eager to be gone, but now, after just a few meters, he found himself regretting his hurry. It was odd, but the one thing that had never occurred to him when he had imagined this day was that he might feel lonely. Already he could feel silence closing in on him, tempting him to turn around—he could always pretend he wanted to check some detail of the plan—but then he heard the car's engine starting up, and glancing back, he watched it slowly disappear down the valley. It was better this way, he told himself. His arm scraped against a tree branch. Nothing at all had gone wrong, and yet, all at once, he felt somehow as if it had. It was early May—not properly hot yet—but the sun seemed too bright in his eyes, while the layers of clothing he was wearing made him sweat and the harness rubbed at his shoulders. He was nagged by a feeling that he was going to do something stupid. Already his sense of serene superiority over Thaher and the others had left him, and he now thought of them enviously: they would never become agitated like this, they would be calm and collected, entirely focused on the task ahead. Yunis tried to anchor himself with their example, reminding himself that all of this was in God's hands—not his own—which meant there was no reason to be nervous. But Yunis had never been the sort of person to see things in a plain, simple way, and already he found himself imagining complications. What if God were displeased with him? He found his thoughts turning against him, like barbs, and into the middle of them all, like an uninvited visitor, came Rachel, standing in the music shop, just as he had first seen her, the sunlight catching her long, auburn hair. Next—and worse—came Uncle Ibrahim, with his weary, amused eyes. Yunis felt suddenly angry. How dare Uncle Ibrahim sully this day, even if just in his thoughts?

Was this the sheep pen? Yunis stopped by a stone wall in the shape of a square. Surely he hadn't walked three kilometers already. He went on hesitantly, keeping to the right of the wall as instructed, and sure enough, after just a short distance, the low hill to his left dropped away and he saw the watchtower peek into sight. Instinctively he ducked but then forced himself to go on, worried that if he hesitated he might lose his nerve. He had walked on some way so he could see the watchtower right down to its base when, far too late, he remembered Hussein's instructions. How could he have forgotten—so stupid—when he had heard them a dozen times? He was supposed to walk slowly, and instead he was hurrying as if he were in a race. If he slowed down now, would that make him look more suspicious? He did so anyway, fighting back the instinct that screamed inside him—run, run as fast you can—and made himself creep along at a snail's pace, his legs stiff like an old man's. A moment later he glimpsed a momentary flash of light from the watchtower. Binoculars catching the sun? Now, for sure, things would go wrong, and he waited for one of the cars parked at the tower's base to speed out toward him. But none did. Moments slipped by, so slowly that it seemed like he was not moving at all but rather was stuck on some dusty treadmill. Gradually the watchtower began to drift beside and behind him until, almost to his own disbelief, he passed over a slight rise in the land and saw the road, just up ahead.

Nothing had gone wrong after all. A few meters farther and the tower vanished behind trees. All at once Yunis felt triumphant. He had done it! This, surely, was the hardest part, to get across the boundary. He wasn't even shaking anymore. Getting rid of the farmer's clothes proved easy, and he waited until the road was empty, then rolled the scarf and headdress into a ball and threw them in the ditch along with the stick. He brushed dust from his jeans and walked on, feeling his stride lengthen, his confidence flowing back. If only Hussein could see him now, so clever and brave. Everything was going to be perfect.

But his mood was short-lived. Here was the line of trees and the bus stop. Waiting there, watching *their* cars slide by, the occupants eyeing him carefully through the windows, Yunis began to feel vulnerable, absurdly so, like an empty bottle on a wall waiting for a stone. How ludicrous this was, the way his feelings changed so quickly. This was never going to work. How had he been so stupid as to imagine that a pair of jeans and a T-shirt would be enough to let him pass for one of *them*? He was the opposite of *them*—he wanted to be the opposite—and this was bound to show, in his eyes, in the way he stood. He felt suddenly angry at Hussein, not for sending him on this mission but for making it so ridiculously complicated. Why on earth had Hussein insisted he go all the way to Tel Aviv, which was asking for trouble, when there was sure to be a perfectly good target here in this little dusty town? Unless he had wanted this to go wrong? Wanted him, Yunis, to be humiliated?

Should he just ignore the instructions and do it here? Would Thaher and the others think him a coward? Then he heard an engine, and the bus was drawing into sight, panicking him into obedience. What if there were soldiers on board? His fingers gripped the cord, even though Hussein had told him he must not, and as the bus slowed down he saw exactly what he least wanted to see: several of the passengers behind the windows were not *them* at all but his own people, and he glimpsed two women with covered heads and a bearded man who looked like a priest. The door swung open, and with a feeling of hopelessness, of falling into the dark, he climbed up. But no, there were no soldiers after all, just anxious looks.

Yunis took a seat, his spirits soaring once again. Something might still go wrong during the journey, of course, but he was aboard and most of his worries were gone, at least for now. Hussein had said the journey took about an hour, and Yunis felt almost relaxed, cushioned by this time. Something strange was happening. As he looked out of the window, he found his thoughts did not flow as usual, one connecting with the next, but instead seemed to jump out at random. Was this how it had been for others at this moment: had they also been subjected to this kind of shock of remembrance, almost as if one's life had been chopped into so many television advertisements? Yunis glanced out at a supermarket and found himself picturing the living room in his parents' house, with its fine carpets and the painting on the wall of running horses. Next, for no reason he could understand, he saw a classroom at his school, and Mr. Mohammed, who had taught him math for only a few months, before Yunis and his brother, Zayid, were sent away to their aunt in Jordan. Now he saw Zayid, looking back with a smile as he walked away at Amman airport for his plane to Canada. Next Yunis was in his parents' sitting room, several years on, and listening to his brother's voice on the telephone. "It's thirty degrees below zero here today." Yunis tried to imagine what that could be like. Could you breathe? Did your eyes freeze? Zayid laughed at his questions: already he sounded like a foreigner. "Everyone just stays indoors."

Somebody in the seat behind Yunis had opened an orange. For a moment the scent, so familiar and sweet, caught him by surprise, and he felt almost as if he were outside the bus, watching himself sitting here, and in that brief instant everything he was doing today seemed somehow impossible, even absurd. Yunis fought back at the feeling. There was nothing absurd about this, he told himself firmly, this was the proudest day of his life, the day that would make sense of all the rest. His thoughts were jumping again, and watching a garden center slip by the bus window, he found himself sitting at his school desk beside Hussein. They were sniggering at Mr. Haroun, whose left eye always seemed to be looking round the corner. "I think someone threw an egg at him from that side, many years ago," Yunis murmured in a serious voice, "and ever since then he worries there may be another egg coming." Hussein—smaller, younger—had laughed too loudly, and Mr. Haroun had sent them both out of the room.

Now they were both in Yunis's house watching soccer—Yunis's father's shop sold electrical goods, and they had a fine television with a large, clear screen—waiting for Brazil to score. "I think they're playing better than I've ever seen them," said Hussein, glancing up at Yunis, as usual, to check that he agreed. "They'll win, I just know they will."

Even Yunis's father had liked Hussein back then—"poor boy, living in that camp"—and when they watched a match Yunis's mother would bring them bread, olives, and cucumber with mint and yogurt. Usually they came from—abruptly Yunis found his remembrance spoiled—from Uncle Ibrahim's shop. Yunis closed his eyes.

The bus was slowing down. Trouble? Yunis fingered the cord,

but no, it was just another stop. The door swung open, and one of *them* climbed aboard, an Orthodox, with his black hat, long beard, and those annoying ringlets. As the man stumbled down the aisle of the bus, Yunis saw there was something familiar about him—in his anxious expression—and a little disconcerted, Yunis realized that he looked like Abdullah, his cousin who repaired shoes near the market. Yunis shooed away the unwelcome thought. What did it matter who looked like whom? At a whim he reached into his pocket to touch the cord again. I can make you white, old man, right now. For a moment he felt strangely warmed by this feeling of power. And why not, he decided. He'd had little enough of it till now.

The bus was speeding up, hurrying past a complex of new houses, and Yunis found he was picturing Hussein's home, as he had seen it on that one strange time he had visited. They had both been out with others from the school, throwing stones at *their* soldiers—the intifada had been going for some months—and Yunis had cut his knee scrabbling over a wall. It had not been such a bad cut, but it bled a good deal—knees always did—and Hussein's home was nearest. Yunis had never been inside the camp until then, and he was shocked by its narrow, crowded lanes, which made him think of a souk without shops. Had his eyes showed their dismay as he walked into Hussein's home? This was hardly worthy of the name *house*: two rooms, both bare, without even a carpet on the floor. Hussein's parents had been kind. "It's so good to meet you at last, Yunis. Hussein's always talking about you." A younger brother was sent out, hurrying back with bandages. "Now you must stay and eat something. No, really, we insist."

Yunis was not entirely sure he wanted to stay and eat in this dusty room, where there was barely space for them all to sit, but he remembered his manners. "Really, it is too good of you," he answered, mimicking phrases he had heard his father use.

But then, without any warning, Hussein got to his feet, looking strangely angry. "He can't stay. It's not safe here for him." Yunis was confused, all the more so as he had never seen Hussein angry until then. Quite the opposite: he was usually eager to impress, hanging on Yunis's every word. Besides, what Hussein said made no sense, as the camp was not dangerous, not back then (though many of the houses had since been leveled by *their* bulldozers). Yunis did not realize it at the time, but that moment was the end of their friendship. The next weekend Hussein dropped by his house, just as usual, but there was an anger in his eyes, and when the soccer match they were watching came to an end, he suddenly declared, "I don't like Manchester United. They cheat." Yunis was taken aback, not so much by the attack on Manchester United— the team they both supported—but by Hussein's unexpected rebellion, challenging the balance of their friendship. They argued and Hussein marched from the house shouting insults. After that they avoided each other at school. At the time Yunis had not entirely understood what had happened, but later he heard that Hussein's family had once been rich, and that before '48, when *they* came and everything changed, they had owned a large house by the sea, roundabout where Tel Aviv now was. It seemed like a clue.

It was not long after Yunis's falling-out with Hussein that a couple of boys from the school were killed throwing stones and Yunis's father decided to send both his sons away to their aunt in Amman, Jordan. "I just want you to be safe," he told them.

Safe? Now the very word seemed almost laughable. As if anyone could be safe in this world: what a pitiful, hopeless ambition. Yunis never much liked Amman, despite his aunt's kindness, as it seemed strangely empty: a city of closed doors. When he finally came back, three years later—soon after his brother had left for Canada—his father had been furious. "Why have you done this? It's so stupid. There's nothing here but trouble and misery." Oddly enough Yunis had been thinking much the same thing earlier that same day, as he waited at the border, enduring *their* searches and *their* scornful looks. He had forgotten how depressing it was here: the feeling of nothing being possible; the sight of people waiting around for something—usually something bad—to happen; the feeling that this whole land was nothing more than a vast, dusty jail. But as Yunis stood in the sitting room with the painting of running horses, listening to his father's anger, he knew he would stay. Bad though it was here, somehow he could not endure the thought of being anywhere else. It was as if he had become an addict of history.

Yunis's eye was caught by something outside the window: tall buildings, just up ahead. Was he here already? He peered at his watch. Hussein had said the journey took almost an hour, and this had been barely forty minutes. For a moment he felt annoyed, as if he had been cheated. What difference did a few minutes make, he scolded himself, turning his thoughts to when he should get off. Hussein had said he must do so before the last stop, but he had no idea how many were left. Abruptly he got up from his seat, hurrying along the aisle behind the Orthodox, and then found himself standing by a gas station, dazzled by the sunlight as the bus pulled away. The tall buildings looked more distant now, so probably he had got off too early after all. He started walking.

There was the sea. Had Hussein's family's house been somewhere around here, perhaps where that building—it looked like a hotel—was standing? This really was *their* heartland. Jerusalem, which Yunis had visited several times during the Oslo peace years, was all mixed up, with his people and *them* brushing shoulders. Here *they* almost had the streets to themselves: young ones in jeans, Orthodox ones, old ones with anxious faces. Probably it was inevitable that Yunis would think of Rachel here, and sure enough, as he glanced up ahead at a music shop, she jumped into his thoughts, holding a CD. He could not even remember why he had been so keen on Brazilian music at that time. Perhaps it was because Brazil always won at soccer: it had felt good to be backing a winner, for once. Just thinking of Rachel seemed somehow unlucky, and he murmured to himself, "Please, God, forgive me my foolishness," but she was obstinate and would not go. Now she was turning toward him, and though he tried to stretch her face and make her ugly, it was almost two years since he had seen her and all he could really remember was her auburn hair. How could you make hair ugly?

"You like Brazilian music?" she'd asked. Her recklessness had taken him aback. He knew exactly who she was, in her jeans and T-shirt—*their* clothes—and she addressed him in English, so she clearly understood who he was, too. Everyone knew that this sort of thing never happened: there was no talking, no smiles, no looks. Was she mad? Her eyes looked defiant, and at the same time somehow lost, as if she was someone who didn't fit. That morning he had felt like that, too. Tell her to go to hell, shout the worst, vilest insults: that was what he knew he should do. He knew some Hebrew (it was so like Arabic) and easily enough for this. Or he should stare through her as if she didn't exist, his eyes like ice. But instead he frowned, unsure. "Yes, I do, especially the new bands."

They had gone for a walk—what if someone had seen?—and stopped for a coffee. The waiter was one of *hers* and had given them a stare. As they sat there, talking about—of all things—what kinds of animals they liked, Yunis had suggested they swap cell phone numbers. Even now he could remember that rich feeling of transgression. A week later he had rung her from the secrecy of his bedroom, and they met soon afterward: the same music shop, the same walk. Several times their arms brushed, and he had toyed with the idea of stopping and kissing her there and then—after all *they* kissed in public without any shame—but he had not dared. That same day, on the journey back, sense finally came to him and he grew scared. Some days later she rang his cell phone, and when he heard her voice he rang off. But the memory of her lingered, alluring, like a story abandoned after just a few pages, and he found himself thinking about her far more often than about Nahla or Sameetha.

Was she here now? He could make her white. He tried to feel pleased by the thought of this power, but somehow the feeling would not come. And then, to his surprise, he saw a café just ahead, not packed but crowded enough. The taller buildings were still some way off, and he had assumed he had much farther to walk. It seemed so sudden. Is this the one, God? He felt nothing, no hint of either assent or discouragement, and was somehow disappointed. But he would be a fool, he knew, to delay, as this would only add to the likelihood that something would go wrong. Why jeopardize his success till now? Feeling dry in his mouth, he strode slowly toward the café door. Good-bye, Father and Mother. Good-bye, Zayid. Good-bye, Nahla. Good-bye, Hussein. He was almost there, his hand reaching for the handle, when to his own confusion, he found he was turning away and walking on down the street.

This was bad, very bad, but it was not a disaster, he told himself. It had simply been too sudden. He summoned up determination. Just do it. What would Hussein think, or Thaher, or Abdul? No, he must beat this, and prove himself, his family. Help me, God, please, as all I want is to serve you. Walking slowly on toward the higher buildings, he decided he would not change his target but would go back to the same café, so that he would not be caught out by surprise. It would be easy. Had he not been preparing for days? This was his chance to even things up, for once. To make everything clean and white. It felt like he had hardly started walking back when there, right in front of him, was the café. He had thought it was farther. His hand found the cord and gripped it, ready to tug, and he strode toward the door. There were the people inside, chatting and drinking coffee. They looked so ordinary. And then, all at once, he found he had again veered away.

Now he felt lost. How could this be happening? He had been so ready, he had read verses of the Koran for a week, he had worn down all his doubts and fears, and now, at the crucial moment . . . He stopped by the window of a supermarket—what nice things they had here—and wondered, Why? Did God want him to live after all? Or was he cursed, unable to cleanse his family's name? Both thoughts led to the same place. The picture that now jumped into Yunis's thoughts was the one he had been most keen to shut out: a crowd was pushing into a shop, past shelves of oranges and dates and cucumbers, and pulling the shopkeeper out into the street, then dragging him along the road, to the waste ground beyond the soccer field. The shopkeeper was Yunis's Uncle Ibrahim.

What had he been thinking of? Yes, times had been hard, worse than ever, and Ibrahim's shop had been doing badly, but still that didn't mean he had the right to do that, the worst possible form of betrayal, selling his country to *them*. Ibrahim had always seemed so shrewd, with his weary, amused eyes, but there had been nothing shrewd about this. The olive grove he owned was a few miles outside the town—he had someone else tend the trees—but it was easily close enough to be noticed. Yunis had been working in his father's electrical shop when a neighbor had come in with the news, his eyes careful. "I heard that part of your uncle's land's been fenced off. There's one of their signs, saying they're going to build there." *They* already had a settlement just farther up the hill. "D'you know anything about this?"

Yunis saw the danger. "No, nothing."

Uncle Ibrahim had dropped by soon afterward, loud in his protests: too loud. "They robbed me. It's a crime, really it is. Now they will steal anything from any man." But when the crowd broke into his shop, two days later, they found a locked drawer with a thick roll of dollar bills.

Ibrahim's funeral was an ending of things and a beginning. It was the end of Yunis's respect for his father. Yes, Yunis knew that he was not a brave man, but still he was taken aback to find he was too frightened to go to his brother-in-law's funeral. Yunis went, accompanying his mother, so there would be someone to protect her from insult. He had hoped that nobody outside the family would come and had been unnerved to see that, standing a little apart from the proceedings, was—of all people—Hussein. Yunis had not seen him for some years, and he looked thinner, his eyes more still and certain. Yunis had heard what he was doing these days. Was he here to gloat? To add to Yunis's family's shame with some barbed remark? But no, instead Hussein had stridden over to him with a sad smile. "Good day, old friend. I am so sorry for all your troubles." When the ceremony was finished and they were walking away, he spoke again. "Come and see me sometime, Yunis. If you choose."

Yunis knew precisely what he meant. Hussein had opened a door. The next evening Yunis's brother, Zayid, rang from Canada and opened another. "You have to get out of there, Yunis, now more than ever. I can help you. You have no idea how good it feels out here, where you can have a real life, with a future to look at and nothing to poison your soul." He wouldn't stop talking, as if to pause would be to lose his chance of convincing his brother. "You know, I don't even hate *them* anymore. I've been thinking about it so much recently. What they do, it's not even their choice, it's inevitable. If a man steals another man's house and lives there with a gun, while the other man has nothing—no house, no gun—then tell me, what will the result be?"

Zayid had always liked puzzles, but today Yunis felt in no mood for one. "I don't know. The man with the gun shoots the man with nothing."

"Worse than that. He fears him." Zayid laughed. "Who knows what we'd have done if we'd won in 'forty-eight? We might be scared of them."

Oddly enough Hussein, who disagreed with almost everything that Zayid thought and did, had said something a little similar. "That's their biggest mistake, that they've left us with nothing. It means we have nothing to lose, and that makes us stronger. That's why we'll win in the end."

For three weeks after Ibrahim's funeral, Yunis went on as before, waking, eating, sleeping, working in his father's electrical shop, but all the while he felt as if he were only half there, while the other half of him was looking at those two open doors. Deep down he always knew which he would choose. Why? Because to turn his back and leave this place—terrible though it was—was exactly what *they* wanted, and what *they* had been trying to make him do ever since he was born.

And now he was here, in *their* town, a harness of explosives beneath his T-shirt, a cord ready to be pulled, and everything was going wrong. Was this what God wanted? Had he felt sorry for the people in the café? Or was it just that it was hard to bring everything to an end like this? He was passing a restaurant and could smell cooking—potatoes, steak?—and never in his life had food smelled so good. Now he saw a girl smiling as she talked into her cell phone, and though she was one of *them,* and though he should make her white, it was such a pretty smile that he wanted to hold it in his hand. He tried to stoke up his determination, thinking of paradise waiting for him, so pure and bright, with beautiful girls greeting him with smiles, and rivers flowing red and green. He thought of how it was to wait at one of *their* checkpoints, enduring *their* scornful looks just to pass across his own land. He thought of that feeling that never quite went away, of being trapped and prevented from doing anything you wanted. But already he knew, deep down, that he had lost this fight.

Should he try to get help? Perhaps there was a mosque somewhere near? But then how would he face Hussein, Thaher, and the others? He stopped, uncertain what to do, and it was then, out of the corner of his eye, that he glimpsed four figures in green. Earlier he had been half expecting to see one of *their* patrols, but now it took him by surprise. He realized he was standing by the same gas station where he had got off the bus. Walk on? That would take him right past them, but it would make him look less suspicious. Then he found he had turned and was walking the other way, his stride stiff and nervous. Now he glanced back over his shoulder— the very last thing he should do, the stupidest thing, but somehow he could not stop himself—and saw that one of them was watching him. It was the tallest of the four, slightly stooped, with a long, serious face: the sort of face you liked, which seemed somehow unfair. Now he was pointing.

"Hey, you!"

Was this what God wanted, that he should make these ones white? They were soldiers, which was the best of all. But rather than go to them, as he should, Yunis found he was darting away behind one of the gas pumps. How could this be happening? He was doing all the worst, stupidest things. He crouched there, breathing fast, and knew he had thrown everything away.

"Come out from behind there, hands high. Come out or we'll shoot."

Was this his final punishment? For Rachel? For his uncle? Everything had gone wrong, and yet even now Yunis saw a choice before him. He could let himself be taken alive—the final humiliation—or he could make himself white, uselessly here by this gas pump. And so, trembling, he reached for the cord, and with a sudden tug he pulled.

ACKNOWLEDGMENTS

I would like to thank the following people for the invaluable advice and expertise they gave me while I was writing this book: James Ashe-Taylor for "Powder," Phillip Cryan for "Leaves," Patrick Reeve for "Metal" and "Seasons," Gilad Atzmon for "White."

I would also like to thank, as ever, my agent, Deborah Rogers, and my editor, Andrew Kidd.

MATTHEW KNEALE is the author of several novels, including most recently *English Passengers,* which won the Whitbread Book of the Year 2000 award and was short-listed for the Booker Prize. He lives in Rome, Italy.

A NOTE ABOUT THE TYPE

The text of this book is set in Minion, a font created in 1990 for Adobe Systems. Type designer Robert Slimbach drew his inspiration from the elegant, readable types of the late Renaissance, combining beauty with functionality to create a font that is suitable for many uses.